CW00430834

ASIN: B0BF93DNZT (EBOOK EDITION)

ISBN: 9798861732086 (PAPERBACK)

PRINTED AND BOUND IN THE UNITED STATES OF AMERICA

FIRST PRINTING OCTOBER 2023

PUBLISHED BY ALIENHEAD PRESS, A DIVISION OF ALIENHEAD ENTERTAINMENT, LLC. MIAMI, FLORIDA, UNITED STATES OF AMERICA

Literally Dead: Tales of Holiday Hauntings

K.G. ANDERSON   RAMSEY CAMPBELL   V. CASTRO

CLAY MCLEOD CHAPMAN   ADRIENNE CLARKE

DOUGLAS FORD   JONATHAN JANZ   JAKE JEROME

JOHN KISTE   DARREN LIPMAN   BROOKE MACKENZIE

TIM MCWHORTER   LISA MORTON   JOHN PALISANO

HAILEY PIPER   ELEANOR SCIOLISTEIN

KATHERINE TRAYLOR   CHET WILLIAMSON

STEPHANIE M. WYTOVICH

EDITED BY
GABY TRIANA

"If I could work my will, every idiot who goes about with 'Merry Christmas' on his lips, should be boiled with his own pudding, and buried with a stake of holly through his heart."

- **Charles Dickens,** *A Christmas Carol*

For Queen Mama

Aug 3, 1939 - Sept 10, 2023

Table of Contents

Introduction

I BURIED MY MOTHER TODAY.

I wish that was the beginning of a fictional story, but it's not. She was 84 and ready to go. Doesn't make losing my best friend any easier. I was with her when she passed. Everyone had gone home after a day of hospital visits that included singing Neil Diamond hits at her bedside and toasting her with Wendy's Frostys.

I knew my mom—she didn't want others to be there when she "left the planet." Some things were private and she never wanted to be a burden to anyone, especially my brother. Which is why she chose to pass when I was there. Because women carry other women's burdens, and she has never felt sorry for me the way she felt sorry for him (Latina mothers and their sons…if you know, you know). So, when she took her last breath and that lifeless honey-eyed gaze stared right at me, through me, possibly at a brilliant light to welcome her, I felt that burden pass to me.

This memory is yours to carry, I heard in my head. *Your nurse brother has suffered enough pain taking care of me—this one belongs to you, daughter.*

The thing is, what my mother considered to be a burden, I considered a gift. Perhaps that's because I've always been obsessed with death and the afterlife, or maybe it's because I write horror. But to me, being present at her transition was nothing short of an immense honor. She was the first to welcome me into the world, and I was the last to say goodbye at her departure.

Now the soil has been tossed, the condolences given, and the sunflowers will soon die, but I will still be here, figuring out where to go without a map. I have never known a life without her. I have never known a season without her. One thing I do know is that she passed on a tremendous love of the seasons to me and my brother, the changes that come with the turn of the great wheel, and the celebration of those changes. My mother loved Christmas. She also loved Halloween, celebrations, and traditions. I call those rituals. Maybe she was witchy and didn't know it. Maybe she knew it damn well but I didn't.

Either way, it's because of Mom I love Fall and Winter. Around my house, we call that "HallowThanksMasKah" and it's the reason with which I knew I had to follow up *Literally Dead: Tales of Halloween Hauntings* with *Tales of Holiday Hauntings*. The two go hand in hand. For a Cuban-American kid who grew up in the '70s in a bilingual household that only really knew how to celebrate Christmas nochebuena-style, this time of year held many wonders for me.

As I grew older and ventured out of my bubble, I realized, like so many other Catholic kids, that Christmas wasn't the center of everyone's world. There were other holidays! And other religions! And other traditions! This only excited me even more, opened my eyes to the possibilities. I've always loved holidays and exploring traditions, and ghost stories that tie it all together during this time of year propel me even further into that cozy vibe. While I adore the classic cautionary ghost tale, I'm also a fan of being surprised, of new twists on the traditional. If you already read *Literally Dead* Vol. 1 and are looking for more of the same, I know you are, too. Within these pages, you will find the classic Victorian ghost tale (or two), stories about mall Santas, pagan witches, geishas who serve up vengeance, grandmas who cannot let go, angry spouses, a haunted collection of first-editions, nuns who watch after us, mythical creatures of Judaism, New Year's Eve club-goers who refuse to go home, and even an ice-ice baby left on a doorstep during a blizzard.

These tales explore what a haunting means to different authors, one of the things I love most about this collection. Whether metaphysical or psychological, ghosts manifest in a multitude of ways, and never more than during the most stressful time of year, when so many of us are under pressure to create happy times for ourselves and others, expectations are rarely fulfilled, and we end the year reflecting back on our successes and failures. It's a melancholy time, to be sure, but to me, that's the experience of the holidays—whether or not you're ready for them, they come. They come and force you to partake, to spiral through the myriad emotions that encompass a time of year that asks so much of us when we have such little left to give.

Be grateful, they say. *Be joyous, prosperous, and jolly.* We shall endeavor to do our best. Oh, and Merry Christmas, Mami, wherever you are. I'll see you on the other side.

Gaby Triana
September, 2023

The Grey Road

LISA MORTON

THE HEATH, KNUTSFORD, CHRISTMAS EVE, 1825

"Oh, yes, do tell us a ghost story, Vicar."

Elizabeth looked at her aunt, surprised; just an hour ago at dinner Aunt Hannah had been gently chiding her niece about her "rather too vivid imagination."

"But Auntie," Elizabeth said, as she rose to stir the embers in The Heath's great hearth, "I thought you didn't believe in such spectral goings-on."

"Well," Aunt Hannah said, "it *is* Christmas Eve. What else would we do on this night?"

There were murmurs of approval from the other guests surrounding the hearth; Vicar Sterling's wife Margaret chuckled, his three adult offspring smiled, and their nearest neighbor, ancient little Mr. North, awoke from his drowsy state long enough to nod. Elizabeth wished that Mary, the serving girl, and Mr. Duncan, the butler, could join them as well, but she understood that Aunt Hannah—as modern as she was in other ways—would never brook such a breach of protocol. Earlier in the evening, Elizabeth had quietly hugged Mary, shaken Duncan's hand, and presented them both with carefully chosen gifts.

The Vicar took a strong sip of brandy, smacked his lips, resettled his considerable bulk in the groaning chair, and began.

"Every village and shire in England has its own ghost legends," he said, his furry brows knotted in feigned apprehension, "and Knutsford's no different. Ours is known as 'The Grey Road.'"

Elizabeth seated herself next to her aunt, who took her niece's hand in a gesture of love and approval, a gesture that Elizabeth returned. There was nowhere else on earth she would rather have been tonight than *here*, in her aunt's great red brick house, with people she'd known nearly her entire life. She missed her father, whom she hadn't seen since the summer, and her brother John, who'd thought he'd share holidays with her but the Royal Navy had other plans. But she was thankful for Aunt Hannah, who'd taken over her upbringing when Elizabeth's mother had died not long after giving birth to her, and she did so love The Heath. She also adored ghost stories; even though she'd heard the Vicar tell the story of the Grey Road before, she snuggled happily against her aunt, ready to surrender herself to the tale.

"This story," Vicar Sterling went on, "comes down from two centuries ago, and has been told in my family ever since.

"On Christmas Eve in the year 1625, a young man named John Harrington was visiting Knutsford. John was just starting out as a solicitor in London but missed his family, who had only recently moved to Knutsford. The great Tudor house that stands on the other side of the heath was the Harrington estate until it was sold thirty years back.

"The family was gathered–just as we are now!–on that

special night, relaxing after a fine Christmas meal, when young John decided to take a stroll. He left the house, walked only a short distance, and came upon a road he couldn't remember seeing before. It was a moonless night, cold and foggy, but this road seemed to glow with its own light. It stretched into the distance in both directions, as far as the eye could see."

"Father," the Vicar's youngest daughter Claire, the perpetually-impatient twenty-two-year-old, interrupted, "*do* get to the ghost, won't you?"

"I'm coming to that, my dear." He offered his child a single disapproving glance before continuing, "As John stood there, pondering, he suddenly began to shiver because the temperature had dropped abruptly. But that wasn't all that happened: the very air itself felt *charged*, causing the young man's fine hairs to rise.

"He was about to return to the warmth of his family and the fire when movement caught his eye. He looked up and beheld the strangest scene imaginable: a great horseless carriage was thundering towards him. It shone from various points of light, and John swore that he could still see his home through it. It traveled directly past him, so close that he could see the faces of the deathless passengers. It all left him so frightened he could barely remember his own name. He tried to turn and run home, but his feet tangled in a briar, he fell, was knocked unconscious and not found until the following morning, half-frozen but still alive and with the tale to tell."

The Vicar leaned back in his chair, assuming an air of satisfied completion.

"What?" Claire asked. "Not even a real ghost? No withered hag stalking the hallways of the ancient castle? What sort of ghost story is that?"

"It's *our* ghost story," replied the Vicar. "And we don't have a castle."

The middle Sterling child, Philip, smirked and said, "I suspect the only spirits involved with this tale came from a bottle."

William, the oldest, added, "Or a knock on the head after tripping in a briar patch. You're lucky, Claire–you've always slept through it in the past."

Elizabeth saw the Vicar about to protest and blurted out, "I think it's a fascinating story."

Those assembled all turned to peer at her curiously. "Do you?" asked the Vicar.

"Oh, quite. There are so many things to consider. For example: why do these ghostly events seem to occur so often on Christmas Eve? Is there something special about the night that causes such occurrences? Perhaps some confluence of seasons, being so close to the winter solstice, and the energy created by gatherings like ours causes shifts in our reality."

Philip cocked one handsome eyebrow at the fifteen-year-old before asking, "And how many spirits have *you* partaken of tonight, dear Elizabeth?"

Aunt Hannah frowned. "Philip, Elizabeth's not the type of girl to sneak sips from the sherry keg."

Philip snickered as Elizabeth felt herself redden, hoping it would be perceived as charming. She added, "Just speculating, for amusement."

"I wonder," asked the Vicar's wife, the dowdy Margaret, "if you are familiar with mesmerism?"

The question caused Elizabeth to blink; she'd never imagined Margaret to be interested in such arcane topics. "Only in passing, I'm afraid."

Margaret said, "Mr. Mesmer's philosophy suggests something not dissimilar to what you're proposing, Miss Stevenson.

He believes the universe is under the control of magnetism, and that we can effect health wonders by learning to properly align our own magnetic poles, something best accomplished in a group that he calls a séance."

"How fascinating. It sounds as if both Mr. Mesmer and I suspect the universe might be full of greater mysteries and miracles than we can imagine."

Aunt Hannah peered at her proudly as she squeezed her hand. "You *do* have a way with words, dear."

Elizabeth hadn't told her aunt that she'd begun writing stories while at school. Since she maintained her status as an exemplary student, she knew that Hannah couldn't truly complain . . . but she also suspected that Auntie would rather see her pretty niece married well than entertaining notions of trying to become a published writer, so she kept her new habit to herself.

Elizabeth abruptly rose. "I'm going out," she announced.

Hannah looked up in mild alarm. "Child, whatever for?"

"To look for the Grey Road, of course."

Elizabeth started for the front entry. Hannah rose halfway out of her seat. "But Elizabeth, it's freezing cold out there!"

As if by magic, Mary was there with Elizabeth's blue floor-length pelisse coat, holding it out for her to put on. "I'll be fine, Auntie. Besides, I shan't be long, I imagine."

Ignoring the protests behind her, Elizabeth opened the front door and stepped out. Behind her, Mary held the door, leaning out to whisper, "Be careful out there, Miss. I do admire your bravery." Mary closed the door, shutting out heat, light, and protests.

The night was quiet, the street lit only by the amber glow from nearby windows; the cold was a physical blow, sudden and sharp, but Elizabeth didn't regret her decision; she was fifteen, and her constitution was more than adequate in defense against the chill. Across Heathside, the open expanse of gorse and marsh sat still, no leaf ruffled by a soft night breeze.

Elizabeth hadn't thought to ask the Vicar if the old tales gave any further instructions on finding the Grey Road, so she arbitrarily turned left, striding along the street with the heath to her right. Her breath puffed out before her and she clutched at herself, chilled despite her coat and fortitude.

Truthfully, she didn't really expect to see anything not of this earth; she was far more interested in the curiosities of society than the oddities of superstition. That, in fact, was really why she was out here, enduring the penetrating cold on a moonless Christmas Eve: she wanted to understand the fact behind the fiction. Surely legends like this one didn't simply come about on their own; Elizabeth was well acquainted not just with the regional ghost stories found all over her own England, but she'd also read German and French tales of spirits and revenants as well. Surely, she'd thought on more than one occasion, there must be *something* that inspired these bits of spectral folklore?

She'd also given thought to writing a ghost story of her own. She was generally more interested in exploring the workings of British society–poor versus rich, employee versus employer, tenant versus landowner, male versus female–but she found no reason she couldn't explore society within the confines of a ghost story. Elizabeth appreciated the way that Mrs. Radcliffe had edged toward questions of wealth and status with novels like *The Mysteries of Udolpho* and *The Italian*, but she thought it was a notion that could be taken even further.

These thoughts consumed Elizabeth as she strode down Heathside, and so she was slow to notice a strange sight ahead, just where her own street spilled out into open countryside: the landscape was bathed in a silvery glow despite the moon's absence. She put aside her creative ponderings to focus on the source of the luminescence. As she walked past the last house and into the wild, the glow increased, taking on shape and definition—a road, stretching diagonally before her. To the left, it wound through the countryside until it vanished behind a wall of trees; to the right, it skirted the heath, disappearing into the distance beyond.

The Grey Road.

Elizabeth stopped, staring in disbelief at the impossible thing that lay before her. She knew this area well, had played here many times as a child, and so she was aware that there was no road like the one she saw now. The temperature had dropped, causing her to shiver as she surveyed the spectral realm. Part of her begged to turn back, to the safety of home and Aunt Hannah, but she willed herself to stay, to see if the rest of the old story was true.

After a few moments of waiting, Elizabeth saw the silver glow moving in the distance . . . or rather, something was moving *within* the glow, something that carried its own light. It approached her, dazzling with sudden brightness. There was no sound as it drew near, but she experienced something like being deep underwater when a boat went overhead, causing everything to ripple. The object slowed as it drew near. It was a metallic carriage with four wheels but no horses, low to the ground, an indefinable color. It stopped a short distance from her, and she glimpsed faces beyond the carriage's windows–two young men. One had dark skin and hair; the other, light brown hair and a short beard.

For an instant, Elizabeth and the bearded man locked eyes. Then the carriage and the Grey Road faded out quickly, as if the wick on an oil lamp had been turned down all the way.

Elizabeth felt the weather shift, gaining at least ten degrees in a heartbeat.

I've just stared into the eyes of a ghost, she thought, before amending, *and perhaps more importantly–it stared into me.*

Her own heart was pounding, yet she was shocked to find herself laughing, nearly mad with wonder. After a few seconds, she turned, still grinning, to make her way back to The Heath. She thought about what she would tell the others and decided on . . . nothing. She would tell them only that she'd had a splendid walk. She would keep this gift only for herself, a Christmas miracle that she knew had just changed her life in ways she couldn't yet see.

HEATHWAITE, KNUTSFORD, CHRISTMAS EVE, 2025

"It's a bit spooky out here, isn't it?" Tony said, before looking down at his phone again.

Amjad crouched over the steering wheel, peering into the darkness beside the road. "I prefer to think of it as simply rural. Did we miss Knutsford?"

Tony turned the phone upside-down before shrugging and putting it down. "Well, we knew it was a long drive . . ."

Amjad glanced at the car's dashboard. "It's almost midnight. God, I'm starving."

"I know, I'm sorry." Tony leaned over to rub his husband's shoulder. "I feel bad, after everything you and David and Maria did to set this up. I've ruined Christmas."

Amjad took Tony's hand, looking away from the empty road long enough to offer a smile. "There's no one else I'd rather be ruined with."

They drove in silence for a time, Amjad concentrating on the search for the missing village, Tony thinking–as he had recently–about his late mum. It had been two months since he'd lost her to cancer; he'd read the books about grieving and understood how difficult it would be, but his most fundamental question–*why her?*–had gone unanswered. Tony had never been religious, and he felt simply hypocritical trying to turn to any god now. Amjad had been there as he'd questioned and raged, bringing Tony more grace than anything else he'd found, but even that wasn't enough. His mind was a closed system, circling around and around his mother's death, an endless Möbius strip. Two weeks ago, he'd become aware of how he was neglecting his beautiful, loving husband of two years, of how he'd denied Amjad any ability to help, and so he'd agreed to this holiday in the country with their friends, who'd rented a house in tiny, distant Knutsford.

Tony was trying to push away (again) that image of Mum, pale and husky, dying in a hospital bed, too sick to even enjoy the beloved books she'd built her life and academic career around, when a sign approached pointing the way to Knutsford. It provoked a victorious cry from Amjad. "At last! I could definitely use a pint or three. David's bringing that craft brew from America that we like."

"I'd be happy with some dinner leftovers myself."

Amjad grinned. "Maria's Christmas goose . . ." He turned onto the indicated road, and both men were relieved to see houses dotting the landscape. This late on a Christmas Eve the windows were dark, the roads empty; for some reason Tony shivered.

"Where do we go next?" Amjad asked.

"Oh, right." Tony picked up his phone, jabbed at the screen to open the map again . . . and frowned.

"What's wrong?"

"That's strange . . . the phone is completely drained. I'd swear it was at seventy percent just five minutes ago."

Amjad slowed down so he could concentrate on reaching into a pocket for his phone. "Here, try mine."

Tony pressed the power button, but the screen stayed black. "It's dead, too."

"That's impossible. I charged it just before we left, and I haven't used it since."

The radio went silent, "Little Drummer Boy" dying in a final burst of static. "What is going on?" Tony said.

"I don't know . . ." The car, a new electric model they'd purchased over the summer, began to slow. Amjad punched frantically at buttons on the dash, but they came to a dead stop. "This isn't good."

"So," Tony said, "I guess we walk from here . . ."

"I guess. I don't think it's that far now . . ." Amjad broke off as he peered out the passenger side window. "What is *that*?"

Tony turned to follow his gaze and saw a strange glow forming outside the car; it had the silvery sheen of moonlight breaking through storm clouds, but the sky overhead was clear, the moon new.

A figure took form in the glimmer–a woman, wearing the clothing of two centuries ago. She was pretty, young, and looking directly at Tony with an expression of shock. Tony realized he could see the surrounding countryside *through* her, except there'd been houses there just a moment before.

"What . . ." It was all Amjad could get out.

Tony's heart thundered as he stared into the young woman's eyes. There was something familiar there, something that somehow reminded him of Mum. He shook, his panted breaths made small clouds on the window.

The glow died, a fast dissolve, taking the girl and the countryside with it. Amjad and Tony both jumped when "Silent Night" burst from the radio as the car started again.

"What did we just see?" Amjad whispered.

Tony realized he was gulping air although he'd felt no fear, no sense of menace from the . . . the . . .

"Ghost," he said, finishing his thought.

Amjad answered, "No. No way. Ghosts don't exist."

"Then," Tony said, turning to look into his husband's eyes, "you tell me what we just saw."

"I . . . need one of those pints."

They were less than two minutes from the house their friends David and Maria had rented for Christmas. When they arrived, their friends greeted them with hugs and concern.

"Everything okay?" David asked, peering at them.

"We just . . ." Tony struggled for words as they moved into the house, still redolent with the scent of food, Maria bringing out warm plates for them. "The strangest thing just happened." He looked to Amjad who could only shrug.

"Eat, and then tell us." Maria indicated two plates she'd set on the dining room table. She and David were seated, looking on curiously as Amjad and Tony sat, still too rattled to eat.

"We saw a ghost," Tony finally said. "Our car failed, and everything stopped, and . . ."

"'The Grey Road,'" David said.

Amjad gulped from the bottle David had set before them before asking, wide-eyed, "The what?"

"It's a local legend–the Grey Road. You know, every British village has its local home-grown horror movie, right?"

Tony, who'd finally recovered enough to begin eating, said around a mouthful of potatoes, "Isn't there one at Ingham about these marble figures that rise from their tombstone every August?"

David nodded. "Right. Well, ours is about a mysterious road that appears only on Christmas Eve, sometimes complete with horseless carriages."

Amjad and Tony exchanged a look before Tony said, "We

saw a road, I think, but not that other stuff. But there was . . . a girl."

"Dressed from two hundred years ago," Amjad added.

"How well did you see her?" Maria asked.

Amjad continued to eat, leaving Tony to respond. "Well enough."

"What did she look like?" David asked.

"Very young–maybe fifteen. Pretty. Wearing a long blue coat." He laughed as he added, "It may be a strange thing to say of a ghost, but she looked as surprised by us as we were by her."

Maria rose, left the room, returned a few seconds later with an old clothbound book. She flipped it open to the frontispiece and showed it to Tony and Amjad. "Does she look familiar?"

Tony didn't need to study the portrait to recognize it instantly, but he turned to his husband for final confirmation before saying, "That's her. Who is she?"

Maria shifted the book slightly, holding the title page up for them to see:*Tales of Mystery and Horror* by Elizabeth Gaskell.

Tony dropped his fork, the loud clatter causing all eyes to turn to him. When Amjad saw his husband's mouth trying unsuccessfully to form a comment, he set down his own utensil and took Tony's hand. "What?"

Tony's eyes watered as he finally got out a hoarse response. "Elizabeth Gaskell . . . she was my mum's favorite writer."

Closing the book and setting it aside, Maria said, "She lived here in Knutsford, right down the street. In fact, they re-named it after her. It's now Gaskell Avenue."

David said, "She also wrote one of the greatest ghost stories of all time: 'The Old Nurse's Story.' It's about a poor domestic in a wealthy household that's haunted by the sins of its past. It's a classic."

But Tony barely heard; he was struggling to reconcile what

had just happened to him with his mother's death. He let the tears drop, squeezed his husband's fingers tighter, and after a few seconds saw the gift he'd been given: to know that his Mum continued somewhere, inside some other miracle.

"Thank you, Elizabeth," he murmured. It was the best Christmas gift imaginable.

...Haunt Me Then

CHET WILLIAMSON

"Go ahead . . . guess what it is. You'll never."

Patricia hefted the wrapped present. "Books," she said to Alec, then ran her finger along the edge of the slab. "*Three* books. All the same size." The lights from the Christmas tree shone on her face, as she smiled wearily. "Do we really have room for another three-volume set?"

"I think we'll find room for this one," Alec said, sliding closer to her on the carpeted floor. "No guesses?"

She cocked her head. "*Lord of the Rings*? No, we have *several* of those. A Library of America set? Cookbooks?"

"No and no. Open it."

Patricia, as she always did, carefully removed the tape from the ends, then folded the festive paper back without tearing it. "What on earth," she said as she exposed the volumes to light. They were uniformly bound in a dark blue cloth with gold stamping on the spines: WUTHERING HEIGHTS I, WUTHERING HEIGHTS II, and AGNES GREY III.

"Lovely!" Patricia held all three in her hands so the spines were facing her. "*Agnes Grey*—that's Anne Brontë's, isn't it? I've never read it."

"Yes, well, you can now," Alec said. "But open the first volume, will you? Um, carefully?"

She looked at him curiously, then set the other two volumes down and opened the first. She saw immediately that the paper was old and knew that the books had been rebound. But she had no idea how old until she examined the title page. When she did, she felt a chill.

"Read it aloud," Alec said with deep satisfaction.

"'Wuthering Heights, a novel,'" she read with a quavering voice. "'By Ellis Bell. In three volumes, Volume I. London . . . Thomas Cautley Newby, Publisher . . . 'Oh, my God . . . '73 Mortimer Square, Cavendish Square . . . 1847?' Alec, this isn't . . . it couldn't be . . ."

"A first edition. Yes. Of your all-time favorite novel. Merry Christmas, my love." He leaned over and pecked her cheek.

"These . . . all three?"

"The publisher," Alec said, "who was a bit of a bastard, liked to issue books in three volumes, but Wuthering Heights was only long enough for two, so he added on sister Anne's novel as well. They're all there."

"Where on earth did you get them?"

"In Dingle."

"What?"

He nodded. They'd toured the west of Ireland for several weeks the previous May. "That little used bookshop I was rummaging through while you were looking in the gift shops for presents? Near the back there was a water-stained box full of . . . rubbish, I suppose. Older books in various states of decrepitude. Musty, some smelling of mildew, damaged bindings, some without bindings at all. I asked about them, and the owner said she'd gotten them from an estate sale. She'd taken out the good stuff and didn't know when she might get to looking through that *junk,* as she called it. Told me I could have anything in there I liked for five euros each.

"You know me, I started digging, even opening the badly damaged ones, just in case. I found volume two of *Wuthering Heights* first. The front board and spine were missing, but when I turned to the title page, my heart nearly stopped. I had no idea it was a first, but the fact that it was by 'Ellis Bell' rather than Emily Brontë told me it was old.

"I kept digging and actually turned up the other two—the *Agnes Grey* first, otherwise I might not have known to look for it. Then finally the first volume of *Wuthering Heights*. All the spines were missing, and what little of the boards were left were in terrible condition, but the actual contents seemed complete. I looked at the other titles and took two more as . . . camouflage, I guess you'd say. A horrible condition reprint of *Tom Brown's School Days*, and a beat-up and *aromatic* volume of Tennyson. I put them on top of the pile, but I needn't have bothered. She just glanced at it, said 'Twenty-five euros then,' and I paid her cash. 'Better keep those out in the sun for a while," she said as I left. 'Get that musty smell out.'"

Patricia tentatively sniffed at the pages. "I can't smell anything," she said, "except old paper."

"It was just the Tennyson," Alec said. "I dumped it in a trashcan along with the Tom Brown as soon as I got around the corner. Then tucked these away with the other books I'd bought."

"And never told me," Patricia said, still looking at the title page.

"I had plans," Alec said. "Soon as we got back I took them in to Brian at Dogstar Books, and he confirmed what I'd found out online—they *were* firsts."

"They must be worth a fortune."

"There were only three hundred and fifty printed of this

edition—and Thomas Newby told the Brontës he'd printed a hundred *fewer*. A bit of a bastard, like I said. Even in the condition they were in, Brian figured six figures. A rebound copy sold over five years ago for over two hundred thousand." Patricia looked up at him, eyes wide. "And *yes*, I called Thome and insured them."

"Oh, Alec, we can't *keep* these . . ."

"We can keep them for as long as we like. If we want to cash in when we retire, we can. But *you*, my love, will get to reread *Wuthering Heights* as it was first issued . . . and as Emily Brontë held it in her hands."

"You had them rebound?" Patricia asked, opening the second volume.

He took the first from her and ran his fingers over the cloth. "I got Tony Haverstick to do it. It's a replica of the original binding and stamping. The little that was left of the original boards wasn't salvageable."

"They're gorgeous." Patricia leaned over and kissed him square on the lips. "It's the best present I've ever gotten. I'm going to start reading it tonight."

"Wonderful. Just not in the tub."

FOR THE NEXT SEVERAL NIGHTS, Patricia curled up in bed and reread *Wuthering Heights* in the edition that had appeared in Emily Brontë's lifetime. The volume, not too large, nestled neatly on her chest, and the paper felt smooth and almost liquid under her fingers, as good, aged rag paper always felt, Alec told her.

It was, she thought, nearly a religious experience, and as she read she felt the presence of something, or someone, perhaps Emily Brontë herself, or the no less real spirits of Heathcliff or Cathy Earnshaw, or the other characters who populated the novel. She was careful not to read too quickly, so as not to reduce the intensity of the experience, and to make that first, thrilling reading last as long as possible.

Still, she could not resist following the story onward, and by the third night, she was nearing the end of the first volume. As the story began to darken, Patricia felt a vague oppression slowly steal over her, and she wished Alec were beside her. But he was in his study, where he preferred to read at night sitting in a chair because his back pained him when reading in bed. He had been reading a book with a horrible title, *The Graves Are Walking*, a history of the Irish famine that he'd bought when they'd visited Ireland. The talk about the Dingle bookstore had reminded him that he hadn't yet read it.

Patricia tried again to concentrate on Brontë's words but had the uncanny sensation that she was not alone in the bedroom. Their cat, Angie, lay pillow-like at the foot of the bed but stirred in her sleep, as little whimpers emitted from her throat. Patricia's eyes went back to the page, but the shadow of darkness beyond the rim of her reading light seemed to thicken, and in the corner of her eye she sensed a slight movement and swung her head toward the darkest part of the room.

At that instant, the cat, ever so placid, raised her head and opened her eyes, and stared directly at the spot where Patricia had detected motion. She looked from the cat to the darkness but could see nothing. The cat leapt off the bed and ran out the door, with the slight snarling hiss she always gave when tussling with a particularly annoying toy. Patricia, her hand trembling, reached toward the gooseneck light on the headboard and aimed it into the dark corner.

For a split second, she thought she saw something, something approximately shaped like a human figure, but then it wasn't there, and she rationalized that it had been imagination, a trick of light and darkness. Still, she looked at the newly illuminated place for a good minute before she finally relaxed. As for the cat, Angie had felt her tension and responded in kind, that was all. She turned back to the book and read until Alec came in to go to bed.

The following evening, she and Alec had done their usual end-of-the-year closet cleanout, putting clothes that they no longer wore into plastic bags to donate to the local Goodwill. There wasn't much this year, just a few winter coats that they'd worn out or had gotten tired of.

"I'll put the bag in the car now," Alec said, "and take it over tomorrow." But when he came back in from outside, he said the car was locked, so he just left the bag by the trunk.

"It's snowing," Patricia said.

"It'll be okay under the carport."

After two episodes of a BBC series they were binge-watching, Patricia took a shower and climbed into bed with *Wuthering Heights*. The cat joined her, while Alec went to read in the den. Patricia tried to shake off the unease she'd felt the previous night and discovered herself quickly immersed in the story again. She was at the point where Heathcliff is told of Catherine's death. His furious response was one of Patricia's favorite passages in the novel, and she found herself saying the words aloud, quite softly, as she read them.

"' . . . May she wake in torment . . . And I pray one prayer—I repeat it till my tongue stiffens—Catherine Earnshaw, may you not rest, as long as I am living! You said I killed you—haunt me, then! The murdered *do* haunt their murderers, I believe. I know that ghosts *have* wandered on earth. Be with me always—take any form—drive me mad! . . .'"

Patricia stopped reading. The room had grown cold, not simply chilly, but freezing, as though the bedroom had no walls nor windows, and the snow was all around her. The cat had gotten to her feet and was standing, spine arched, the fur on her back sticking straight up. She hissed and spat and dashed from the room.

Something moved in the relative darkness of the corner, something tall and angular and pale. Patricia wanted to close her eyes against it, but she couldn't. She couldn't move at all. She could only watch as the thing encroached upon the small, weak circle of light the bedside lamp produced. And then she saw it fully.

It was as pale as paper and naked as birth, neither male nor female, adult nor child, but a gaunt and stark combination of all. Sparse hair as white as its flesh framed its long face, a face with cheeks so hollow the ridge of the jaw jagged against the thin flesh, eyes deep and sunken, twin pools of yellow rheum in shadowed craters, the nearly toothless mouth agape, pale tip of tongue hanging over bloodless lower lip.

The body was worse. The muscles of arms and legs had thinned to bands under the ivory flesh so that the bones stood out, making the figure appear to be constructed of sticks over hide. Two dried, long useless breasts dangled on either side of the visible breastbone, which served as the keystone for the ribs that arched above the concavity of the stomach, through the flesh of which Patricia could see the spine. Shriveled genitals hung like dried fruit from between thighs around which she could have wrapped her fingers. The creature seemed at once of great age and great youth, child, crone, babe, dotard; laden with sin, filled with innocence, worthy of scorn, deserving of pity.

But the emotion Patricia felt most emphatically was fear. If the thing before her had been more ghostly and less substantial, had it glowed with a light of its own, or had the wall and furniture been visible *through* it, she would have felt terror in the presence of the supernatural. But it was as real as she, as real as her surroundings. It was solid and reflected light. It was there in the room with her, at the foot of her bed, and she knew that if it came closer, she could reach out a hand and touch it, just as it could touch her.

That thought, of those white bony fingers reaching out and coming into contact with her flesh, freed her, and, for some reason she couldn't name, with her first voluntary movement, she closed both the book she was holding and her eyes. Then she prayed.

When she opened her eyes, she was alone in the room. She lay there, head against the pillow for some time, trying to slow her breathing, waiting for her beating heart to cease its heavy pounding. When it did, she began to cry, not out of terror or even relief, but tears of pity for that most sorrowful thing that had shared her room.

Her crying grew louder, until at last, it became great, heaving sobs that brought Alec into the room, his book still in his hand. "What is it?" he said, alarmed. "Pat, what's wrong?"

Trembling and weeping, she told him what she had read and how she had read it aloud, and then what she had seen, and tried to make him see it too, in everything she had felt as she observed it.

"Naked?" Alec asked. "It was naked, and you were cold?"

"It was freezing in here, I swear, and it wasn't a dream, it *wasn't*. Look!" She opened the book. "The bookmark is still there where I was reading—see?"

He took the book and read the words silently: *You said I killed you—haunt me, then! The murdered do haunt their murderers, I believe.*

"Naked," he said again softly. "And cold."

"Yes," she whispered. "And *so* sad. So pitiful."

"Pat," he said, and she had to strain to hear. "I was reading, just now, in the book about the famine . . ." He held up the history book with the horrible title. "The people in all parts of Ireland were starving. Dying of hunger. You knew that. But it got so bad that they actually pawned their clothing for money to buy food. It says that in Mayo in December of 1846-47 people were publicly naked, wrapped in whatever rags they could find. Barefoot in the snow, crawling, too weak to stand."

Though the warmth had returned to the room, Patricia still shuddered.

"There were whole families *completely* naked," Alec went on. "And instead of only starving, they froze as well."

"What . . . happened to the clothing?" Patricia asked.

"Nearly all of it went to England. Where it was pulped. In paper mills." Alec reached out and touched the pages of her open book. "Rag paper. And I doubt that anyone, least of all a man like Thomas Newby, cared about where it came from as long as it was cheap." He picked up the book and turned to the title page, where they both looked once again at the date. 1847.

After a long moment, she looked at Alec and said, almost desperately, "Did you . . . see it? Did you . . . hear anything?"

"Just before I heard you crying . . . I thought I heard the back door close. I thought maybe you were looking out at the snow."

She shook her head, her eyes widening. "It wasn't me."

They both had the same idea at once. She got out of bed, and he helped her into her robe and slippers. Then they walked through the house to the back door where they turned on the outside light and looked through the window.

No one was there. But the plastic bag that had held the coats they had planned to donate the next day was lying next to the car, open and empty, like a skin discarded by a snake.

"Someone took it," Alec said with a certainty Patricia knew was feigned.

Not replying, she put on her coat and handed Alec his own, then slipped her feet into some shoes. She unlocked and opened the door. They stepped outside onto the carport and walked across the cement to where the still gently falling snow lay on the uncovered ground. There was not a single footprint anywhere.

A wind came up, blowing cold. It filled the empty garbage bag with itself, and blew it out into the snowy night, a dark ghost that fluttered and rippled and lifted and vanished into the black.

A Geisha's Christmas in Kyoto

ADRIENNE CLARKE

Chiyo watched the lights twinkling outside her window with a kind of weary resentment. Another Christmas Eve. Once, the brightly lit lanterns lining Kyoto's streets would have made her want to jump up and dance. She would have put on her most luxurious kimono, the blue silk shot with gold threads, and fastened a scarlet obi around her waist. She would have dressed her long, silky black hair in an elaborate updo of coils and glittering jewels that would have made her the envy of the other geishas. Everyone knew she had the most magnificent natural hair. No false pieces for her. But that was many years ago; so many she'd lost count.

Now Christmas Eve was just another day. She still wore her kimono, but there were tiny holes at the hem and her once bright obi had faded to a dull brown, the colour of dried blood. She no longer put up her hair or even brushed it. The shining crown she'd been so proud of hung down her back in dull, lank strands like rivulets of black water. Her once porcelain skin, buffed and powdered to geisha white perfection, was cracked and yellow. The face, adored by so many, had begun to peel around the edges. A forgotten masterpiece left to rot. She had devoted her life to beauty, but in return, it had brought her nothing but misery and destruction. She avoided all mirrors, but when she occasionally caught sight of her reflection in the window, she felt a stab of horror, followed by a strange sense of satisfaction. All vanity was behind her now. Only her soul remained.

Tired of the lights, she moved away from the window and glided through the teahouse, invisible to all its inhabitants. The sharp clacking of her wooden clogs against the floor were soundless to everyone but her. It would be especially busy tonight. In Japan, Christmas Eve was a time for lovers. No one wanted to be home alone on a night like this. Happy couples strolled the cobblestone streets looking for the most elegant place to sit down and stare at one another over steaming cups of matcha. A few early birds had already stumbled inside, looking for the best tables. In the old days, guests would have sat on tatami mats carefully arranged on the floor, but the new owner preferred the more relaxed ryurei style.

Chiyo watched the arrivals with a mixture of curiosity and envy. The envy had lessened over the years, but tonight she felt its sharp edges surge beneath her breast, cutting grooves in the heart that had long since ceased to beat. The sight of so many men and women–their dark eyes alight with the promise of love and romance–still had the power to stir her. Once, she had the power to ignite such a look in the eyes of any man. How she'd delighted in that first glance! The expression of hopeless longing that would come over their faces and the tingling of excitement she felt knowing they were wholly in her power. Their lovesick gazes made her feel strong, invincible. Now she understood how vulnerable she'd been all those years. Men had paid thousands of yen for the pleasure of her company, but in the end, she'd paid the highest price of all.

She scanned the room and was reminded yet again that her flower-and-willow world no longer existed. Through discipline and talent, she had learned how to conjure an air of mystery and fascination. Born a poor farmer's daughter, Chiyo had transformed herself into a living work of art. Men craved her company because she took the threads of an ordinary life and spun them into something rare and beautiful. Reality had no place in a geisha's house of dreams. Geishas didn't have sad stories, until, suddenly, they did. Most nights the past seemed far away; a half-forgotten dream, but on Christmas Eve it came back to her, as vivid as her cherry-lacquered lips. She studied the couples seated across from each other, admiring the way soft candlelight gently erased lines and shadows, creating a soft radiance in even the most ordinary face.

The screen door slid open, and a new couple entered. For a moment, the room seemed to tremble around the edges, and Chiyo felt herself caught by the couple's bright aura. She watched, transfixed, as the couple sat down at the table in front of the window. They wanted to be seen. And why not? Beauty was her business, and it had been many years since she was in the presence of such exquisite perfection. They were young, enjoying the first blush of dewy youth that lasts only a short time before maturing into something different. She tilted her head to one side, admiring them. Both man and woman were lovely, but his beauty was the more intoxicating of the two. And he knew it. She could tell by the way he sat down— his awareness of the other eyes in the room, taking in his artfully tousled hair, immaculately cut white shirt, his flawless pale-skinned complexion. In another time, he might have been a geisha himself.

His companion leaned across the table to whisper something in his ear, but he pretended not to hear, and Chiyo noted the arrogant tilt of his chin. She also saw the hurt in the young woman's eyes as she pretended to study the menu. When the man finally deigned to speak to her, she was all smiles again, like a puppy eager for her master's approval. *She's used to this*, Chiyo thought. Used to being his creature. To smile when he smiles and be afraid when he refuses to smile. She'd known men like this before. Men who couldn't love women for themselves, only for the light of admiration their presence shone on them. She continued to watch, interested now. The couples seated at the surrounding tables gazed at each other over bowls of fragrant tea and plates of flower-shaped sweets. Lost in the exquisite magic of being young and in love, they had come to celebrate. But not this couple. The young man with the handsome face and cold heart had come for something quite different. A scent of danger rose from his soft, unblemished skin. Trained from girlhood to understand the ways of men, she never failed to spot a beetle among the blossoms.

He continued to speak, his voice low so only his companion could hear, and Chiyo watched the colour fade from the woman's cheeks and rosebud lips until she seemed as much a ghost as Chiyo herself. The woman must leave him before it's too late. Chiyo remembered how it felt to want to be everything to everyone–like you might cease to exist if you failed. She put a hand to her hair, an old nervous habit, and was disgusted when it came away coated with grimy black strands.

Chiyo drew closer, debating whether to allow herself to be seen. It required so much energy. In her time, a geisha was like the sun. When she walked into the room it became brighter; but now her powers of illumination came with a cost. She'd likely become ill and exhausted for days, but something about the man would not let her go. He reminded her of someone; the memory flitted around the edges of her mind without quite taking form. A former customer, perhaps? She stared at one of the lanterns, summoning its energy, trying to draw the light into her chest. She closed her eyes and took a deep steadying breath before approaching the table and giving a graceful bow. "Konbanwa. Have you made your choices?"

Too distressed to speak, the woman took no notice of Chiyo's formal greeting. She stared at the table as though the answer to her troubles was written there. The man, on the other hand, smiled widely, his lips too full and too red. On a woman, they would have bestowed a look of sensuality, but they gave him an unpleasant, hungry look. She could imagine those lips and the teeth behind them, devouring, always devouring. Afterward, he would smack those lips in a kind of sated satisfaction. "I'll have the matcha, a plate of manju, and of course, some of your famous wagashi."

"And for you?" she said gently to the woman who remained transfixed by the table.

The woman raised her head slowly, and when she finally looked at Chiyo she had a dazed look in her eyes, almost as if she'd forgotten where she was. "Just tea," she whispered, her voice barely audible. Chiyo treated the couple to another geisha bow before drifting towards the kitchen. She sighed deeply, fatigue already tugging at her human form. Nothing was more draining than the emotions of the living.

Chiyo went to a separate room where she whisked the finely milled matcha powder with hot water. She closed her eyes as she worked, soothed as she always was by the tea's grassy and subtly sweet scent. When the tea and sweets were ready, she brought them to the couple's table where she continued to observe the man's calculated dance of kindness and cruelty. A half smile followed by the slight down-turning of the mouth. Sometimes, he would lean his body into the woman's, and she would half-close her eyes, anticipating a kiss, then he would pull away from her as if repulsed.

He ate his food with gusto, red lips fastened greedily around the sweets while the sipped her bowl of tea as if the healing drink was liquid sadness. *Why does she put up with him?* Chiyo wondered. Women had all the world before them now, yet the attraction to bad men had failed to lose its power. The man continued to eat and Chiyo frowned at the careless way he held his chopsticks. There seemed to be no end to his bad manners. Someone really ought to teach him a lesson. If he'd been one of her customers, she would have refused to eat with him. Beauty alone did not secure your place in the world. She should know.

The couple pushed away their tea, and Chiyo gave a gentle sigh of relief. Such an evening for sighing! Weary of their sad romance, she was for ready for them to be gone so she could rest. Still, she resolved to hold onto her physical form a while longer. It was Christmas, after all. In the absence of friends, family and brightly wrapped presents, she might at least enjoy the suppleness of her limbs. The man stood up to put on his soft leather jacket and tie a white scarf around his slender neck. The woman, still flustered and ill at ease, struggled with the buttons on her own jacket, but he made no move to help her.

Finally, the unhappy couple left the teahouse, but instead of watching them go, Chiyo gave in to an impulse to follow them. She couldn't go far; her physical body must obey certain rules, but she might follow them to the end of the street. Far enough for her to . . . what? She hadn't decided yet. A scare? Or something more?

She slipped through the door and joined them outside where they'd already begun to quarrel. The woman cried softly into the sleeve of her jacket while the man shouted.

Chiyo's heart fluttered. Many years had passed since a man had screamed insults at her, but she remembered every cruel word—the shape of his lips curled into a sneer, the rank scent of stale beer that seeped from his pores. She wasn't afraid. Believing herself untouchable in her geisha armour of jewels and paint, she'd laughed in his face. How dare he, a mere craftsman, imagine himself entitled to her company? But when he pulled a long, shining knife from his belt, she knew she'd misjudged him. There were no limits to a man's ego, no matter how lowly his status. She had paid for her laughter that night with her life.

The man still shouted, and the woman still cried as they made their way down the street. Chiyo hung back, not wanting to see any more. She would have let them go, returned to the teahouse for a glass of sake in front of the fire, if the man hadn't made one final mistake. Just as Chiyo turned away, a tiny whimper snapped her attention back to the couple. The lanterns overhead illuminated the man's form as he reached out and struck the woman so hard across the face, she fell to the ground.

Gifted with a dancer's step, Chiyo moved soundlessly, her clogs barely touching the ground. Neither the man nor the woman, who lay crumpled at his feet, heard her approach. They didn't see the long, shining silver hairpin in her hand, sharp as a dagger. In one thrust, she stabbed the man with all her remaining strength in the side of his neck. Blood cascaded onto his snowy white scarf, turning it scarlet. It surprised her, really, how quickly all that anger and arrogance faded away to nothing. Now he, too, lay on the ground where the woman screamed as if it were her blood staining the ground. Chiyo briefly laid a comforting hand on the young woman's shoulder before moving away. *The girl should count herself lucky. She'd had a narrow escape.*

When she reached the door of the teahouse, Chiyo paused, stopping to admire the twinkling streetlights. How pretty they were. Like stars. How could she have grown weary of their brightness? She went inside the teahouse, her elegant head held high as she carved a graceful path through the room. When she reached the mirror, instead of turning away, she stopped and stared. Her porcelain skin shone with a youthful radiance not even the most flawlessly applied powder could conceal. Her lips glistened with dewy softness, like a ripe cherry, and her dark eyes glittered. Not only had her beauty been restored, but she possessed the young man's, as well. Satisfied, she turned away from the mirror, grateful for unexpected gifts.

The Coat Closet

DOUGLAS FORD

On a trip home from college during the winter break, I lost my coat on a train.

I would never have taken the train in the first place, if not for the fact that my car showed signs of falling apart completely, everything from worn brakes to leaking gaskets, and my parents worried that I'd never make it alive if I drove from Virginia to Florida. My father came up with the idea of the train—specifically the Auto Train, where passengers could load their automobiles into special oversized cars and take them along for the journey.

I'd never traveled by train, but my father assured me I'd enjoy it. "I'll even pay for a sleeper," he said. "It's a unique experience, one you'll never forget. And you'll be happy you won't have to sleep in coach."

I didn't understand why I'd need to sleep at all, but he explained that the train took a full day to make the trip from its starting point in Virginia to the Sanford station in Florida. "Trust me, you'll love it," he said. Dad preferred trains over flying, and, I suppose, he expected everyone to share his sentiments. "Get the car here safely, and we'll work on it together over the holiday. You and me, like old times."

I didn't bother to ask what old times he meant. We never did much together, and I suppose that fact led to feelings of regret on his part, resentment on mine. But we never talked about such things. On top of that, a heart attack over the summer scared him, and he resolved to work less and make up for lost time. I saw no reason not to indulge him and let him make my travel plans.

I did enjoy watching the crew load my car onto the train, marveling at the sheer size of the auto carriers, as well as the length of the train. Nearby stood a family, and I overheard the father proclaim that as far as anyone knew, this train was the largest in the world. "Europe might be smoother and more efficient, but leave it up to Americans to come up with something this audacious."

Either way, I felt happy I didn't have to drive the car, especially since it developed a new rattle on the way to the station. Plus, snow began to fall, adding an additional road hazard. I imagined myself breaking down then freezing to death while I awaited help.

No fear of that on the train. In fact, the heat worked all *too* well. If not for the garlands of holly hanging from the handrails or the notes of "Jingle Bells" playing over the staticky speakers, no one would ever guessed that winter had long ago arrived. All attempts to make things feel festive seemed in vain, foolish. The porter even apologized for the temperature as he led the way to my compartment. "Isn't supposed to be this hot," he said. "You'll probably wish you brought a fan along with you." Sensing an inexperienced rail passenger, he showed me how the tiny bathroom stall functioned as both a shower and toilet. Then he asked me what time I planned to go to sleep.

I didn't expect such a personal question, and my expression made him laugh. "I ain't trying to get up in your business," he said. "I just need to know when to come back and fix your bed." He tapped the bench, pointing out how he needed to unfold it and get it arranged so that I'd have something to sleep on.

Laughing at my own embarrassment, I provided him with a time. Beads of perspiration formed on my face, so I took off my outer garment, a light brown coat I'd owned since high school. That prompted the porter to show me another feature of the compartment: a tiny door I failed to notice at first. A closet, roughly the size of an infant's coffin. "Most folks don't even notice this is here," he said, holding open the door as I hung my coat inside it.

"I wouldn't have seen it," I said.

"Nice and compact, you bet," he said, shutting the door that now contained my coat. Then he indicated the opposite wall. "Normally, you could open that up and double your space, but someone's bunking in the other side."

"Oh?"

He nodded. "A sick old lady. She's the reason for all this heat. She boarded early and started complaining about how cold she was. Even now she wants me to raise the thermostat. I say, 'Lady, it can't go no higher.' She says she understands, but then two minutes later she rings me again and tells me she can't get warm. I suppose she forgets."

I wiped the sweat from my brow, and after the porter left, I settled down to wait for the train to begin moving. Outside the window, I could see the snow falling harder while bundled passengers continued to board the train. Maybe because of my own restlessness, the heat seemed only to increase. I couldn't imagine sleeping under such conditions and I considered not even trying. I thought of the sick old lady in the compartment adjoining mine and the miserable conditions she created for everyone. I wondered if the porter gave in and found a way to make it even warmer for her. Maybe I ought to lobby for cooler temperatures, no matter how absurd that notion seemed considering the snow falling outside.

Moments later, I heard a knock at my compartment door.

Expecting the porter, I instead found a diminutive woman with white hair, nearly half my height. Her pale, mottled skin hung from her face like soaked rags, and her eyes looked rheumy and unwell. Around her shoulders hung a thin shawl.

She spoke with a faint backwoods accent and offered no introduction or greeting. "I'm cold."

I stood there, wondering how to respond, feeling tired, and vaguely irritated at this elderly woman for making it almost unbearably hot on the train.

"Is there a coat or sweater I can borrow? I'm freezing," she said, and as if for emphasis, her body shivered.

I have no justification for what I will say next. Confessing it here now brings only shame. Even a self-absorbed college student should garner sympathy for someone obviously very ill. But I resented her for the misery she brought on me and everyone else on the train. I didn't even consider my coat hanging in the tiny space of the closet. Had I offered it to her, she would have vanished inside of it, her stature so small compared to mine. It would have warmed her for sure. So selfish I was in those days, so uncaring and focused only on my own needs. The freezing temperatures she felt only existed in her mind, I believed.

I don't recall exactly what I said to her. Something about not having anything I could offer her. Maybe I wished her a good night. I'd like to think I did. Then I closed the door, leaving her shivering outside my compartment.

Sweltering, I sat there, doing my best to put her out of my

mind. Eventually, the train began moving, gradually picking up speed. From the window, I watched the snow continue to fall. I fantasized about what it would feel like to bury myself in it. The porter came and went a couple of times, once to bring me my dinner, and once to arrange my bed.

"These windows don't open, do they?" I asked before he left the second time.

He laughed and shook his head. "Don't we all *wish*."

Remembering the advice of my father, I tipped him. After he thanked me, I asked, "What's wrong with her?"

"With who?"

"The woman next door," I said, wondering how he could possibly not know who I meant.

"Oh," said the porter, "just old and under the weather. Happens to us all." Then he left.

Sleep didn't come easy that night. The train's jostling and its clacking wheels helped keep me awake the entire night. But the heat alone was enough to keep me tossing and turning all night. Even stripped down to my boxers, I perspired heavily, soaking the sheets. I gazed out the window, searching for some indication of how far we'd traveled. We would reach the Sanford station at some hour in the morning, but that seemed like an impossibly long time to continue suffering. Outside, the snow continued to fall.

Once more, I heard knocking at my compartment door, followed by a slight voice I knew belonged to my elderly neighbor. "Hello," she called out plaintively. I thought she might go away if I ignored her, but she kept knocking and calling out with that warbly voice of hers. "Hello. Hello?" Unable to take any more, I opened the door while muttering curses under my breath. At the sight of her, my volume rose. The words I spoke next should never have left my mouth. I don't recall them exactly. Or maybe I don't want to. I probably said, "What can you possibly want now? You're making everyone miserable. Absolutely fucking miserable."

No reply at first. She simply stared without comprehension. To an observer, it would have looked like a strange stand-off: a tall young man, sweating and wearing nothing but boxers, looking down at a shivering old woman. From the speaker in the passageway, the absurd lyrics to "Frosty the Snowman" became audible.

Finally, she said, "But I'm cold."

"I heard you. I truly did. But you know what? I don't think you're cold enough." My voice rose into a cruel laugh. "Not even close. Maybe when you're finally stone-cold dead, the rest of us can have some peace."

I'll always remember how she looked at me then, her expression finally registering recognition. She finally saw me for the first time. She nodded, showing she understood the individual before her. Not a good person at all.

Without another word, she turned, and I watched her walk away. Already the guilt began to surface, but I ignored it, instead slamming the door closed and walking back to the bed where I let my body fall onto the soaking sheets.

Still, sleep still refused to come. With the heat, I now felt nagging guilt.

In the morning I would apologize, I told myself. I would make it better.

Not long after, the train started to slow. Finally, it came to a dead stop.

With fresh irritation, I sat up, certain the woman had something to do with the train halting.

Sure enough, I heard voices outside my compartment door, along with the static of walkie-talkies interfering with the piped-in Christmas music, as well as the patter of anxious footsteps.

Bleary-eyed, I opened my door. That brought me face to face with the porter.

"Sir," he said. Nothing else, just *sir*, as if that word contained both a statement and a question. He looked nervous.

"What's going on?" I asked. With him standing in the way, I couldn't exit the compartment, and he made no effort to get out of the way. In the narrow passageway behind him came the source of the walkie-talkies, two paramedics squeezing past him. Through the window above them, I saw flashing emergency lights illuminating the snow.

He took a breath before answering my question. "Something pretty bad."

"The old woman?" I asked.

He stared at me. "Mrs. Hazel. She has a name."

"Oh," I said. "I didn't know her name."

"I thought I told you."

He hadn't said anything about her name, but I conceded I'd forgotten.

"Did she come to you at all?" he asked. "For help?"

"No," I said, attempting to convey concern with my eyes. "At least I didn't hear her if she tried."

Studying my face, he nodded. I held my breath, wondering if he'd detect the lie.

"She died," he said, "right here in the passageway. No telling how long she was lying here."

I couldn't imagine how that could be true. Only moments ago, I'd spoken to her. I made a sound of protest, almost admitting my lie to the porter. But then he reached out and squeezed my shoulder, a very fatherly gesture that brought forth a surge of regret. "It's good you didn't come out and find her this way. She looked . . . well, in pain. And when I touched her, she felt so cold." A pause before he added, "I should have increased the temperature for her."

I didn't know how to reply to that statement. The paramedics completed their work and lifted a gurney that held her body. It looked as if they carried nothing at all, her form underneath the sheet so slight that one could barely perceive anything at all. To make room, the porter stepped into my compartment, where we watched them carry away her corpse. Once they departed, he tipped his hat to me and promised the train would move again soon. We said goodnight.

I returned to my bunk and stared at the ceiling. Eventually, as promised, the train began chugging along again, but sleep remained impossible. With the woman gone, I wondered if the porter would lower the temperature, but it only grew hotter. A bit later than scheduled, we crossed the state line into Florida. I continued to lie there awake and watched the sunlight work its way through the window. Finally, we arrived in Sanford, where I disembarked with the other crabby passengers, all of us scowling and ill-tempered as we watched the vehicles slowly unloaded, one by one.

Because of these delays, I forgot all about my coat hanging in that tiny closet.

I FINALLY REMEMBERED it on Christmas Day after exchanging gifts with my family. We'd just sat down to the first home-cooked meal I'd enjoyed in weeks, and I found myself relating the story of the dead woman. Already, I'd revised my narrative and perhaps also my memory of the event, casting myself in a more sympathetic light. I described how I did my best to find her something to wrap around her shoulders, and my parents congratulated me on my self-lessness.

"Is that where your coat went?" asked my mother during dessert. "Did you give it the woman to keep her warm?"

That stopped me cold. My expression must have become readable because they showed concern. I wonder what they saw more of, the guilt or the sense of loss.

"What is it?" my father asked.

I confessed to them that I'd foolishly left the coat on the train.

"They have a lost and found," said my father. "Or they should." He reached for his phone and began dialing the station. But because of the holiday, he reached a recorded message.

"No matter," he said. "We'll call Monday. I'm sure someone found it."

But I thought about the small dimensions of the coat closet and how easily one could overlook it. I had doubts I would ever see my coat again. If I could so easily leave it behind, why hadn't I given it to the dead woman? Another even worse thought nagged me: that if I'd given it to her, she might not have died. But I would never know that, not for sure.

My pessimism about ever again seeing my coat only increased then next day, when we finally reached someone at the station. They did have a lost and found, but no one turned in a coat. Recovering it, they said, depended on the train schedule and someone finding the time to check the compartment I'd booked. Did I remember my car number? I did not. I left a number for them to reach me on the off chance it ever turned up.

But it didn't. Eventually, I came to accept the fact that I would never see that coat again.

A FEW YEARS after I finally graduated, my father experienced his second heart attack, the one that finally killed him. At that time, I'd just taken a job at a consulting firm in

Virginia. While sitting at my desk, I received the tearful news from my mother.

"That car," she said. "What do you want to do with it?"

She meant the automobile I'd transported on the Auto Train all those years ago. Dad and I never could get it running properly, so it just sat in their garage for years. Every so often, we talked about working on it, but we never found the time.

Now my father was gone forever, and my mother wanted rid of it. Though she never told anyone before, it turned out that she never liked that car or what it represented.

"What do you mean?" I asked.

"It killed him," she said, almost matter-of-factly.

I thought I misheard and asked her to repeat herself.

"That car killed him. He wanted to keep working on it with you, but you never had time. All that worrying and planning on his part. He thought it wasn't about the car. He thought you didn't want to spend time with him. He talked about it all the time."

I felt sick. "Well, he never said that to me." Instantly I regretted those words.

"Well," she said, "he said it to me. Come get the car."

AT THE TIME, a winter flu made its way through the office, but thus far, I'd managed to avoid it. The date for the funeral luckily coincided with management's decision to close the office a little early for Christmas in the hopes that the extra time would give everyone a chance to recover. That gave me more time to work out how to get the car from Florida to Virginia, and after considering several options, I decided to take the Auto Train, regardless of the unpleasant memory of the last trip.

Or maybe *because* of that unpleasant memory. Maybe I

intended to punish myself. Maybe I hoped it would offer penance for the terrible things I'd done or, even worse, not done. The lies I told.

So, on an unseasonably warm day in December, I boarded the train. Hours before, my nose started running and my throat was sore, but I attributed these symptoms to the unusual weather and not the flu, which I felt certain I'd escaped. Even when I felt myself shivering, despite everyone around me complaining about the heat, I thought I was experiencing an allergic reaction of some kind. I regretted not bringing anything heavier than the sweater I wore, and I tried hugging myself to retain as much warmth as I could.

The train felt even colder as the porter showed me the way to my compartment. My hands trembled and my teeth chattered, causing me to fumble for my wallet as I handed him an extra twenty-dollar bill and asked him if he could please lower the air conditioning.

He raised an eyebrow, showing none of the affability of the porter from the first trip. "It's not even on," he said. "In fact, it hasn't been working well."

I trembled. The air felt freezing. I pointed to the wall dividing my side of the compartment from the other. "Maybe I could go in there," I said. "Maybe it's warmer."

He shook his head, but he accepted my money. "Afraid not. It's all on the same system."

"It wouldn't hurt, would it? Just to find out?"

Again, he shook his head.

"Is someone on that side?" I asked.

He continued shaking his head. "It's empty. And you paid for one compartment, right?"

We both knew the answer to his question.

"I'm afraid it stays closed sir," he said. And then he left.

Through the window I watched the boarding process

continue. White hot sunlight filled the scene, but I felt colder still, so I sat on the bench seat, drawing my legs to my chest in the hopes I could generate more heat. I continued to sit in this position as the train lurched into action, my teeth chattering and my sore throat worsening. No more denying I had the dreaded flu that went around the office. I debated calling the porter and asking him to raise the heat on the train, but I clearly annoyed him before.

I recalled my previous trip and how I treated that elderly woman with contempt. If I believed in that sort of thing, I might have attributed my current state to recompense of some sort. Punishment I deserved.

I thought also of the coat I left, and its long absence filled me with fresh regret. Shivering, I wanted nothing more than to feel its thick, reliable fabric against my body. I could think of nothing else except the paralyzing cold as the train clattered on and night began to fall outside. At some point, the porter delivered a meal, but I didn't tip him, though I asked him once more about whether he could increase the temperature on the train. He looked at me with an expression of half worry and half disbelief, and he left without making arrangements to lower my bunk so that I could go to sleep.

Not that I could sleep, not with that pervading chill. My growing sickness made it impossible to eat, too, so I left my meal untouched. At one point, flies buzzed around the plate, an unbelievable thing to see in a freezing atmosphere like this one. Not only that, but I detected a noxious odor and wondered if the porter had served me spoiled meat.

But maybe I could no longer trust my senses, because next came the sound of knocking, along with a small voice that sounded eerily similar to the one I heard years ago on that journey. Despite my stuffy ears, I clearly heard the voice say, *"I'm freezing."*

I thought I must be hearing things, but I managed to gather myself and check the passageway outside my compartment.

Relieved, I saw no one there.

After sitting again for only a few minutes, I once more heard the knocking, followed by the voice. This time, I thought I heard the word *coat.*

No question it any longer—whatever ailment I suffered from must be causing hallucinations, I reasoned.

At that moment I heard the knocking again, only louder, more insistent.

The door between compartments, I realized. The sound must have been coming from there. Maybe too the bad odor only seemed to worsen. Maybe someone let a meal go bad in there.

Once more, I struggled to my feet. Placing my ear against the dividing wall, I listened.

And listened.

Finally, I heard it again, but realized the sound didn't come from there at all.

Instead, it came from *within* my own compartment.

Again, I worried the flu caused my hearing to go haywire. But then my eyes found *it*, and I remembered how, long ago, the other porter showed me the closet. How he paternally assisted me with taking off my coat and hanging it up inside.

There, off to the side, barely visible, I once more beheld the slim door.

I dared to imagine the impossible—that I could open the door and find my beloved coat hanging there. But what chance of that? It seemed inconceivable that I occupied the same compartment as the one from all those years ago. Even more inconceivable that my coat would still be hanging there after all those years. Someone would have found it and claimed it as their own.

Nevertheless, as my hand reached out to open the door, I clung to some distant hope.

Once open, darkness seemed to spill forth from the closet, along with stale air, clearly the source of the odor filling my compartment. My eyes burned and struggled to adjust, but gradually, my vision cleared.

And there it was. My coat. The same fabric, the same light brown color. Even a coffee stain on the sleeve looked familiar. Still doubting, I reached out to feel its texture, as if that alone would verify it belonged to me.

And touching the sleeve, I knew. In every way, I was witnessing a miracle. I no longer cared about the terrible smell. My coat was still there, exactly where I left it years ago.

I would wear it, use it to blot out the cold.

But as I continued to touch the sleeve, it happened. Something terrible and inexplicable.

I froze with my hand outstretched, once more in a state of disbelief. The coat moved on its own. Not only had I rediscovered a lost possession, but I found it animated somehow.

Or so I thought. Until I saw the roaches emerging from the sleeve, four of them, wiggling their way out, each one as black and angry as the grave. Then I saw the skeletal worms attached to them, and realized that they weren't roaches at all, but fingernails, each one followed by a gnarled finger. A gray, bony wrist followed.

Then I saw the legs curled up inside the coat, extending themselves so *she* could crawl out of that tiny closet, and I recognized the body wrapped inside my coat. I remembered the features of the wrinkled face, as well as the eyes that locked upon my own, no longer rheumy but completely black. Her lips bore the same color, and I imagined if she used them to kiss me, they would feel as cold as the hand gripping my arm with an iron firmness.

Instead, the lips formed a smile as the thing in the closet spoke in a scratchy voice. "It's my coat now, but I'll share it with you." As I sunk to my knees, feeling the arms enfold themselves around me and the odor of the grave envelop me, I felt no relief from the cold, only a bitter iciness that remains with me still.

Mordecai Weiss: Monster Hunter

DARREN LIPMAN

My grandfather's journal said the story of Hanukkah was a lie. There was no miraculous oil that burned for eight days; it was the rededication of the Temple that took this long. More than mere cleaning, he wrote, it took time to exorcise the demons.

The Syrian-Greeks desecrated the Temple to its core, sacrificing pigs and smearing their blood upon the walls, floors, and ceilings. They prayed to their gods at our altar, burned our holy books, and spread the ashes amongst the blood. Such hatred stirs the spirits, taints the sparks of holiness inside all things, and births terrible beasts we call demons and monsters.

I'm named after my grandfather, actually: Mordecai Weiss, though my friends call me Morty. It's lucky I've got any friends at all in this line of work: monster hunters rarely live long.

Though maybe that's an outdated trope. After all, there aren't many big baddies left in the world, so the hunts are fewer and farther between. Doesn't matter, I suppose, when you're finally facing one of them big baddies, one of those Temple demons sealed away so long ago.

. . .

MORDECAI SLAMMED SHUT his own journal, a keepsake should he not survive all eight nights of Hanukkah. He looked across the room of the small cabin he was holed inside. His dad used to bring him here when his mom and sisters needed a girls' weekend, and now he was here for more sinister purposes, the seclusion offering security his apartment in the city didn't allow.

Mordecai's gaze settled upon the mantel where the hanukkiah sat. It was old, thousands of years, carved from the white stone of the Holy City. A friend of his, Miriam Taylor-Friedman, worked at a world-renowned museum, archiving antiquities. She recognized the obscure symbols engraved in the stone, but she wasn't a monster hunter—she was a scholar. So, she smuggled the hanukkiah home and sent it to Mordecai.

That was months ago, during the summer. Mordecai had spent every day since studying the clues in his grandfather's journal, deciphering apocryphal texts and trying to piece together the forgotten—or hidden—history of Hanukkah. Murder in the Temple was not permitted, so the priests sealed the demonic forces in the hanukkiah, one each day for eight days. But every door has a key, and lighting the Hanukkah candles each night would release them.

For thousands of years they had remained entombed. Now Mordecai was unleashing them one at a time, to slaughter them once and for all.

The first night had been a petty thing, a small specter destroyed by a single blast of salt from his shotgun. The second night had brought twin demons that tried to encircle him with their wit and wisecracks; a few verses of Torah brought them to a smoldering heap, which he swept outside before saying *kaddish*. The third night conjured a massive swine, spewing its guts as it charged at Mordecai; he hacked it to pieces then burned the remains. The greasy smoke that filled the cabin was suffocating, and he kept the windows open all night to dissipate the smell.

The fourth night summoned a half-woman, half-serpent creature with claws as long as scythes. They battled in the small cabin, overturning the table and shattering one of the wooden chairs. Finally, Mordecai drove his dagger through the beast's heart, and it shrieked as it collapsed, consumed by a pillar of fire.

On the fifth night, a cloud of bats descended through the chimney, spiraling around his head with their high-pitched cries. Mordecai managed to knock a few from the air, but he couldn't keep them from coalescing into their true form: a fanged man with talons for hands and ghastly white skin. He swooped in toward Mordecai, but he was faster: a slash severed the vampire's head, and one of the broken wooden chair legs pierced its heart. He buried the pieces in separate graves and only returned inside as morning rose again.

Now the sun was setting, and soon Mordecai would light the candles once more. He had no idea what new horrors might face him as the wax burned low.

I WASN'T ALWAYS *a monster hunter. In fact, I didn't believe in monsters most of my life, even after I found my grandfather's journal and started learning about his life as one himself. Werewolves, ghosts, demons? It sounded too fantastic, too much like popular books and TV shows, to be taken seriously. I deemed him a man ahead of his time, writing fiction that would've landed him on best-seller lists if he were alive today.*

I never knew him growing up and only chanced upon his journal after cleaning things away when my father passed. I wondered why my father had never mentioned Grandpa's interest in writing. I had been a bit of a storyteller myself those days, mostly inspired by

Saturday morning cartoons that I had to record and watch later to attend Shabbat services. Rewatching them again and again filled my mind with the magical. It was all I could think about. I knew magic wasn't real, but sometimes I wished it was so I could have adventures like they had.

Youth wanes, however, and as a teenager, I began volunteering with our synagogue's Sunday school, teaching the children of our congregation how to read and write Hebrew, how to sing our prayers, how to observe our customs. Slowly I learned that Judaism offered far more than I had learned when I was in their shoes as the teachers I worked with became mentors of my own. Myths and legends, folklore from across the world, all these things filled my mind, and as the world of the spiritual grew around me, I grew closer to my faith.

My days as a madrich, *a teacher's assistant, compelled me to study education in college, and soon after graduation, I was head of my own second-grade classroom. I was content for six years, building my repertoire, enhancing our curriculum, being the best I could be. So devoted to my work, however, I began to lose touch with Judaism and drift away, becoming more secular.*

Discovering my grandfather's journal reinvigorated my interest in faith. The pages upon pages of stories added to the rich culture I had learned as a madrich, *made me see yet another facet of this ever-evolving religion. Still, though, I didn't believe these myths were real.*

The world must have laughed at me because soon enough my mind was changed.

THE CANDLES WERE grayish-white in the shape of knobby fingers. They'd been found in a wooden chest near the hanukkiah, and Miriam's analysis showed they were formed from the rendered fat of swine. The antiquities department had wondered why Judaeans would have made candles from pork tallow, but Mordecai had a suspicion: they were the keys to open an impure door, so why would they be made of purer sources of wax?

He placed six candles in the hanukkiah, and added a seventh, the *shamash*, the helper candle designated to light the others. He chanted the prayers and struck a match to the *shamash*, then used its flame to light the candles from left to right. Once they were all burning, he placed the *shamash* in its holder and took a step back.

The demons never came right away; sometimes they waited until all the candles had burnt out, other times they came sooner. Mordecai sat down in a wooden rocking chair near the hearth and grabbed his bible. He would study the Hebrew beneath the candlelight until the demon appeared to feast upon his piety. Then the battle would begin. Yet as he read, the candles burned lower, and nothing arrived. No ancient Greek beast, no Syrian specter. He was alone.

No, not alone: the hairs on the back of his neck stood up as he sensed another presence.

"Reveal yourself," he said, then repeated himself in Hebrew.

A dust mote swirled on the floor, tangled up with a shadow that seemed to slide across the floor like a pool of expanding ink. The darkness coalesced in the corner, and a small figure began ascending from inside. She was small, barely seven or eight, her skin marked with horrific burns, her hair still smoldering in tight strands of glowing filament.

Mordecai gasped and stumbled back. He knew this child. Even through her disfigurement, he recognized Sarah Taylor-Friedman, one of his former students. One he had lost in the incident that made him a monster hunter.

Her mouth twisted into a sneer. "Mr. Weiss, why didn't you save me?"

His knees shook. "I—I didn't know how."

Her eyes widened, a spark alighting inside them that grew to a roiling flame, filling the entire socket. The frown she wore deepened; charred teeth poked out from behind her lips.

This couldn't possibly be Sarah. She had been a sweet, curious child, without a single maleficent bone in her body. This was a trick. The demon was taunting him. His stomach roiled, old scars threatening to tear apart. He wouldn't give it the upper hand.

Mordecai began chanting, snippets of prayer and verse, whatever came to mind. "*Adonai li v'lo ira.*" The Lord is with me; I shall not fear.

His legs tightened and stopped shaking; he stood up taller even as the child in the corner began wailing. Tears discolored by ash rolled down her face and splattered at her feet, but even these did not freeze Mordecai in his tracks as he strode toward her.

He reached his hand past her flaming eyes and set his palm atop her head. He recalled the *Shabbat* blessing his parents had said over him and his sisters, and the words echoed from his mouth as the memories of sitting around the dining table came back to him. *May God make you like Sarah, Rebecca, Rachel, and Leah.* The girl trembled beneath his hands; hers shot up to grab his arm and yank him away, but he held firm. *May God show you favor and be gracious to you.* She shrieked, the cry splitting the air and drowning out his voice, though he pressed on. *May God show you kindness and grant you peace.* The small hands on his arm loosened, and as they fell away, her body crumbled to ash. A soft wind scattered the dust and faded into the shadows of the cabin. Stillness fell over him and he sank to his knees, weeping.

· · ·

I HAVEN'T THOUGHT *of Sarah in years, especially not like that: the way she looked that day after the explosion. The city claimed it was a gas leak, but I had seen the flaming beast moving through the classroom, right toward me. Afterward, if I dared describe the burning figure and its gaping maw, everyone told me I was seeing patterns where there were none, that I had simply witnessed the cloud of fire filling the classroom, but I knew better. I had seen one before.*

In the pages of my grandfather's journal.

It was an ifrit, *a spirit of the dead reborn from the flames of its passions.*

I still don't know why it didn't touch me, why it fled, why it was there in the first place. More than half of my students were seriously injured, and Sarah was killed. The only good thing to come of it was that her mother Miriam and I became close friends. Her work in antiquities had always predisposed her to belief in the supernatural, and she confided in me that Sarah had been having dreams of fire monsters for weeks before the incident.

"I should have known something was coming," she told me, showing me all the pictures Sarah had drawn, "but I just—I didn't want to believe."

I showed her the drawing my grandfather had made, and its similarity to Sarah's sent shivers down my spine. Miriam started crying, clutching the pictures in her hands.

I vowed then to destroy the ifrit *that had destroyed our lives, to hunt down and obliterate the world's greatest evils so they could never hurt anyone again. I found catharsis in my first few hunts, thought I'd finally set the past behind me. Maybe I was wrong.*

THE SEVENTH NIGHT, the hanukkiah was lined with eight candles, ready to be lit. Once more, Mordecai chanted the prayers, struck a match, and lit the *shamash*. There was a certain sameness to the ritual each night that made him feel warm inside, although this year was different. Never before had lighting the candles come with so much danger and trepidation.

Mordecai wondered what demon this night would summon and tried to see a pattern in the ones that had already come. The specter could represent the dead among Jerusalem when the Syrian-Greeks attacked; the demons the next night could have been those who had forsaken their faith and turned to the Greek gods. The swine? Remnants of the sacrificial beasts that had soiled the Temple and stained it with their blood. The half-woman, half-serpent was certainly an echo of Greek monsters, perhaps even the Greeks themselves.

Then there had been a vampire. Perhaps it had been born by the blood in the Temple, but that didn't feel right. Perhaps it wasn't its bloodlust, but its flight that held significance: vampires were creatures of the air, and surely the Temple air had been tainted by the miasmic smoke of heathen sacrifices and needed purification. Then the girl? Whatever demon had conjured her must've been able to peer inside him, to dredge her up from his memories and remake her body. That's all it had been, though: an empty body, an empty husk.

"Dust and ashes," Mordecai said, suddenly doubting everything. Perhaps there were no patterns in the mix, just dark forces eager to consume the light.

Now the candles were low, and the *shamash* flickered out.

Mordecai looked up at the hanukkiah, surprised by how much time had passed without him noticing. He stood and turned around slowly, trying to discern anything out of place that might indicate the arrival of the penultimate demon, but everything was as it should be.

He walked to the small kitchenette and grabbed a bottle of water. He pulled off the cap and took a swig. It was gritty on his tongue, bitter. Mordecai stopped drinking and looked down; the water was full of black specks suspended like sand. As he held it, they multiplied and a gush of black water gurgled out at him—he tossed the bottle aside, the liquid splashing onto the floor. Wherever it spread out, the entire world seemed to vanish beneath its glossy surface.

Mordecai glanced at the other bottles, and each darkened just like the first. He ducked to the side as they exploded, sending a torrent of dark water across the room.

And as before, everywhere it touched became a mirror reflecting the last flickering flames of the Hanukkah candles.

Mordecai began chanting a verse from Genesis in which God created the seas and proclaimed it was good; another from Noah, proclaiming the end of the flood. The words did nothing to calm the spreading deluge, and soon he was backed against the hearth.

The water's smooth surface began rippling, white crests atop sparkling shadows, and Mordecai saw a coiling shape beneath the waves. He saw it coming just in time to fling himself to the right; the tentacle smashed into the fireplace, scattering broken bits of brick. The next tentacle was already flying toward him, and he pressed himself to the left to dodge it, carefully wedging himself between both of them to avoid falling into the water. But with nowhere else to go, the tentacles wrapped around his body and pulled him in.

He expected the water to be frigid, but it wasn't. In fact, it was pleasantly warm, and for a moment he felt the impulse to stop struggling, to let go and just bask in the warmth, let it swallow him and wash away all the dark memories he carried.

Then he breached the surface and gasped for air, and the thought of succumbing to this monster vanished at once. He filled his lungs before the tentacles pulled him back under, but this time he kept his eyes open as he reached for the dagger strapped to his side. He stopped struggling against his captor, and after its grip upon him tightened, he felt it dragging him through the water toward its underside. A moment later he saw its beak opening.

Mordecai jabbed the knife into its maw, thrusting forward as much as he could, hoping to connect with anything on the other side. He felt the blade snag on something, and he pressed harder, slicing through the flesh. He was shoulder-deep, and any second the beak might close around him and sever his arm, but he kept slashing.

Then there was a jerk backward as the monster realized his plan and tried to pull him out, but at the same time, one last slash slaughtered the beast. The water gushed outward, and Mordecai landed on his hands and knees in a puddle in the middle of the cabin.

He sat there panting for a long minute, then he stood to grab the mop. He wasn't sure if any of the taint remained in the water, but he wasn't keen on finding out either. One glance into the kitchenette confirmed his suspicion: all the water he'd brought was now lost, and he'd have to survive the last day and night without anything to drink.

Mordecai wiped the sweat from his brow after he finished mopping the water. He'd never had a hunt last this long before, and his whole body ached. He was still shaken from seeing Sarah the night before, and if not for the relief journaling gave him, he'd have lost his mind already.

I BELIEVE *the first four demons represented the people inside the Temple, so the next four must represent the Temple itself. A winged creature for the air, and now a watery abyss; Sarah's reappearance must have been an earth spirit, makes me think of the saying "dust to* dust" in a whole new light. Of course, that means there's only one element left.

Fire.

I can imagine the victorious Judaeans, slowly cleaning, purifying, rededicating the Temple. How they must have waved blankets to clear the smell and then purified the air with smoky incense. How they must have swept the floors, time and again, scattered them with salt to consecrate the Temple stones. How they must have emptied the urns and vessels and refilled them with purpose and intention, the high priests offering their blessings. And at last, how they must have purified the menorah's flames, finally burning the sacred oil.

It's no coincidence that it was a fire demon that brought me to this life, and now a fire demon I must vanquish to finish the job started in the Temple so long ago. I know it's impossible that whatever demon I meet tomorrow is the same one that decimated my classroom and took Sarah's life; but perhaps if I can defeat this one, it'll make up for never finding the other.

That is, after all, why I haven't stopped hunting: because that first one is still out there. Spirits come and go, and if I'm honest, there's a chance it's gone back to hell, or wherever it came from, and will never resurface again.

So, this, then, is my last chance to vanquish my past once and for all.

MORDECAI RETURNED the *shamash* to its holder and took a step back to admire the nine burning candles. There was always a moment of awe on the last night of Hanukkah when the entire hanukkiah was lit. Doing so represented the completion of an eight-night ritual, the coming of longer days, even the rededication of the Temple itself.

Tonight, however, the candles burned almost too bright.

The flames began to bulge, to billow upward until they

were twice the height of the candles they sat upon. Mordecai stumbled backward, swallowing the lump that had appeared in his throat as he watched the flames soar higher, and higher still. Soon they spread outward along the ceiling, though the cabin itself did not burn.

He vowed to stand there and wait for the beast to emerge, but as the heat fell upon his skin, his mouth already parched from the lack of water, his conviction crumbled. He turned and dashed into the kitchen, grabbing the salt from the counter. He spread it in a circle around him, and once it was complete, he turned toward the burning hearth.

A fist formed of raging flames pressed through the fire, and the wall of burning candles parted as the human-like shape stepped out. Where its feet fell, the wood darkened and smoldered, smoke wafting upward like small white clouds. The *ifrit* walked toward him, its face a stoic sphere of fire. A single spot of blue sat at the center of the flame, and from the way it moved side to side before finally facing him, Mordecai knew the blue flame must be its eye. Now it was only a step away from the salt circle, and though it wouldn't be able to reach Mordecai, he wouldn't be able to reach it either. It took another step toward him, and the flames curled around an invisible dome. Mordecai sunk to his knees, his whole body shaking, as the roiling flames encircled him. It was like watching his classroom burn all over again.

"*Adonai li v'lo ira*," he said again and again until the words sunk in. *The Lord is with me; I shall not fear.* Though his legs trembled, Mordecai stood. He squared his shoulders, tried to ignore the searing heat all around him. The only way forward, he thought, is through it.

Then he felt something inside himself, his own spark of the divine, smoldering inside him. He felt angry, anger the likes of which he had never allowed himself to feel, and the anger empowered him, turned to indignation and awe. He pressed his palms together and pushed them forward, throwing his hands apart like Moses before the Red Sea—and the flames split down the middle, granting him safe passage from the furnace.

Mordecai whirled, walking backward to make some distance. The *ifrit* curled around, the conflagration taking its human shape again.

Power coursed through him; perhaps the Lord truly was with him. Mordecai saw his hands glowing, and though it could've been the firelight, he swore it came from within. He faced the monster and raised his hands, made the signs of the priests, and started walking toward it. With every step he took, the *ifrit* grew smaller and smaller, and finally, it was barely a candleflame flickering on the floor: Mordecai snuffed it out with his foot.

His face was tearstained, and his hands shook. He grabbed at his collar and ripped his shirt down the front. A part of him had died that day in class, a part he had never known, never mourned. Now he knew the emptiness he had felt for years was due to its loss, a hole perhaps that a greater power could fill. He threw his head back and screamed to God, blamed Him for all the loss and bloodshed, then cried and thanked Him for seeing him through this ordeal.

Mordecai awoke the next day on the floor where he had been the night before. The morning light from the windows revealed the scorched footsteps of the *ifrit*, though there was nothing he could do about them now. He put on a new shirt, packed his things, and locked the cabin behind him. It was about a mile's hike to where he'd parked his car, but something about the crisp air and a light dusting of snow made him forget how far it really was.

Perhaps the real Hanukkah miracle wasn't the one

everyone remembered, but maybe that didn't matter. Every year, every time he lit the hanukkiah, it meant something, and this year more than any before, it meant both death and rebirth.

The Temple had been rededicated, and so, too, had he.

The Fewer the Better Fare

JAKE JEROME

The apartment downstairs won't shut up.

She lies in bed with a pillow pressed over her ears and tries to sleep through it—big day tomorrow, she's presenting enrollment numbers to the board and hopes the results land her a cushy role in admin—but the apartment below them just won't shut up. Constant chattering. Howling laughter. Doors banging against their frames and a never-ending shuffle of feet.

Now they're caroling.

Silent Night.

Her husband rolls over and sits on the edge of the bed, head in hands. "I'm going to go down there."

"It's the holidays," she says. "We're just going to have to put up with it."

"You've been prepping all week for that meeting."

"Please don't, they just moved in. We'll have to see them in the hallway eventually. I don't want it to be awkward."

"I'm not going to crash the whole thing. I'm simply going to ask them to keep the noise at a respectful level."

"Fine, be quick."

He grabs some clothes from the floor. A pair of jeans and a Christmas sweater with Rudolph on the front, nose adorned with a red puffball. Same outfit he wore to the office party earlier.

"They're going to think you've come to join them."

"Well, I'm not changing," he says. "Who knows, maybe they will, and I'll get a free shot of Maker's."

Before she can tell him he's had enough for one evening, the caroling ends. Cheers and applause erupt from under them. Her husband says he'll be back and closes the apartment door. The *tap tap* of his footfall descends the stairwell until it dissolves into the greater commotion as if he's been absorbed by some other world.

She removes the pillow from her head, stares at the oblong shapes of streetlight on the ceiling. A cool air brushes against her cheeks. Feels like no matter how high they set the thermostat the place never gets any warmer than above freezing. The building was constructed in the '30s, long before the institution of insulation standards. Guess neither of them really figured out how bad it could get when they moved in over the springtime.

Part of her wants to go visit the party. Soak in the warmth of other bodies.

She also doesn't want to be alone. Not here. Truth is she isn't worried about any awkward hallway encounters. Could really give a rat's ass about neighbors who appear overnight and don't even introduce themselves. She only said that to stop him from leaving.

But he did, and she wasn't going to fight it any further. Didn't want to risk raising concern. Didn't want any more of his good-natured chauvinism. That look on his face. The words, "Are you sure everything is better now? We can get you back on the panic meds if you need them."

She pulls back the comforter, walks to the window. Her finger traces a parabola of snow on the outside sill. No one is walking the street. Not one car on the road. Would be unusual for such a big city if it weren't for the blizzard. The flurries shimmer through the beams of neon storefronts. Sparkle on the flawless blanket forged from their own advent.

Would have been a peaceful scene if not for the party. When the news called for seven or eight inches, she envisioned a night without interruption: no sirens or car alarms or the desperate cries of drug withdrawal below their bedroom windows. Just a quiet storm.

And a chance to catch up on sleep.

IT STARTED after the events of last Christmas.

"Insomnia is a natural reaction to post-traumatic stress," the doctor had said. Natural or not, it eventually made the world look synthetic. Like things appeared real, but slightly off, as if closer inspection would reveal all of it as nothing more than clever artifice. People became unfamiliar. First, it was the faces who shared her commute. Then it was acquaintances and colleagues, her family and friends. In time her husband, too.

Even herself.

Whenever she tried to sleep, her heart would beat like the slow boiling of water, an imperceptible rise until the moment it tipped into a full-blown rage. She'd breathe. Grind her teeth. Ball up the sheets in her fists and let them go and grab her phone and scroll and scroll through its infinite depth.

Sometimes, on the nights when she *did* fall asleep, she

would hear things, like an abrupt clap in her ear or a sack of quarters smacking the ground.

"Exploding head syndrome."

The doctor said it as if the annihilation of her head was rather unremarkable.

So, she had chalked up the eerie noises in their old house to the auditory hallucinations. Every creak in the ceiling. The drips of water from the bathroom sink that never leaked. The whispers in the downstairs hallway.

Were they saying anything? Or were they merely susurrations without language? It didn't matter. They had gotten so loud she could no longer attribute them to a product of her own mind but instead the manifestation of an actual haunting. Like what happened that Christmas forever imbued a negative energy in the walls too strong to dispel.

But the voices whisper here in the new apartment too. A little less loud, a little less often, but they're here.

She hasn't told him. He wouldn't say what he really thought. That they upended their entire lives overnight and relocated to the only shit hole available on short notice just to discover it didn't solve the goddamn problem. No, he's too nice to do that. So nice he'd make it worse. He'd play along, rub her shoulders, and say something he thought would help her feel a little less crazy.

"This city is full of ghosts."

BUT WHAT'S the common denominator?

"Me," she says. Her breath sticks to the window, and she draws her finger through it, bisects the perfect circle. He's been gone longer than expected. Much longer. The party is no further away than a flight of steps, and it shouldn't take more than a minute to negotiate a noise complaint.

Perhaps they can't hear him knock.

She reaches toward the nightstand to grab her phone and bangs her knee on the radiator. Right at the joint. She bends it back and forth, massages the tendons, and curses, but the sting fades as fast as it came. Not a big deal.

Come back, she texts him.

Within seconds his phone pings from the other side of the room. It lights up, casts a blue glow on the wall.

Figures. He never worries about anything, never considers the worst could happen and they might need to reach each other. He seizes every moment without anxiety. Exudes confidence and thrives in social situations.

It's this attitude that makes her love him.

It's what makes them polar opposites.

It's also what makes her realize the truth: he joined the party downstairs. Couldn't resist. One shot of free liquor for the road turns into another and the road is forgotten, and no one cares because everyone loves a cheap date.

They're caroling again. *Joy to the World.* Voices in chorus, for he has come and come without her. She sighs but notices the exhalation she hears isn't her own. It's the whispers in the hallway again, their indecipherable gossip.

She didn't attend his office party today. Opted to stay late at the college instead, told him there were more reports to compile. Which was true, but only because she made it so. She wasn't ready to partake in any festivities with the wounds of last Christmas still tender to the touch.

Better to blame work for her absence. It's easier that way.

For the past decade, they hosted the party at their old house. And even though he rearranged the venue this year and they ordered catering from her favorite restaurant and that woman—the one she could only refer to as Moon Tattoo— no longer worked there, she just wasn't ready.

But how long would it take?

"Enough."

She turns on the light, and the whispers retreat into a low sibilation, like the voices of schoolchildren when the principal finally takes the stage.

There's no need for a fancy outfit, just something that won't invite judgment. She opens the closet and grabs a pair of distressed jeans and a red and green flannel and puts them on along with some sneakers.

She fixes her hair and brushes her teeth and takes a deep breath before opening the door.

"The more the merrier, right?"

Her footsteps echo down the stairwell, trundle over the planks of old oak. When she was a child, her grandmother said knocking on wood releases the good spirits trapped in the grains. Now she stands outside the party and hopes the march of her feet did the trick.

Chatter and laughter, so much of it, fills the hall right outside the door. The voices are indiscernible from one another. Can't even single out the sound of her husband's usual exuberance. She reaches out. All of a sudden her skin feels slightly hot. Her throat a bit tight. The back of her tongue like a sponge. But she fights through it and knocks.

And knocks.

Nothing. No one can hear her. Maybe this wasn't a great idea after all. Her grandmother wasn't just a believer of superstition but also a practitioner of basic etiquette, and she can hear her now, scolding her for being so uncouth as to show up somewhere uninvited.

No, she's tired of it. Tired of being confined behind walls of her own creation. Of arresting herself for crimes defined by laws written nowhere but inside her own head.

She knocks again, this time loud enough for the whole party to hear.

And the door opens.

Standing there in the same stupid Santa hat he wore last year is one of her husband's colleagues. She can never remember his name no matter how many times they've hosted him in their own home. Something common and without personality and therefore the perfect fit.

"Oh, good to see you," she says. "Can I—Can I come in?"

"Of course? It's your party."

SHE STEPS INSIDE. Everyone is drinking wine and eating charcuterie and wearing the same outfits they wore last Christmas. Ugly sweaters with LED lights. Headbands with elf ears and reindeer antlers. They're all from his office with names that don't matter because none of them are her friends. They're all his. Always have been.

And they're sitting on her couch.

In her home.

Gorging themselves on the food she's prepared. Breathing pine-scented air from the candles she's crafted. Leaving presents with bows and wrappings of greens and golds under the tree she's decorated. All for themselves, maybe one for her if she's lucky.

Foolish to think she could leave her old house behind. The first home they bought. The place they painted and furnished and imparted so much of their love. Where they were supposed to spend the rest of their lives.

Wherever she goes, this home will follow.

It's here.

The painful memory returns.

•   •   •

HER HUSBAND HAD COME into the kitchen while she was slicing oranges for the winter sangria. They'd split the cooking duties. She made the ham, sweet potatoes, and mac and cheese. He made the turkey, greens, and rolls. But afterward, she always made the drinks and baked the dessert alone. Something to occupy herself with while everyone else talked about work and collectively griped about things like key performance indicators, disrupted supply chains, and excessive micromanagement. She didn't know the language of their trade. Her mother tongue was College Recruitment. Similar in drudgery, different in jargon. Sometimes they'd break topic to include her, but it usually resulted in small talk that forced them back into the conversation that excluded her to begin with. So, she manned the libations and baked goods. Not out of passion but distraction.

"How long are you going to be in here?" he said.

"Still got to finish this up, and I haven't started the other stuff yet. Maybe thirty minutes?"

"Ah, heck. You're missing the party."

"Well, this has to get done."

He went back out into the living room. She sliced more fruit. Dumped it into the pitcher and added the pinot noir. Someone started to play her grandmother's piano in the living room. Another began to sing. Soon enough the rest of them joined the caroling.

She rinsed the knife under the faucet, citrus sluicing off the blade, and cut a few apples into little chunks for one of the desserts. Maple walnut apple crisp. She could have crushed the walnuts herself, but part of the recipe required such a fine grain it made more sense to use the coffee grinder.

Besides, she never used the thing. Not once since they bought it.

After a failed search of every kitchen cabinet, she finally

remembered it was in the garage's storage closet. The place where all their unused gadgets went to die. She could even see it sitting on the second shelf from the top.

She walked out and didn't notice the knife was still in her hand until she traipsed on past the party. Blade pointed out, combat position, like she was on her way to save them from some intruder. Her husband wasn't with them. In fact, a couple of heads were missing. Probably out front with the smokers.

Nobody saw her. Too busy clapping and laughing and starting up a new song. She turned into the hallway leading to the garage, looked at the photographs on the walls, remembered how the nails were so loose when she hung them, and the further she got from the party, the lower the chorus got, the more the sounds from the garage became clearer.

It sounded like whispers. The sharing of rumors or the planning of a conspiracy. Probably the latter, since no one would have any reason to venture into the garage, and wasn't the door locked? That's how they kept it. No. It locks from the inside, not the outside. The whispers were like rats behind the walls of her head, chewing on the circuitry of rational thought.

She placed her ear against the door. Tried to make out what the whispers were saying knowing full well they weren't saying anything at all.

Just the sound of deep, lustful breathing.

She opened it.

It was him and the one with the moon tattoo. Right behind the ear. The one who always overstepped boundaries. Constant inappropriate comments. A touch that lingered a bit longer than it should. But come on, you can't invite the entire office over every year except for one person in particular, right? That's just rude.

They let go of each other and stared with their mouths still open. Moon Tattoo tried to say something, maybe apologize. Her husband tried the same but couldn't. Then Moon Tattoo brushed past her. Hurried down the hallway, out the front door, and down the street to her car.

Moon Tattoo didn't mean to push her against the wall.

It was an accident.

But it happened. The knife turned inward and entered her below the opposite wrist and bifurcated the pathways which carried her blood.

She lost a lot of it.

"COME," the man with the Santa hat says. "Sit down."

She turns around to leave, but the apartment door is no longer there. It's been replaced with the hallway that leads to the garage. The picture frames lay scattered across the floor. Nails must have finally given. She reminds herself she needs to buy those adhesive hooks from the store, the ones so strong they can hold a full-body mirror.

The man pats the seat next to him on the sectional. "Come on, take a break from the dessert real quick."

The guests stare at her, all ten, fifteen of them. Most of their faces are clear and recognizable, just as she knows them. Some are blurry and featureless. Others are scrambled, have mouths where there should be eyes, noses where there should be chins.

"No, thank you," she says. "I better get back and finish the crisp."

The man kneels on the floor and reaches under the tree and pulls out a box wrapped in red. "But we're giving out the gifts now. This one's for you."

Someone starts to play her grandmother's piano, a familiar holiday tune. *Carol of the Bells*. Another one tells her to take a load off. She's been working too hard.

They're right. She has. She steps forward and joins them.

"We all pitched in for this," the man says. "Hope you like it." He hands her the gift. It isn't too heavy. She traces her fingers over the edges, the wrapping, the tag that bears the name that means nothing to her, hasn't for a long time.

"You shouldn't have."

She rips the corner, peels, and tears it away. The wrapping falls to the floor. What's left in her hands is a plain shoebox. The guests nod, and the ones with mouths smile.

"Go ahead," he says. "Open it."

She removes the top, pushes aside the tissue paper, and almost drops everything when she sees the knife. Still covered in her blood. Fresh and wet and soaking the tissue beneath.

"We thought you might want to finish the job."

One of the guests stands up and places a hand on her shoulder. Presses his lips right to her ear with a voice like ice water and tells her to finish it. Another one stands and says it, too. Then another. Soon they're all urging her to finish it. *Finish the job*. The one at the piano sings it.

She picks up the knife, considers the blade, how it had pierced her so smoothly like a splinter in the fingertip. How it disarticulated the web of muscle and tendon. The surgeons reattached the connections as best they could, brilliant minds they were, but God, there was so much rehab, learning again to expand and contract the hand.

They chant and sing and implore her to reinsert the knife back where it belongs, right in her arm, as if it were its natural sheath. Louder. And louder. Discordant and so deafening her eardrums begin to throb.

Finish the job!

"No!" she shouts. She closes her eyes and yells it again and again, each shout a negation of them, every *no* an affirmation of herself. Screams it until she can't anymore.

When she opens her eyes, the guests have vanished. The tree, the living room, all of the old house is gone. She's standing in the middle of the downstairs apartment. It's vacant like it's always been. Cobwebs hang from wall to wall and glow yellow in the streetlight. The pattern of her shoes are imprinted on the dust-covered floor.

Nothing is left except for the gift. The one her guests had so generously given. It's tangible, real. The edge so sharp, formed with the intent of its natural function.

HE'S SLEEPING on his side of the bed when she returns to their apartment.

She stands at the window next to him. The snow is still falling. The lights still shimmer and refract across the white blanket like a pearlescent gem.

It's clear. Undisturbed. There aren't any tracks in the streets or marks of trespass upon the sidewalks. Should have known it was the ghosts who paid a visit.

She looks down at him, innocent in his slumber. For the past year, he's been a saint. Forgiving. Patient. Generous and considerate. But none of it atones for the sin. Deep down she knows he's selfish, someone who takes what they want and whose every action stems from that impetus. Every good deed and kind word spoken is nothing but performance, like some child desperate to land on Santa's nice list.

He took her from her friends. Took over the house. And when that wasn't enough he took the woman with the moon tattoo. Took more and more and no doubt plans to take again and leave nothing left for her.

"The more the merrier, right?" she says for the second time tonight.

She can't remember the latter half of that phrase—*the fewer the something*—but it doesn't matter. Words are symbols, and symbols are hollow. The real meaning of it is found when her husband opens his eyes and stares at the blade coming down.

psychic santa

CLAY MCLEOD CHAPMAN

Their faces tend to blend together. You may remember a few, sure. The peculiar ones. Could be a birthmark or a bruise that sticks out. Something they wore, maybe, or something funny they said. Even that tiny squeak in their voice lingers a little . . . But after those first few years, believe me, their features all melt in your mind, a never-ending strand of taffy full of eyes and gap-toothed smiles stretching on and on for as long as that line of kids, every last one of them patiently waiting their turn to sit in your lap, staring vacantly back at you the entire time.

I'm always gonna remember Benjamin Pendleton, though.

That kid just sticks. His robin's egg complexion. Palest blue skin I've ever seen. The ice crystals clustering along his eyelashes. The pockets of frost in each socket, both eyeballs totally frozen over, the vitreous humor gone all gray. That boy's face is gonna be with me for as long as I live. I'm never forgetting him.

My first ghost.

Most Santas only last a couple Christmases. They're just not cut out for the costume. These guys ain't got the motz to slip on this suit day after day. Some fellas stick it out for a few years, sure, hitting up the holiday blitz wherever they can find work, but they burn out on these rugrats kicking their shins and simply call it quits.

It's a rough business, let me tell you. We're punching bags in black boots. Folks sure like to joke about how many Santas are alcoholics, but after a twelve-hour shift of getting your beard pulled, kicked, punched, pinched, sneezed on, screamed at, clawed, jabbed, stabbed and pissed all over—multiple times —believe you me, you'd probably make a bee-line to the bar for a boilermaker or two (or ten) to unwind, too.

Judge not, lest ye be Santa . . .

I haven't had a drop of alcohol since I first met Benjamin. That's the God's honest truth. That kid cleaned me up. You'd think it would be the other way around, but no, he scared me sober. The way he waddled up to me made my blood run cold. Just listening to the squish in his rubber galoshes, full of river water. I can still hear them now. *Sqush-sqush* with every step. *Sqush-sqush.* He'd been patiently waiting for his turn amongst all the other boys and girls, never cutting in line or creeping up on me.

That's the thing: He didn't pounce. Didn't bite. All this kid did was stand in line along with the others, his frost-ridden eyes focused on me the whole damn time. *Staring.* I swear the temperature dropped the closer he got. There was this chill coming off his skin. I could feel him before he even reached me, my breath fogging over . . . while he didn't have any breath at all.

Did anybody else see this kid? Was I the only one?

What did he want from me?

I couldn't afford to lose this gig. Turnover is pretty swift here, so I had to keep my composure. Don't scream. That'd be enough to send me packing. Shops like Balkins cover their asses. They don't even hire the same Santa year after year anymore. It's got everything to do with liability. Parents aren't as eager to let their kids sit in some stranger's lap. Mom and Pop are afraid of . . . *you know*. Whether Santa's got a rap sheet or whatnot. They want to know if he can live within a thousand feet of a playground. Sign of the goddamn times. Everybody's scared of the things that're supposed to be safe. *Clowns*? Come on. Don't get me started on clowns . . .

But *Santa*? Why do we got to be afraid of *him* now? Ain't nothing sacred?

What'd I ever do to deserve this?

Should be the other way around, you know. It's us Santas who should be terrified of the kids. Lord knows I used to be.

The dead ones, at least.

This is my sixteenth Christmas working the department store circuit. Where does the time go, you know? Damn right, I'm a man of the cloth. Got my own suit and everything. I've clocked a couple Christmases at other stores, sure. I've done them all. JC Penney's. Did a quick stint at Dillard's. Made my way up to Macy's, if you can believe it. Hitting the big time.

I've always had the physical disposition for this gig. Born with a bowl full of jelly and all that. It's a bit chicken and egg: *What came first, the job or the belly*? Who knows. My doctor keeps warning me I'm borderline diabetic, but I simply consider it an occupational hazard. Comes with the turf.

I got my routine down pat. The laughter. The banter. The whole kit and Christmas kaboodle. *Ho Ho Ho! Merry Christmas! So . . . have you been a good boy this year?*

Who am I the other three-hundred and thirty-five days out of the year, when I'm not donning the suit? Good question. I'm not so sure anymore. I'm collecting disability. Got myself an apartment. Nothing too fancy. Just a two-bedroom unit close to I-64. Had a wife but we separated over a decade ago now. No kids of my own—that I know of—but that's okay. I've had plenty.

Used to be a bus driver.

Sorry, *school* bus driver. Precious cargo and all. I had my route for some twenty-odd years. Same circuit for nearly the whole time. Same neighborhoods, same streets, practically the same kids for all that time, sending them to the same school. It got to the point where I could pick them all up with my eyes closed. By the end there, I practically did.

I had driven after a bender before and done just fine. Technically I wasn't drunk that morning. *That morning*, Christ . . . Listen to me. A little coffee was all it usually took to get in working order again. Christmas was right around the corner. Only a few more days left before the holiday break, and I wouldn't have to slip behind the wheel of my bus until after New Year's.

I mistook some Christmas decorations for a green light, running a red. Never saw that FedEx truck coming. The second it slammed into the side of the bus and spiraled us out, my head met the windshield, and I was out. I remember hearing it—that fracture of glass, like ice cracking under my heel. You know that feeling? When you're walking over a frozen pond? You don't just hear the crackle, you feel it, too, reverberating through your foot and all the way up your leg, your bones becoming a tuning fork. My head went right through the windshield. There was water waiting for me on the other side—cold, black water—swallowing me all up.

When I came to in the hospital two weeks later, I could see.

Not with my eyes, but with my mind.

Yeah. So, I'm a psychic Santa. Maybe I should've mentioned that up front. After coming out from the quick little coma, I didn't have a job anymore, but I did have second sight.

When I wear the suit and sit here, I feel—I don't know—

like I'm doing *something*. Something that matters. Making up for my mistakes. Lord knows I've had my fair share.

Growing a beard began as a means to cover up the scars along my cheeks and chin. That windshield sure did a number on my face. Now I just wear it for the job.

The gig. The kids. The ghosts.

Everybody remembers their first time sitting with Santa. I know it's not me who these kids are thinking about. All they see is the suit. The hat. The beard. I'm a means to an end, the guy who's gonna get them what they want.

Still me, though, you know? Underneath the outfit. I'm making this memory that'll last for them.

I just want to do something that'll sink in, that they'll hold onto for the rest of their lives.

Or afterlives.

Benjamin Pendleton came to me. Out of all the department stores in town, that kid had to wander into mine. Of all the Santas he could've sat with, he crawled into my lap. He took one look at me with those iced-over eyes, splitting open those pale, purple lips, and said . . . and said . . .

Cold.

That's it. His first word—only word—slipped out from his mouth with a little river water.

Cold.

That kid had been dead long before I asked him what he wanted for Christmas. I had a sneaking suspicion something was off about that boy from the get-go, but there's always a couple of kids who give you pause. Little weirdos. Home-schoolers. You just have to take it in stride. Not break character. You smile, do your laugh—*Ho, Ho, Ho*—and just go through the pre-scripted spiel: *Have you been a good boy this year? What would you like for Christmas, l'il fella?*

What did Benjamin Pendleton want? Someone to find his

body, that's all. Wherever it was. That's not so much to ask for Christmas, was it?

So, I've got this ability to see dead kids.

Long story. Bear with me.

It's not just anywhere, though. Only in these department stores. Only when I'm in the suit. I don't know how this all works, if there are—I don't know—*rules* or whatever, but that's just how it all seems to play out. These ghosts get in line like all the other boys and girls, simply waiting their turn to sit on my lap. I'll ask if I can help put their spirits to rest. Sometimes that means finding their bones, wherever their remains are buried. Other times it means dealing with some unfinished business. Sometimes I send a message to their loved ones. Just depends on the kid. How they died.

Our day always kicks off when the department store opens. Back in the good ol' days, you might get a line that winds around the whole store. Sometimes it even reached out into the parking lot. Not so much anymore. The first few kids in line are always the overachievers. The parents who want to get their picture all done. I'm granting kids all kinds of gifts. Rocket ships. Teddy bears. Bikes. You name it. Who cares if they're naughty or nice anymore? I feel like a governor offering pardons to death row inmates, doling out reprieves left and right: *You get a toy and you get a doll and you get a stuffy and you get a . . .*

Then I'll spot a kid just standing there, minding their own business. No parent. Looks like they're all by themselves. They usually got this vacant stare. Never blink. I'll never know if anybody else can see them or not. When this holiday phenomena first started, I asked one of my little helpers—just some pimple-faced greaser squeezed into an elf costume—if he saw what I was seeing, he just looked back at me like he wasn't getting paid nearly enough to deal with my crap. He didn't see this kid, no matter how close he got. Only I could. Lucky, lucky me.

Best thing to do is play it cool. Keep calm. Don't panic.

I'm keeping an eye on them as the line keeps ticking down. Each living kid brings them closer and closer to me, until finally, it's their turn to sit on my lap.

Well, hello there, young lady . . . What's your name?

Sometimes they'll talk. Other times they just stare. You just got to roll with it.

Have you been a good girl this year? What would you like for Christmas? Is there some—

The girl's gone. If she was even there at all. She's too shy to share her secret with me. Maybe she'll come back tomorrow. The kids in line—the live ones—all stare at me like I've been mumbling to myself. Got to play it off. Act natural. Can't let my little helpers think I'm sauced up or something. They'll tell the manager and that's not something I need right now. That guy's been breathing down my neck every damn day from the moment I first clock in. Taking piss tests nearly every other shift. I get it, I do, but I'm clean. I've been clean for years now.

It's this gift. These visions. It's not like I'm looking for them. These kids find me. They come to *me*. I know how that makes me sound. Believe me, I know. For the longest time, I tried to avoid them. Act like they're not there . . . but that just gets them angry. They won't go away.

Like Benjamin. Since he was my first, I didn't know what the hell I was supposed to do. Wasn't like he came out and said it. That's what's so frustrating with these ghosts. They don't tell you what they want for Christmas. They just stare at you. It's up to you to figure it out. Thought I was going out of my goddamn mind, seeing this dead kid in line, all bloated and blue.

He was wearing a puffy blueberry snowsuit. One of those slick nylon outfits that covers your whole body, arms, and legs. When you walk there's always that synthetic *zip-zip-zip* sound from the friction between your knees. This kid's skin was the same tint as his snowsuit. He drew closer to me, from across the room, and I swear I could hear the sound of his suit. *Zip-zip-zip* . . .

He's wet. Not dripping wet. Just . . . moist, I guess. The water is soaked inside him. If I squeezed him too hard, all that water might come dribbling out. *You feeling okay, son?*

Cold . . .

Where's your mother?

Cold . . .

Maybe we get your parents over here. See if we can't get you a hot chocolate or —

Cold . . .

Cold . . .

Cold . . .

I paid my dues. I did a tour of duty with the March of Dimes, clanging that goddamn bell outside of nearly every grocery store this side of the highway. I pray to God I never go back to that godawful gig. Standing out in the cold for hours, begging moms for pocket change. Nothing but a panhandling Santa. I'd always get a migraine from that bell after the first hour, just *ring-a-ding-dinging* that goddamn thing all day. Really sets your teeth on edge. Sinks into your skull by the end of your shift. No amount of ibuprofen is gonna take that chiming away. Some nights, I swear, I still hear it. Even years later, it's still ringing, pealing away in my ears —*dingadingading.*

I can't even begin to tell you the number of migraines I had after my accident. Most days my head felt like it was still underwater, still under that sheet of ice, my mind frozen over.

But a gig is a gig is a gig. I'd slip into my Santa suit and ring that damn bell all day. Started noticing these kids clustering around me on the sidewalk. Not saying anything. They'd just stand there, almost like they were in a line, waiting their turn. I'd try shooing them away with my bell, but they'd always wander back. I had to explain I wasn't *that kind* of Santa. If they wanted to sit on my lap, they'd have to go to Balkins and bug one of my brothers. *Go on! Shoo!*

Every Santa is desperate for a department store. That's as cushy a job as you're liable to land these days. The pay ain't all that grand but the perks make it worth it, trust me. You get to sit on your keister all day, inside, where it's warm and toasty. Not on the curb. Not in the cold.

Not with these dead kids trailing after you.

I'd happily take a shop like Balkins any ol' damn day. So it's not Sak's Fifth Avenue. What the hell is? Even Sak's isn't Sak's anymore. Every last damn department store is going the way of the dodo, you know? Thank Walmart for that. Box stores don't give a shit. You think Target's gonna bring in Kris Kringle? Forget about it . . . And it ain't like Amazon's offering up a spot for guys like us to earn an honest living. You think they want us delivering gifts to kids on Christmas morning? Wouldn't that be a fucking hoot? Nah—all we got left are department stores. The ones that're still around, at least, clinging on for dear life at the strip malls and town centers.

So, you never heard of Balkins. No surprise. Balkins is one of these third-string retailers cropping up along the southeastern corridor like canker sores, clustering around the Carolinas. A couple spots are still open in Georgia. None in Florida. Last one got mowed over by Hurricane Whatshername. I forgot. It's cheaper to just take the insurance money and never reopen again.

My Balkins beat is the Chesterfield Towne Centre, right

here in Roanoke. It's pretty much the only store that hasn't shuttered in this place. Whole mall is practically a ghost town. The food court's closed. Victoria's Secret pulled up stakes months ago. Just us and the Dippin' Dots kiosk. Don't ask me how this Balkins is still limping along. Not like they're stocking up on the latest fashions. The clothes on the racks are from five seasons ago. Most folks do their holiday shopping online now. Not here. The writing's on the wall, clear as day, just like the graffiti spray-painted all over the façade. I give this place until the end of Christmas before it shuts down. Pink slip by New Years. *That's all, folks* . . . Swan song for Santa. Gotta find a new gig.

Somebody better tell that to all the ghosts.

Used to be these spirits would sprinkle themselves amongst the living, shuffling along with the rest. Nowadays, though, there are more of them than there are flesh and blood boys and girls. What's gonna happen when the only kids coming to sit in my lap are all dead?

I've learned to live with it. Used to be I'd nearly shit in my drawers, but now . . . now I just treat them like any other kid. Talk to them. Everybody wants something for Christmas, right?

Jenny Schumacher needed her mom to know it was her uncle who strangled her.

Tommy Watkins just wanted his younger brother to have his old baseball card collection.

Keisha Quinn needed someone to look for her body, even if the cops had stopped searching.

So, this is what Santa must feel like. I'm granting these ghosts one last gift for Christmas.

I'm giving them peace.

Santa's workshop is just a cardboard backdrop pulled out from storage every year, its edges wilting. Looks a little soggy, to be honest, like the whole building got soaking wet one winter and now it's about to collapse. Rolls of the same cotton carpet get unfurled over the floor, so it looks like sheets of snow. Styrofoam candy canes sprout out from the linoleum. Silver tinsel. But the chair, my God, let me tell you about this chair . . . Fit for a fucking king. It's all varnished wood and red velvet cushions, studded with copper buttons. It is the most comfy chair I've ever sat in. Don't even need a donut for my hemorrhoids, it's that soft. Makes the hours slip. I could sit here year-round and never leave. Maybe I will.

If you want your kid sitting on Santa's lap, get your picture to stick on your fridge, you got to actually get off your ass, hop in the car, drive down to your local Balkins and pay me a visit. That's the one leg up this brick-and-mortar shop has over Amazon: flesh and blood Santas.

The Christmas crunch is upon us. It's the last Saturday before the 25th, so we've got a bit of a blitz. There are kids cordoned off behind a red velvet rope, waiting for this show to start.

Gonna be a grind today, I can tell. Kendra called in sick so I'm down to two elves. We'll just have to make do with a skeleton crew. One elf escorts the kids up. He's my bouncer. Whenever we've got an unruly rugrat, it's up to him to kick them out.

Each kid gets about forty-five seconds in my lap. When we're firing on all cylinders and really got our rhythm, we're clocking in thirty seconds, in-out. It's all about the picture. The other elf snaps off the shot. The elf behind the camera fancies herself a photographer, I can tell. Not like there's anything to master at this. It's just a Polaroid. Snap and shoot.

I know most Santas complain about catching whatever cold these kids carry. Doesn't bother me. I've got a strong constitution. It takes a lot to knock me down.

I glance out at the line and try to decide who's alive and who's dead. Getting harder and harder to tell the difference these days.

Benjamin Pendleton came back the very next day. I recognized him right away: Same blue snowsuit. Same moistness. Same chill. I spotted him a few kids back, waiting his turn like all the others. Nobody else seemed to pay him any mind. Most parents hover around their kids. They're not paying attention, per se, focusing on their phones while they move up the line...

Benjamin was all alone. No parents by his side. Nobody holding his hand. There were four kids between us before it was his turn.

Then three.

Now two.

I was hardly paying attention to what these kids were even asking for, going through the motions while my eyes always drifted back to that boy in the blueberry snowsuit.

Now it was his turn.

I had to maintain myself. Keep my breathing even and not panic as he slowly waddled up to me. The nylon *zip-zip-zip* of his scissoring legs. The *sqush-sqush-sqush* of his galoshes.

I couldn't run. Couldn't move. My entire body was screaming for me to bolt. Just leap on out of my chair and head for the exit. But I was frozen. Bones locked in place. I couldn't escape.

Benjamin Pendleton waddled up. One hand grabs my knee, using my leg for leverage to hoist himself up and climb into my lap. His puffy blue snowsuit feels like a soggy pear. Some soaked piece of fruit. I was terrified that if I wasn't careful, one misplaced hand would tear right through his flimsy skin and I'd see the bones underneath. The gray muscle tissue.

This kid climbs into my lap. *Slowly.* Everything about him

moves at a stalled pace, delayed by a second or two. I can smell him now. There's a funk coming off him. River water.

His eyes meet mine. There's barely even a foot between our faces. I swear he's not breathing. His skin is blue. Glassy eyes. A purple latticework of veins reaches through his cheeks.

Hello, little fella . . . M-merry Christmas.

Nothing.

Have you been a good boy this year?

His lips split and I can see that his gums are purple. His tongue. His tongue is blue. *Cold*, he says. Gray water trickles out from his mouth, dribbling down his chin.

What do you want from me?

Cold . . .

Just tell me. Tell me what you want . . . I was gonna tack on: ". . . for Christmas," like I always do, but this wasn't about a brand-new bike or a dolly.

Cold . . .

Cold . . .

Cold . . .

Benjamin Goddamn Pendleton.

That kid kept coming back. Patiently waiting his turn in line. He would come and go out of nowhere. Sometimes I'd notice the cold before I'd see him, this precipitous drop in temperature, as if somebody was futzing with the thermostat. Then I'd spot him in line. Waiting his turn. Waddling his way up to me. The squish-squish of his water-logged galoshes.

His body was still out there, somewhere. Needle in fucking frozen haystack. He'd be in a body of water. That much I knew. Everything else was pure intuition.

I needed my head examined. This was crazy. I was crazy. What the hell was I thinking? Coming out here? Trudging through the gray snow . . . I'm not some police officer. Not some CSI-whatever. I'm just Santa Claus, for Christ's sake. Just another goddamn department store Santa.

Cold . . .

I swear, I could nearly hear his voice, pulling me through the snow. Leading me downriver. With every step I took, trudging alongside the frozen riverbank, I could hear the squish of his rubber galoshes. *Sqush-sqush-sqush-sqush.* The river itself was nothing but a sheet of gray glass, frosted over, so there was no seeing through. But I was getting closer. Closer . . .

Cold . . .

Cold . . .

Cold . . .

The newspaper would report the following morning that a local man who preferred to be unidentified found the body of Benjamin Pendleton trapped beneath a sheet of ice. That kid had been pirouetting through the water. His body drifted further downriver about a mile away from home. He was wearing the same blueberry snowsuit.

He'd been in a bus accident.

Benjamin Pendleton always sat in the back. Always in the very last row, right there in the rear, where the emergency exit is. His body must've slipped through the shattered glass, whisked up by the river, swirling for a murky eternity until somebody finally came upon him.

What was left. Bones in a blueberry suit.

That man who found him? The newspaper never got his name. He preferred to remain anonymous. Some folks said he had white hair. White beard. Bowl full of jelly.

You want the truth? There's no grind. The department store is empty. Nobody comes in now. Blame it on the economy, blame it on Amazon or whatever the hell you want to wag your finger at. Doesn't matter anymore, now, does it? Not really. Not when nobody's around.

This mall has been shuttered for months. Balkins went bust. The store's all empty. Somebody propped a maintenance door open and must've forgotten, so it was simple enough to slip in when nobody was looking. The holiday decorations are in storage. The suit was waiting for me. I've got the whole place to myself. Just me and the kids. All of the kids.

Funny thing is . . . the line never dies down. It's only gotten longer since I found Benjamin. Word must've gotten around about my abilities. That line of children just stretches around the aisles, the clothing racks, out the front door and around the building, on and on and on . . .

Look at them all.

Just look.

You see them, too, don't you? Hard to tell who's alive and who's a ghost anymore.

Who am I kidding? It's nothing but ghosts now. These spirits all line up, waiting their turn to sit on my lap and whisper in my ear what they want for Christmas. What they need.

I've really got my work cut out for me. Gonna be a busy one this year.

Merry Christmas to all and to all a good night . . .

The Solstice Guest

K.G. ANDERSON

Angry gusts and fitful rain worried the manor house eaves and rattled the panes of the upstairs windows. On the second floor, Tick Wiltshire moved through the rooms of her ancestral home, checking the window locks and letting curtains fall to shut out the dark December night. Her delicate lace-up boots clattered as she hurried down the broad oak staircase.

It was nearly midnight. Almost time. Her heart missed a beat as she imagined herself coming up the staircase in just a few minutes with Ethan at her side. Once again.

The ring of the phone in the front hallway startled her. Without thinking, she snatched up the receiver. "Hello?"

"Tick? You're home—"

"Alberta!" Tick swallowed hard. "Alberta! How are you? Everything all right?"

"Of course. But we were worried about you. I thought you were going to your aunt's in Sidmouth for the holiday."

Damn. Tick hated to lie. "Oh, I wasn't feeling well. Couldn't face making the drive."

There was a silence at Alberta's end. Tick kept silent as

well, licking her lips and glancing about the dark, chilly hallway.

"All right." Her mentor spoke slowly. "I wished we'd known! We could have brought you over to our place so you wouldn't greet the dawn alone. Well, I am so sorry to have bothered you. But all evening I've been worried, and Leonard suggested that I call."

"Oh, no need to apologize," Tick said, wishing the phone call would end. "Leonard's student is taking my place, yes?"

"He's here. We're almost ready. But, Tick, the Solstice just won't be the same without you…"

Alberta paused, and Tick wondered if she'd been about to say "—and Ethan." Her mentors had never approved of Tick's involvement with Ethan Camber, a young magician who'd claimed descent from the Anglesey Druids. Ethan's death in a road accident last summer had, Tick suspected, relieved their concerns.

Now Tick just sighed. "I'll miss you, too, Alberta. And of course, I'll call in the morning to wish you the joys of the Solstice."

After she hung up, Tick stood for a moment by the phone. Alberta's call had thrown her off. A draft brushed her cheek and she shivered, trying to remember what she'd been about to do when Alberta called. She'd practiced for days, of course, but this was the first time she tried casting the spell. She didn't dare forget a step.

Tick flipped the entryway switch and the chandelier came on, filling the room with light and color. She crossed the red Persian carpet to the front door where she tested the deadbolt. *Secure.* She'd be safe from any interruption.

But with the doors and windows locked, how would Ethan get in? The books she'd studied hadn't talked about that, had they? And she hadn't wanted to ask anyone, even Alberta and

Leonard. *Especially* Alberta and Leonard. The two senior members of her triad were old-school witches. Conservative.

To reassure herself, Tick smoothed her velvet skirt over her hips. The gesture soothed her nerves and coaxed a quick smile to her round face. Ethan had always liked the skirt. She bustled into the library to check the white votive candles she'd set among fresh fir boughs in front of the fieldstone hearth. Then she crossed the room to the tall bookshelves, where she carefully turned the photos of friends and family to the wall.

"I'm entitled to do this," she said defiantly. "This is why we have spells to bring back the dead. Spells that I've studied." *Though perhaps I'm stretching the definition of—*

"No!" Tick snapped. This was not the time to be thinking that way. She hurried to the record player and set the needle on the disk. The pipes and drums and bells of the old tunes began. She kindled the Yule log on the grate. And as midnight neared, she set a long match to each of the white votives, lighting the passageway for Ethan's return.

The summoning spell itself was simple. Thirteen words, repeated three times. Then three simple gestures. Finally, ashes from beneath the smoldering Yule log would be sprinkled over one of the white candles.

Slowly, deliberately, Tick began.

"Lord of the Otherworld, I beg return for one who left without farewell," she whispered. With each repetition, her voice gained strength.

Her hands trembled only slightly as she lifted the worn spellbook that had belonged to Ethan. She raised it to the sky, then held it to her heart. Finally she lay it beside the hearth.

With a silver spoon she lifted ashes from the fire and showered them onto one tall, flickering candle. Now all she—

"Tick?"

She startled. All these months spent refining the spell to

bring her lover back on the longest night of the year—so why was she surprised it had worked?

Ethan was there now, in his chair, the old one beside his reading lamp, the one she'd always been sure didn't give him enough light. He'd always been thin, but now he seemed painfully so, wearing stovepipe pants and a black corduroy jacket over a black shirt. His wavy black hair, swept back off his forehead, had that one stripe of grey. He was just the same. And yet, he was different.

A clap of thunder shook the house. It startled Tick but Ethan seemed not to hear it. He looked around the room, clearly puzzled. Tick had imagined their reunion many times, but in her imagination her lover had not looked confused.

"I brought you back," she said, her voice so soft she wondered if he'd heard her.

He still seemed puzzled. "Back?"

"It's the Solstice. I found a spell. I've missed you so much since you were . . . since you . . . died. I brought you back."

Ethan stiffened and his eyes went wide. Then he closed them for a moment. When he opened them again, Tick saw they glistened with tears.

"Tick." At last he stood and opened his arms wide in the embrace she'd dreamed of. Tick ran to him and leaned into his strength. He was real. But when he let her go, she was horrified by the somber look on his face. She had done something wrong. What had she done? "L-let me pour us some wine," she said.

"Please."

She turned off the record and poured from the bottle she'd left to breathe on the sideboard. They sat down with their glasses, he in his armchair, she on the square ottoman beside it. As they'd so often sat . . . before.

"What's it like, where you've been, Ethan? Where you are?"

"In the afterlife, we live on memories," he said. "My memories are good. Thanks to you." But his smile left as quickly as it had come. "Tick, I'm afraid there are going to be problems." Ethan's voice was low and calm, but he swirled his wine in the glass—a nervous gesture she'd never seen before. He had always been so still. "Those spells you used weren't designed to call back someone who's been—" Ethan looked around the room, anywhere but at Tick "—involved with magic."

Tick swallowed quickly. "I thought about that. I tried some modifications. And look, it worked!"

Ethan shook his head and closed his eyes. "Do Leonard and Alberta know what you're doing?"

Tick hesitated. Then, "No."

Ethan sighed. He set down his wine, hardly touched, on a side table and turned to her, then placed both his hands on her knees. He gave a smile at the feel of the velvet skirt, but it was short-lived. "Tick, the crash I died in was no simple roadway accident. A spell had gone wrong, and a powerful spirit was pursuing me. We were fighting, and I lost. I died, and I took that spirit with me."

Tick read horror in Ethan's eyes as he recalled his final minutes of life. "No!" she protested, and threw herself into his arms.

He pulled her close. "Tick, when you brought me back, I'm afraid you brought that spirit back as well. Listen."

Beneath the wail of the night wind, she thought she heard a voice calling Ethan's name. Tick's hands twisted her velvet skirt. *How dare they!* Her carefully crafted spell had worked. Ethan had come back. But now, everything was ruined. Their joyous reunion was anything but. She wanted to smash her wine glass on the stone hearth but was afraid to disturb the flickering candles lighting the pathway to the spirit world.

"I must go back and take that vile creature with me," Ethan said. "But Tick, that's not the worst of it. You see—"

A pounding on the front door made both of them jump from their seats.

"Can't you make it go away?" she wailed.

Ethan shook his head. "Tick, that's not the spirit. The ones at the door are Alberta and Leonard."

"That's not possible. I didn't tell them I was summoning you!"

"Of course you didn't. Because you knew you shouldn't have." Ethan sounded bitter, even angry. The hammering on the front door grew louder.

"I have to answer." Tick gave a ragged sigh. "They could probably magick the locks."

Ethan pulled her into his arms and whispered into her ear, "Alberta and Leonard have your best interests at heart, Tick. Whatever happens tonight, I want you to remember that."

She pulled back, trying to search his face in the flickering light from the fireplace. But Ethan wasn't meeting her eyes. Out in the hallway there was a slam as the bolt broke and the door flew open. Alberta and Leonard were in. Alberta's powerful voice rang out. "Tick? Tick?"

"I'm here!" Tick ran out to meet them.

Leonard was stamping his feet on the hallway carpet, looking about with brows furrowed, shaking off rain. His grizzled jowls were flushed with cold. Alberta, usually so bold, clung to his arm. They both looked older than she remembered. Alberta's heavy black cape appeared torn.

"Did you cast a summoning spell?" Leonard said. "What manner of creature have you brought back?"

Tick stood with her head bowed in shame. She gestured to

the library. "Come in and I'll ex—"

She screamed. Leonard had seized her by one arm and Alberta had taken the other. They dragged her out of the house, the great doors slamming behind them. The front steps were slick and black with sleet. In the darkness, Tick could just make out Leonard's ancient Bentley parked in her driveway, facing out toward the road.

"If you value your life, you'll come with us," Alberta shouted over the wind.

Tick stumbled along between them, her boots clattering along the path's cold flagstones. When they reached the car, Leonard yanked open the door to the back seat and Alberta shoved her in. Tick saw that any possibility of escape was blocked by Leonard's familiar, a massive Newfoundland dog. It sat sullenly beside the window.

Alberta leaped into the back seat beside Tick and pulled her door closed. Leonard sprang into the driver's seat, started the engine, switched on the headlamps, and they rattled down the drive. Only then did Alberta relax her grip enough to allow a panting, soaked Tick to look back at the manor. A light was on in her second-floor bedroom and Ethan stood at the window, watching them drive away. Tears filled Tick's eyes. "Where are you taking me?" she asked as Alberta bundled her in a lap robe.

"To our house," Alberta said. "Out of danger."

"No! I have the spell to send them back!"

"Them?"

"Ethan. And the spirit that pursued him. The accident. That was why he crashed the car."

Alberta gasped. Leonard was silent.

"Then this is even worse than we thought," Leonard spoke slowly. "Tick, do you know why there are no spells to call a magician like Ethan back from the dead?"

"Because it's never been done before?"

"No! It has! You are not the first witch to try it. And every single one of them has paid the price."

"Which is?"

Leonard broke in, "Tick! By the gods. You don't know?"

Tick shook her head, damp curls lashing her skin.

Leonard pulled to the side of the road and stopped the car. He stared straight ahead as he spoke. "If a witch summons a practitioner of magic back from the dead on the Solstice, a witch must return to the dead with them."

Tick gasped. "Nothing in the books said anything—"

"You read the wrong books," Alberta snapped. "Stupid, stupid girl."

Tick's anger flared, but the sight of Alberta's tear-stained face sobered her. In some dark corner of her mind, she'd known there'd be a price. That was why she hadn't told any of her fellow witches about her plans. All she had thought about was the prospect of seeing Ethan again, the prospect of being able to bring him back every year on the Solstice. Why hadn't she waited? Why hadn't she been more careful? Albert and Leonard were horrified—and Ethan must think her a fool.

"This is so much worse that we'd imagined." Alberta's tone was bitter. She twisted her hands in her lap. "We need to call the Council, we need—"

Leonard interrupted. "There's no time."

"Take me home!" Tink sobbed. "I have the spell to send Ethan back. And I . . . I'll go back with him." Through her tears, Leonard became a blur of bushy white hair and gold spectacles. A violent gust of wind rocked the car. "I've practiced for months," she said. "I can do it."

"All right." Leonard started the Bentley. He drove to the next crossroads, where, ignoring Alberta's protests, he turned the car around the headed back toward Tick's. In the glow of the headlamps the road seemed rougher, narrower, and darker. It had begun to snow, fine, dry flakes. Beside Tink, Leonard's familiar growled.

When they reached the manor house, Leonard stopped the car well back in the driveway. "Wait," he said. The witches peered through the falling snow. "Look there."

"It's Ethan!" cried Tick.

Ethan stood on the steps, his long hair whipping about his dark face. He'd spread his arms wide as if to gather someone, or something, in. When Leonard cracked a window in the old car, Tink thought she heard voices arguing. Then Ethan fell to his knees.

"Ethan!" Wrenching free of Alberta's grasp, Tick leaped from the car. She stumbled through the snow to the doorstep where Ethan had collapsed. The wind had subsided, but the snow was coming down in ever larger flakes, spangling his thin jacket. Tick called his name and his eyes opened—great dark orbs in a face that seemed even thinner. His body convulsed.

Tick looked back at the car. Alberta had climbed into the front seat with Leonard, and the two of them sat there. Black-robed. Like judges. Tick knew she was on her own, and deservedly so. She held Ethan until he was able to rise to his hands and knees.

He pulled himself upright using the great bronze handle of the door. "Time for me to go," he rasped. His voice and face were devoid of any expression.

Was he angry? In pain? Tick didn't dare ask. She helped him into the library, looking back at the front door and wishing she could bolt it behind them. But the wrought iron bolt, wrenched from the door by Leonard's spell, lay useless on the floor.

Ethan collapsed into his armchair and gestured weakly at

the raised hearth. The stout Yule log still burned, but the white candles Tick had employed for the summoning were flickering out. Now she replaced them with the black votives she'd prepared for his return. *For our return,* Tick thought, and the hairs raised on the back of her neck. She cast one last look around her beloved library. Then she knelt and lit the black candles, moving carefully, slowly, thinking about each step. She had not rehearsed this well.

Ethan came to the hearth, stood beside her, and raised her up. "Goodbye, Tick," he said. "I'm afraid it's forever this time."

No, it's not, thought Tick. *I'll be coming with you.* But she said nothing.

They embraced, his cold lips on her warm ones, and she wondered if their love would come with them to the other side. But she couldn't ask. Slipping from his arms, she began to whisper the spell of return. *Thirteen words, three times.*

She knelt, took ashes from the hearth and sprinkled half of them over one of the black candles, snuffing the flame. Carefully blocking Ethan's view, she used the rest of the ashes to smother a second candle. *My light has gone out, too,* she thought.

When she turned, Ethan's face and fingers were becoming translucent, his clothing fading from black to gray. Tick looked down at her own hands and waited to be taken. But her fingers remained solid. She spread them wide in panic. "Wait!" she shouted. "Wait! I'm supposed to go, too!" She spun to face the hearth, just in time to see all the black candles go out. The passage was closed for the year. Ethan vanished. She was still here. But she was not alone. Alberta stood in the doorway.

"He's gone," Tick said, her voice rising. "But I'm still here. Leonard's books were wrong!"

"Leonard's books were right." Alberta walked forward, her

fine-boned face grim. "It's just as Leonard told you: If a witch summons a magician from the dead on the Solstice, a witch must return to the dead with them." The elder witch paused. "It doesn't need to be the same witch."

Tick gasped. She looked wildly around the library, then ran to the front hall. There was no sign of Leonard. She and Alberta were alone in the silent manor house. "Blessed goddess!" she wailed. "No!"

Alberta, who'd followed her, gave a shuddering sigh. "Any spell you could have concocted to send Ethan back would have been far, far too weak to have returned the spirit that pursued him. Leonard knew the proper spell, and he used it."

"Oh, Alberta," Tick sank to her knees. "This is all my fault. I am so, so sorry."

"Hush." Alberta closed her eyes, pressed her long, elegant fingers to her lined face, and murmured the words "next year." When she removed her hands, she looked up and pointed to the hallway's high window. The black of the longest night was giving way to the silver gray of dawn.

"Get a warm coat, Tick," Alberta said. "And hurry." The old witch gathered her heavy cape around her and headed out the door, her voice rising with an ancient song. "The dark is fled. The light returns. We who survived must bid it welcome."

Like a Million Points of Light

JOHN PALISANO

"Anything but Christmas songs." Ivy nudged the Sam Adams Winterfest bottle in front of her. A finger tapped its side. "In keeping with us avoiding the holiday." She nodded to the big fellow standing behind the bar.

"Reggie M. Jackson," he said. "Like the ballplayer. With an 'm.' Pleased to meet you. Welcome to The Dark Spot."

"Weird place," she said. "A bar hidden behind a bowling alley. But hey? Thanks for the invite."

"We're in that awful time when Christmas still hasn't gone away and everyone else is still happy about it, and even worse? New Year's, which is the absolute, most depressing holiday in my book."

"Indeed." Ivy scanned the room. There were only two other folks sitting at a table near the back. "Well, this place seems pretty lonely."

"What we don't have in numbers, we make up for with personality."

"M'kay." She used the moment to take a big swig of the beer.

Reggie pressed a few buttons, and The Dark Spot came to life with the first punchy notes of Ricky V's "All Alone in the Zone." The walking, hip-hop beat and distinct distorted rhymes sounded like they floated inside her skull.

"Damn thing should come with a volume control. Can't even hear myself think." The woman behind Ivy hollered.

"You'll be okay, Erica. Just for this one song. Makes me feel like when things were perfect—back before I needed to forget." Reggie turned his back and moved to the beat ever so slightly as he polished a glass.

Ivy made it halfway down the beer. Her throat was sore from being outside. *He said the folks that come here are all grieving. Guess he is, too.*

When the song finished, Reggie turned around. "So, Ivy. We need to break the ice. We have a tradition here." He waved to Erica and the man to join them.

Ivy took another big sip. "Not sure what's happening."

"We are going to share our stories with you." Seeing she'd nearly downed the beer, he put another one on the bar.

"Speaking of books . . ." Reggie handed her a loose-leaf notebook. "We take down everyone's names. Helps those who come after. Helps you to look back later when and if you feel better about it all."

Ivy opened the battered thing and saw a few pages of names with dates. "This goes back about twenty years," she said.

"The Spot's been here longer than that, helping people let go. We are always in search of new broken souls."

"I don't know if this will work. I kinda think I'm always going to be a Grinch this time of year," Ivy said. "Just something about all of it that makes me sick. Just so phony. All the cheap, plastic decorations. You have to buy presents for everyone. So stressful. Who do you buy for? Who do you exclude? I don't want to be an asshole, but I always feel like I've disappointed everyone, so I'd rather just go away and hide."

Erica sat next to her. "We're all hiding here as far away from the holidays as possible." She swirled her whiskey and Coke on the bar with her finger.

"The family keeps nudging me to come and be a part of the festivities," Ivy said. "I think it's their way of keeping a little bit of Jake alive. But he's dead and I feel like I'm dead inside . . . like I'm walking through life like a ghost of who I used to be."

"I get that. I do. You get used to the new, awful, brutal normal, though. Over time. But it's never the same," Erica said. "And I hate every goddamn, rotten, stinking person that posts pictures of themselves smiling with their families. Wearing their little winter hats. Like everything's all perfect for them. Fuck them." She lowered her head. Put a hand to her face . . . her eyes. Stemmed back tears. Took a deep breath.

"I hear you," Reggie said. "I do. It's no fun to have that shoved in your face. No one wants to hear from us and deal with our feelings, like how it makes us feel like broken toys that haven't been thrown out yet."

"Amen," Erica said.

"We can learn to control our feelings instead of letting them control us," José said. "It's something I've been working very hard on."

Reggie smirked then traded a knowing look with Ivy. "I'm so happy you're doing better, my friend. Working through grief is one of the hardest things we can ever do."

"It is." José took a baby sip of his drink.

Then what the hell is he doing here if he's so happy? Ivy stared at him, looking for a cue. She saw it right away. The hand not holding his drink was at his side, shaking like a leaf. *Keeping the dark way the fuck down, aren't we?*

"We're all ghosts here. That's the motto," Reggie said.

"Well then, I should fit right in." Ivy pounded her beer. When she came up for air, she started in. "Lost my fiancé. Jake Campion. Fentanyl. Messed up thing is he was a straight arrow. Was at work at the hospital and got a migraine. Someone gave him an Advil. At least that's what he thought it was. Counterfeit. He was gone before anyone figured it out. And he was right there at St. Joseph's, and they still couldn't save him in time. Sucks." Everything went hazy as though a veil made of countless wiggling black spots covered her face.

Erica put a hand on her back. I'm so sorry, darling," she said. "That's just plain awful. You're so young, too."

"He was twenty-seven. Denver's been dark for me ever since." Ivy curled her hands on the bar like an eagle perching on a branch. "Dark as pitch."

Erica sighed. "Another round for us," she instructed Reggie. He obliged. "Lost my husband. My kids. Thirteen years since the accident. Feels like yesterday. Still raw as the night it happened. It's not better but I've learned to live with it."

"I wish the feeling would go away," Ivy said. "I'm tired of living with it. Sometimes it feels like my insides are being eaten alive by a swarm of little black bugs."

They all exchanged a nervous look. José broke it. "You're still standing, Ivy. There's a lot to be said for that."

"Hopefully I'll be stumbling pretty soon." She realized José was sitting until it clicked with her he was in a chair. A wheelchair. How had she missed that? *Too wrapped up in myself.*

"At least you can stumble. I can only roll." He tapped his heart. "Stray bullet. Friendly fire. Not even real combat. No one wants to be with a queer Marine." He looked down at his knees. "Not even the one who'd been with you for seven years. Didn't want to be a caretaker. Like I can't take care of myself."

"I'm sorry," Ivy said.

"Dropped the bomb on me Christmas Eve. Let me suffer with that. I'll never forget it. Or forgive Miguel. This is a self-ish, cruel world."

"Amen," Ivy said.

"I lost my wife, too," Reggie said. "Fuck cancer. In its eye."

"Cheery bunch, aren't we?" Ivy said. "'Tis the season."

Her head buzzed. Ivy finished the round and got up. On her way to the head, she noticed the decorations around The Dark Spot. Odd items were displayed on shelves. A wallet. A beaten-up copy of *Hitchhiker's Guide to the Galaxy*. An Employee of the Month Award for someone named Stanley Brown. She shrugged it off and made her way. *Probably tokens left by the people who escaped their grief. Like an actor who leaves a headshot once they get their big break.*

When she sat on the can, her head spun like she was on a ship. *I better slow down with the booze. Don't want to end the night early.* She thought back to how she'd first met Reggie through social media. She'd made posts about losing Jake. He made supportive comments, but they'd never met in person. Just one of those people that comes into orbit that way. Then, a month back, he sent her a DM.

"I go to this place that helps people with grieving. Especially this time of year. It's pretty quiet and out of the way. We help each other. You should stop by," he'd written.

She scoffed at first. It sounded like a support group. She was intrigued when she found out it was a bar. "But you have to be invited. And the drinks are free. It just costs your time."

Splashing her face to try and sober up a little, Ivy tried to steel herself. *You're strong. You'll get through this. Jake would want you to be okay and be happy.*

Rage rose up. *Fuck that self-help shit. This sucks. No way around it or psyching yourself out of that factoid. You got a raw deal.*

She knew it was most definitely time for another drink. Leaving the bathroom with an empty tank and a renewed purpose, Ivy rushed back.

When she got back to the main room, someone new stood dead center. His pale gray and blue eyes stared at her. It was as if he was expecting her.

Who's this asshole? She looked around to try and find the others. Erica and José had their backs to her. Reggie met her gaze and nodded. "We have a new friend," he said. The Dark Spot was small enough that she easily heard him. The music was back on, but it was low enough that she couldn't even figure out the song, let alone the genre.

"All right," she said. "Welcome to the I Hate the Holidays Club."

She approached him and put out a hand. He didn't reach back—just stared right at her, his otherworldly eyes unblinking.

And I thought I was damaged goods. This guy's a basket case.

Looking away, she made her way around him. "M'kay," she said to Reggie. "Can you set me up?"

"Same thing?" he asked.

"Maybe something a little stronger. Whisky and water."

"You're not messing around," he said.

"Nope." Ivy sighed. "Booze is one of the few things that helps quiet the bugs eating me up." He was acting a little different; his hands shook ever so slightly. What was he hiding?

She found her same seat next to Erica and watched Reggie pour.

"Hello."

Ivy jumped. The fellow with blue-gray eyes stood next to her. *How'd he get here without me even hearing him?*

"Your sadness . . ." he said. "Your pain." There was something off about his voice. It was like he had two tones fighting for prominence.

"What about it? What's your story?" Ivy looked to Reggie for an out; she didn't want to make eye contact with the dual-voiced man.

"Mr. T has got a lot to say," Reggie said. "You should listen to him. I was hoping you two would meet."

Ivy shook her head. "I'm being punked, right? Mr. T? Reggie Jackson? Is Madonna going to deliver us a pizza from 1986?" She wondered if the man had been wounded in an accident—maybe a fire? Why wasn't anyone else mentioning it? Maybe everyone was just used to damaged people and were accepting, but she still sensed something very off.

"My name is Tenebrous," the man said. "Reggie gave me another name."

"Fine," Ivy said. "Tene . . . something. Whatever. I'm listening."

"There's a way to manage your grief," he said. Again, his strange voice unnerved her.

"And I suppose you've managed yours?" she asked. "What's up with your voice? Were you in some kind of accident?" She didn't mind being brash and turned to him, aiming to look him in the eye and see what he was made of. She expected an older, lecherous man, but found his face smooth and unblemished, yet he still gave off late middle-aged vibes.

"I don't have feelings of my own, usually," he said. "Not like you. But I know a way to take them away."

Ivy slammed on the bar. They were all in on it, whatever was happening. "All right. Something's really fishy here. I'm being scammed. I don't know what kind of weird cult you all are . . ."

His fingers touched the top of her right hand. Gentle. Light. An electrical pulse surged through her, to her wrist, her elbow, under her arm, down to the area of her kidney. She felt warm in a similar way to being buzzed, only deeper.

"What the . . .?"

He clasped her hand in his. The pulse turned into a surge, racing through her nerves to every tip of her body. Her head felt tingly. Ivy's mind became impossibly lighter. Her anger lifted. She felt good.

Too good.

"What are you doing? Is this some sort of contact high? You're drugging me with something on your skin. That's what this is." Even as she spoke, she somehow knew it wasn't true. *Don't be stupid. Use your brain, Ivy. This is how they make you vulnerable. Get out of here. Now. Run.* She looked at Reggie; he didn't look concerned for her at all. *I've been set up. He's in on it. They all are. Fight or flight says to flee.*

"Excuse me," she said, summoning all the willpower she could. Pushing his hand off hers, she jutted away from the bar, off her stool, and ran to the door. She was outside just as someone . . . she couldn't tell who . . . shouted for her to wait.

The cold hit her. The weird buzz Mr. T or whatever his name was wore off, but she was happy to still feel a little high from the booze. "What the fork was that all about?" She looked out at the dark Colorado sky and could just make out the top of the Rockies above the bowling alley building. She patted her pants pocket and felt her phone. "Thank God for small miracles." Reaching inside for it, she knew she was going to call an Uber and go home. Block Reggie's profile. Report him. Report what they'd tried.

Before she had a chance, Mr. T was outside, standing only a

few feet from her. How had he moved so quietly and fast? She would have seen him moving out of the corner of her eye.

"Get back," she said.

"I'm not here to hurt you." His weird, dual voice. "Just help take it away."

"No. Not interested."

In a blink, he charged at her. No. Flew at her, his arms outstretched.

She saw dark bat-like wings unfold. Wrapping around her, Tenebrous flew upward. She faced his chest, smelled the leather vest. Felt the cold night air. *I'm tripping eyeballs. That's what this is. How'd it hit so fast? Usually takes hours to kick in to hallucinate.*

She tilted her head back. The world was painted white with snow. Lights glowed, visible even high up. It was remarkable seeing Colorado from such a vantage. They approached the slopes of Pike's Peak, and she remembered going on the incline train with Jake. At the thought of him, her guts knotted. *I wish he could see this with me.* And there it was, in the pit of her stomach. Her grief got her, even as she soared through the air. Nothing was worth it without Jake.

Sharp needles pierced Ivy's sides. She looked down and saw claws connected to her, pulsing. She felt woozy. *It's taking my essence from me. That's why it took me. To feed off me.* She felt faint and looked away. *Never look when they take your blood.*

Her face flushed, angry at the breach. *How dare this thing do this to me? Steal from my body.*

Warmth spread from the points, numbing her from the tip of her head to her toes. The pain fell away, and her guts unknotted. Her anger turned into complacency.

They flew higher and she felt frozen. She couldn't shiver. She couldn't do anything. *I'm like a lifeless doll.* She couldn't see anything below them; all she saw were clouds. Endless, gray clouds. She fought against it, but she couldn't keep her eyes open. All she felt was a pleasant tingling throughout her entire body. She blacked out. At least the anguish had settled.

IVY WOKE and looked up at a clear night sky. Lying on her side, she blinked several times. She saw the man in front of her, lying down, too, and on his side. He was breathing, a good sign. *Where am I?* She didn't recognize the landscape. Barren of any plants, the ground was made up of brown soil and brown rocks, all the same color. Ahead of them, she noticed a short ridge. Powerful moonlight illuminated the area. She made out every detail, the light putting everything into high contrast.

She pushed up and sat. Her head hurt. *It's like a hangover.* She stood, fighting against dizziness. Stepping toward the flying man, she saw him splayed out. His wings looked like a dark blanket. His eyes were shut.

Ivy thought it best not to wake him. She tiptoed past him and walked carefully toward the ridge. *Is this like a place where the Three Wise Men found Jesus? Is this where the Jews hid from the Egyptians? It feels sacred here.* When she got to its edge, she gasped as she stood on the edge of a massive crater. The bottom had to be several stories down. She couldn't see to the other side of the hole, either. Inside, it was forged from the same dull brown soil and rock as the area around her. Below, she spotted several holes like cave entrances. *He . . . it . . . brought me to its home. That's what this is.* She wasn't sure how she knew, but she was sure.

"Ivy."

She jumped. Turned around. The thing stood only a dozen steps away, upright, awake, its eyes fixed on her. A deep chill went from her chest to her guts.

"We are here."

Its skin shimmered as though infused with metallic flakes. It reminded her of the seats on the ski lift from when she and Jake went to Aspen. Oh, to be near the snow-covered hills, the amazing downtown, to hear his laughter again as they tried to ski . . . she'd give anything. That was the best Christmas ever.

"Where are you?" it asked. Again, the strange, double voice jarred her.

"I'm here." Ivy met its gaze again. "Why?" *What was its name again? Mr. T? No. That's just what Reggie called him. Tenebrous. That's its real name.*

"To make you an offer. To take away your pain." Tenebrous opened its middle. From its sides, long, finger-like appendages slipped outward, their needle tips pointing toward her.

"With those things?"

Tenebrous nodded. "I will consume it for you."

"You already took some. When we were flying."

"Just enough."

"Just enough for what?"

The appendages stiffened, eager to poke, anxious to draw from her.

"A taste so I knew your darkness," Tenebrous said, his gaze never faltering. "And it is quite a lot. Just a small amount took a lot out of me."

"That's why you slept, too," she said. "Now I get it. Wouldn't more hurt you worse?"

Tenebrous nodded; the appendages looked like snakes about to strike. "Consuming your darkness would be like gorging and I would sleep for a long time."

Ivy got it. "So, you feed off this stuff. Off people's darkness."

"Yes." Tenebrous didn't hesitate.

"And what happens after? How do I get back? Will I be cured?"

"You'll remember nothing. You'll be free."

"And you'll be full," she said. "And what do you mean by remembering nothing?"

"The root cause . . . the fluid and electricity that makes up these memories will be flushed out."

"So, I won't remember Jake?"

Tenebrous paused. The appendages softened their stance. "You won't."

"I don't want to forget him." She lowered her head, taking a moment to think about the offer. " Is that what the others did? Back at the bar? They all seemed to remember their loved ones. Did you make them the same offer?"

"Those left refused me. But there have been many others they've brought to me who have agreed."

That's what Reggie meant when he said a lot of people came and went. "If they don't bring you someone each year to feed off of? Then what?"

Tenebrous lowered his head. "Enough talk." He charged her, his movement impossibly fast.

Ivy screamed, "No!"

The appendages pierced her sides once more, only it was not smooth and gentle, but violent. Pushed down onto her back, Tenebrous pushed her shoulders down with his hands. "You can't do this. I didn't agree."

Her sides felt filled with liquid fire. She felt fluid being sucked out. "I don't want to forget Jake. He's mine to keep alive."

Drained, she felt dizzy, but in a more painful way than before. *This thing is killing me. It will leave me to die and wither to dust.* She tried to push up and fight, but her strength had gone. She felt like she couldn't even control her blinking. *It's drugged me. Made me incapable of fighting back.* Ivy wanted to kick. Punch. Bite. But nothing worked.

Her throat felt so dry. Her eyes hurt. Her lips. Everything. Her eyes shut but she didn't sleep. She cycled through as many memories of Jake as she could. *Don't forget. Don't forget.* As she did, her stomach felt so tight. His loss made her feel scooped inside. *How can I even carry this much and not have just died from it all?*

She went back to her favorite memory, in Vail, on the slopes just as the night had fallen. Jake, his breath white clouds, his eyes glossy from the cold, his cheeks as red as Santa Claus's, smiling at her, looking at her in a way she thought no one ever could. "Merry Christmas, Ivy. I love you so much."

No. No. No. He can't be gone. And this thing on top of me can't be real.

She passed out, the image of Jake burned into her brain, faded into a remnant, and then into the dark, his voice echoing.

IVY COUGHED. Her throat was filled with substance. She rolled on her side and spit up. The dark, oil-like fluid soaked into the dirt. She felt her sides, burning from the piercings. As she sat and then stood, she saw Tenebrous laid out, too. *Didn't this just happen?* She walked toward the creature. The appendages were strewn out and weren't moving. When she went up to Tenebrous, she noticed his eyes were open, but they were dull and lifeless. So, too, was his skin. It'd turned pale and chalky. She kicked his back lightly. No response. She tried again. Nothing. *He's dead.*

But how?

My darkness.

"Bit off more than you can chew, didn't you?" she said, laughing.

Ivy felt compelled to grab his arms and drag him to the lip

of the crater. She looked back several times to make sure it wasn't a trap, but he didn't resist. He'd died. "Don't know why I'm doing this, but whatever." As much as it hurt her to push and roll him on account of her wounds, she did.

"Ah!" she hollered as she finally tumbled his body over the lip of the crater.

He fell for a short bit. Halfway down, his body exploded like a nest of spiders, a thousand pieces breaking apart, disappearing into the brown soil.

There was nothing left she could see.

Ivy laughed. "Got you." She laughed again. It was the first time she remembered laughing since before Jake passed.

She looked down for a while, expecting Tenebrous to reappear from the lip of the crater, to manifest itself once more. It didn't. Spotting something near the ridge, she went to it. The tip of one of the appendages had been ripped away from its host. Ivy picked it up and regarded the piece, confident it wasn't alive. She put it in her inside jacket pocket. "A little souvenir."

Turning away, she stepped first four times, then more, and more until she came upon a hill. She climbed the hill. At its crest, she looked out and saw light. Homes. Cottages. Roads. Above, in the sky, a large, lone star shined. Ivy smiled. "You're with me, Jake," she said. "In my heart. Always."

She nodded and made her first steps toward the village, toward home, and felt the little dark spots she'd carried inside fall away, vanishing into the dirt, buried and gone.

Ivy raised her face to the winter star and beamed. *I'm going to let my pain explode like a million points of light and watch it all vanish into the winter night like the falling gunpowder of a New Year's firework, for a moment, so bright you have to squint. But then? A faint impression, all that's left behind.*

She sighed. "I'm going to be okay," and kept walking.

"Finally." She had to make it back to the bar—to The Dark Spot—somehow, from wherever she was, to share the news and to leave behind her token for the wall—the severed tip— proof she'd defeated Tenebrous. They were free and she was free. Ivy patted her heart and pictured Jake. *And I get to keep all of you that's still alive inside me. It'll never be the same, but it doesn't have to hurt like hell anymore.*

The North star shone down from the clear sky so brightly she felt like she could cup it in her hands.

FROM THE SKY, a snowflake fell. The dry, oppressive air chilled and dampened. She crossed her arms in front of her and walked to the top of the small hill. The snow increased. Within moments, the ground was covered.

Ivy turned but could no longer see where the land stopped and the crater began.

She scaled the hill, her feet slipping. She had to find shelter fast. *I don't even know where I am. Somewhere in Russia if it's snowing like this?* Her heart quickened at the idea.

Below, she saw lights. Roads. The edge of civilization. She hurried toward it. Details were scarce, and the whipping snowstorm made visibility quite low. Her hands were freezing. Her nose felt made of ice.

It felt like she was walking downhill forever before she reached the bottom. She had to follow the amber glow of the streetlights to find her way.

Reaching the road, she gasped. Ivy read the signs on a building she approached. "Rocky Mountain Storage. Wait a second." She turned and looked from where she'd come and saw a towering snow-covered slope. "That was a hill. It could not have been that big. I swear it wasn't."

She kept going and found a gas station with a convenience

mart inside. She recognized everything. Coca-Cola. Donuts. Coffee. Blessedly, coffee. She went to make a cup and warm up.

"¿Qué pasó?" There was a young man speaking into his phone near the back. "¿Me compraste las entradas para los Broncos?"

The Broncos? How was she back in Denver? She had just flown halfway across the world to a crater. She checked her phone; she had service. The weather app and map confirmed she was home.

"How can I be on Colfax Avenue?"

Calling an Uber, Ivy had the driver drop her off at the bowling alley just outside of Cherry Creek—the address was still in her history. When she made her way round the back toward The Dark Spot, she was surprised at how dark it was. "What happened to the lights?"

The door to the bar was open, so she went inside.

It was nothing like she'd remembered. It was empty—looked like it'd been empty for years. The bar was covered in dust.

"Hello?" Ivy checked everywhere for signs of life but found none.

The tokens were still on the walls. She looked at them and found a photo of Reggie she hadn't noticed before. In it, he had his arms around a smiling, bright-eyed lady that must have been his late wife. In front of the photo? The same Broncos hat he'd been wearing in the photo. His token. *Now they're all just ghosts.*

Ivy remembered her own token—the tip of the appendage—and reached into her pocket.

She pulled out a handful of dust. She spread her fingers and watched it sift through and fall to the dusty floor. She went to the door and took one last look around. "We're all free now," she said and walked back into the cold, Denver night, eager to get home, glad to say goodbye to The Dark Spot, as grateful as she was for its gift.

And for the first time since she could remember, the knot in her stomach unraveled and she felt her grief finally slip away.

The Angel

KATHERINE TRAYLOR

She knew the recipe by heart. Oven at 300°F. Flour, sugar, baking powder, salt. Cinnamon, nutmeg, cloves, molasses. She'd had to bake in Pyrex before, but Aunt Alex had left her Grandma's prized cast-iron loaf pan along with most of the Christmas decorations. Her sister would kill her if she knew Marie had the pan, but Marie wasn't giving it up. Grandma's spice bread never quite tasted the same without it.

And with the spice bread baking, it was Christmastime. Marie wasn't Christian anymore, but the feelings of warmth and excitement from childhood still echoed through her adult heart despite the darkness that had sometimes haunted those days. Sometimes she managed to isolate the good memories from the bad and just be happy in the memory of what she'd once had. Sometimes she wanted to put the past as far behind her as she could.

As the aroma of spice bread floated through the house, Marie wandered into the living room and looked at the Christmas tree. She glanced uneasily at the handmade angel at the top. Rumpled and creased (though she'd tried to press it), it was made of reddish patchwork, with brown yarn hair and a gold pipe-cleaner halo. It looked out of place on the tree, but she couldn't quite bring herself to leave it off now that she had it.

Her eyes roved over the metal snowflakes she'd bought in a local art shop, the cinnamon-stick bundle Holly had made in kindergarten, the green plastic Grinch from a fast-food restaurant, the string lights shaped like ice cream cones. It was an eclectic mess: less elegant than the witchy kitsch she and Holly had filled their home with, less important than the altars and the embroidered hymn to Brigid. It was a fun way to connect with their pasts, a place to display their ornaments. The cats enjoyed the ornaments as much as anybody; she'd chased them from the branches twice already this morning.

Mixed with the clutter of modern ornaments were older, more fragile ones that had belonged to her grandmother: glass orbs and spindles, starched-lace snowflakes, tiny wooden carousels, a wreath of glued-together seashells. Aunt Alex, her mother's sister, had inherited them when Grandma Booth had died, and in turn, left them to Marie. Alex had been estranged from her family for pretty much the same reason as Marie herself: religious differences and a "lifestyle" her mother couldn't come to terms with. She'd have known better than anyone that holidays were the most difficult, the times when you really missed being home.

But this year the tree wasn't entirely comforting. Since putting up the ornaments, she'd been bothered by a hunted feeling, as if something unfriendly were watching her. For the last few nights, just as she fell asleep, she'd heard low, vicious snarling at the edge of her consciousness—a voice she recognized. Grandma Booth had been an ogre in her worst moods, angry at the world and sure everyone was teaming up to spite her. She'd snarled the same way when Marie's mother told her they wouldn't be visiting anymore, and again when Marie (still closeted in multiple ways) said she wouldn't go to Bible college. She wondered uneasily what Grandma, a devout life-long Christian, would think of her precious ornaments being hung in a house of witches.

Mood souring, Marie sat on the couch and hugged a cushion, thinking of those childhood visits. She could picture Grandma Booth without closing her eyes: her wispy hair; the men's shirts she wore; her stumping walk and the quick, decisive way she did things when she wasn't flustered. On gray days, Marie imagined herself back in the Smoky Mountains, following her grandmother through the woods in the chill wet wind of a North Carolina December. She could smell the fragrant pine straw underfoot, hear her grandmother's footsteps in the leaves mixed with the rustling of nearby animals.

Even now, far east of the mountains, she could look out the window into the woods and imagine herself there: twelve or thirteen again, ready for Christmas. Spice bread baking meant it was time to hang suet balls for the birds, time to skip stones on frozen creeks and gather pine cones for the windowsills.

But Grandma's moods had always changed like lightning. One moment she might be showing Marie and her sister Jessica how to make ginger snaps. The next, she might slap them for wiping their floury hands on the wrong dishcloth.

That was why the visits had stopped. Even their mother, sometimes violent herself, had had enough when Grandma had thrown a shoe at Jessica and cut her forehead. After that, there'd only been phone calls and a few stiff lunches.

Grandma had died while Marie was at school. The fight over Bible college was never resolved, the relationship never mended. Marie had been too angry to go to the funeral, though she'd regretted it later. She wished she and her grandmother could have had one good sit-down conversation as adults, if only to get the feelings out.

She was looking gloomily at a picture of her sister Jessica and her kids—a niece and two nephews Marie hadn't seen in months—when her partner, Holly, came in with the dog.

"Why so cloudy, sunshine?" Holly said, kissing Marie's forehead. Beside them, Dis threw herself onto the couch, rubbing eau-de-squirrel all over the cushions.

Marie shrugged. "Miss everyone." She and her sister still talked but rarely at Christmas. Jessica still hadn't quite come to terms with Marie's new religion.

Holly scooted in beside Dis, rubbing the pit bull's belly and kissing Marie gently on the neck. "I'm sorry. Are you still up for the ritual tomorrow?"

She'd almost forgotten. "Definitely. Wouldn't miss it." She wondered what Grandma Booth would think of her patchwork angel having a front-row seat for a pagan celebration.

There was no point in worrying about it. The timer was ringing. There was dinner to make and lots to prepare for tomorrow. Accepting Holly's hand off the couch, she went to take the bread out of the oven.

That night they sat in the living room with the lamps off and a small fire burning. The Christmas tree was a nest of soft-colored lights. They sparkled on the chalices and candlesticks on the altars, the glass of the night-dark windows, the varnish of Holly's brown guitar.

Holly was in a good mood: today had been her last day of work before vacation. She bumped Marie's shoulder affectionately as she tuned her guitar.

Cozy with the cats and Dis around her, Marie held up her glass to the firelight, admiring the rich darkness of the mulled wine. The same beauty glowed in Holly's dark eyes as she began to play a soft, intricate melody on her guitar.

Listening, Marie was suddenly overwhelmed by gratitude for this house, this happiness, this absolute acceptance of who and what she was, the incredible love Holly showed her every day. These were blessings she'd never thought she could receive back when she was cowed and frightened, sure all kinds of things were wrong with her. Though she missed her family, she didn't miss the smallness of her former life: stuffed into an evangelical shell, told over and over again how "joyful" she was while she felt more miserable day by day. If she'd known how happy she could be, she would have—

In the kitchen, a cupboard door slammed.

Both women gasped. The cats bolted in opposite directions. Dis let out a long howl and started barking. Putting down her guitar, Holly rose to investigate. Marie followed a second later.

As she passed the Christmas tree, something pinched sharply into the crook of her shoulder, tightening and tightening until she cried out in pain.

Holly spun. "Marie? What's wrong?"

The pain stopped as suddenly as it had started. Bewildered, Marie hurried into the kitchen, still rubbing the abused spot. "Nothing," she said. "Bumped into the door. What happened?"

"Don't know." Holly flipped the light on. "Did something fall?"

They looked a little longer, but all the cupboards were neatly shut and nothing seemed out of place. Reluctantly, Holly turned off the light, and they went back to the living room.

But the peace was gone. After a few more strums, Holly put the guitar away. The cats stayed hidden, and Dis paced fretfully all night, searching in corners for something that wasn't there.

They sat there for a while longer, neither speaking, both watching for threats though neither admitted it. There was nothing in the house to fear, she knew, nothing she didn't love and didn't want there. But for just a moment, as they stood to go to bed, she thought she saw a dark silhouette against the shadows of the kitchen doorway. Suddenly, she didn't feel nearly as safe as before.

They were busy all the next day cleaning and decorating, buying groceries, and cooking for nine hungry witches. Marie had almost forgotten what had happened the night before, though her shoulder still tingled. She was rolling out sugar cookies when a jingling crash sent her right out of her skin.

Of course, she knew the sound. The tree had fallen over.

"Dis!" she shouted, exasperated. The dog was usually well-behaved, but so many baubles would have tempted a canine angel.

Footsteps clicked on the kitchen floor behind her. Stomach sinking, Marie remembered that Dis had been sleeping under the window. The cats, always hopeful she might drop something tasty, were in the kitchen, too. They sat bolt upright, watching the doorway. None of them moved to enter the living room.

Marie desperately wished Holly were back from the grocery store. She looked all over the living room for anything that could have caused the tree to fall. The stand had been full. Water was leaking out in a spreading puddle. The weight should have kept the tree stable. As far as she could see, there was nothing else that could have made it topple.

Luckily, only two glass balls were broken, but ten or twenty ornaments were on the floor. The angel lay apart, cloth arms spread as if to drag itself away. Uneasily, Marie picked it up and set it on the piano.

She didn't put the angel back, but it didn't seem to matter. Ornaments kept falling from the tree, sparsely at first and then every other minute. Holly, always sure a problem could be fixed if you looked at it right, spent half an hour fiddling with the tree stand, but the ornaments kept falling. Dis and the cats wouldn't go near the room.

That night, Marie did her best to relax, greeting the guests in their solstice regalia and trying not to think about the tree. After a dinner to rival any she'd had at her grandmother's Appalachian table, she followed her friends outside and stood barefoot in a circle with the others, waiting for the ritual to begin.

It was a mild night. Though the patio was chilly under her bare feet, her long green dress kept her from getting too cold. They'd laid a circle of greenery around the usual salt, and the massed candles in the center of the circle cast warm golden light on faces that had become dear to her over the last few years. It was the highlight of her years now, she often thought: standing hand in hand with Holly in the circle, singing the darkness to an end, calling for the light.

Still, this year she was a little distracted. The lights of the tree glowed through the window, and the remembered aromas of their meal (roast meat, stuffing, green bean casserole), hung in the air with the incense. It was, she thought suddenly, as if the feast of Solstice present were being haunted by the memory of Christmas past.

With difficulty, she drew her attention back to the ritual. Roxanne was leading a call-and-response sequence, guiding their visualizations through winter into the light. "Who sleeps through the cruel seasons, deep under snow, but goes forth when the sun begins to brighten?"

"It is the young year who wakes," they answered.

"What threads through rivers, climbs high mountains, lodges in the dens of beasts, waiting till a warm season calls it out into the world?"

"It is life that waits!"

"Who—"

The loud *pop* from inside would have been audible even without Dis barking, without the faint crash of the Christmas tree falling once again.

Rossana and some of the others remained in the circle, trying to maintain some of the energy, though the ritual would have to be restarted. Everyone else helped salvage the tree, which was in much worse shape this time.

"You'd think at least a few of the ornaments would have stayed on." Autumn frowned at a little drummer boy on a velvet ribbon. "Look how short the loop is. It shouldn't have slid off like that. You'd have to pull it pretty hard. And . . . oh, no."

Marie looked where Autumn was pointing. "Oh, no," she groaned. "Holly, baby, look."

She and Holly had picked out one set of new ornaments this year, blown-glass baubles shaped like sweets: an ice cream cone, a cookie, a donut, and so on. All but the donut were now broken, a chaos of pink-and-silver shards where the tree had lain.

"What a shame," Sharon murmured. "Were they all on the same side?"

Marie and Holly exchanged glances. "No," Holly said slowly, "they weren't. We'd spaced them out so we could see them wherever we were."

"But they were all under the tree," said Sharon.

Everyone was quiet. "Could it have been Dis?" Autumn ventured. "Or one of the cats?"

"They're still in the bedroom," Holly said. "And Dis was with us." They could faintly hear her barking, upset at being locked outside while they cleaned up the broken glass.

Everyone looked at the tree. Shadows played eerily in its branches. The lights had shorted out so violently that the room still smelled faintly of smoke. There had been an eerie few minutes in the dark before Holly reset the breaker.

"I can do a cleansing if you'd like," Sharon volunteered. "Just in case, you know . . ."

Autumn shivered. "Probably a good idea. This happened to my mom once when she bought a doll at a yard sale. She still hears noises sometimes."

Marie thought of the shape in the doorway, the painful pinch.

Holly was already agreeing. "That would be incredible, Sharon, if you don't mind. I've been feeling something skeevy the last few days. I didn't want to mention it, in case I was imagining things," she told Marie sheepishly, "but I haven't wanted to be in the living room alone. Maybe just a nice smoke cleansing . . ."

"Of course," Sharon said. "I can come tomorrow, if you'd like."

Marie was about to accept. Then her eyes fell on the angel.

She knew whose ghost this was (no point denying it was a ghost). She imagined Grandma Booth's spirit being swept out of the house and banished from the property. Despite all the problems she'd had with her grandmother, she didn't like the thought of treating her so roughly.

"We really appreciate the offer," she said. "But can we try something else first?"

"Of course," said Sharon, looking surprised. "As long as you're safe."

"We will be." Seeing Holly's startled look, Marie squeezed

her hand, wordlessly promising to talk about it later. With a last uneasy glance around, they went back outside. Marie tried not to see a dark shape watching them through the window as the ritual resumed.

THAT NIGHT, Marie dreamed that the Christmas tree was on fire.

It was the most vivid dream she'd ever had. Heat scorched her face as the flames climbed higher. The crawling burn of smoke slid through her lungs. As the flames licked the ceiling, she heard faint music: Burl Ives singing "Have a Holly Jolly Christmas," Grandma's favorite Christmas song. Below that, she heard the faint angry muttering that had troubled her sleep for days—an unhappy old woman confused by death, railing against things she couldn't understand.

As the dream ended, the fire spread, consuming the house and filling the air with smoke and pain. Marie woke in a sweat, heart pounding and mind diamond-clear. "That's it," she said calmly, getting up. "We're dealing with this today."

When Holly woke, Marie asked her to take Dis to the lake for a few hours. Amazing as she was, Holly agreed, though Marie knew she'd want an explanation later. When they were gone, she cleaned the house thoroughly and locked the cats in the bedroom. Then she went to the kitchen, took out Grandma's loaf pan, and made another loaf of spice bread.

As she slid the pan into the oven, she was suddenly overwhelmed by a memory: herself, five or six, standing by an oven with Grandma, each wearing one of a matching pair of oven mitts as they put the spice bread in to bake. She remembered Grandma's laugh, how jovial she could be, how much fun their visits had been. She remembered how Grandma had shown her frogs in the creek and taught her how to crochet—

how she'd sung with total concentration on Sunday nights, sitting with her Bibles and her hymnal by the fire. Her voice had been harsh but strong, her energy uncontainable.

The memories were so intense that Marie teared up. Closing the oven quickly, she wiped her eyes and pulled herself together. She made a pot of tea, poured two cups, and set them at opposite sides of the table. "All right, Grandma," she said. "You wanted my attention. Here's your chance. Sit down. We'll talk about things like grown-ups."

The air grew heavy. Marie strained to listen, almost expecting to hear footsteps, but the silence was absolute. So it was even more shocking when, just when she'd started to relax, the second teacup spilled across the table. Every hair on her body stood up. Her muscles locked with the effort of not screaming. Though she was terrified, she put on the bravest face she could.

"You're acting like a child, Grandma. I don't know if you get this, but I'm offering this conversation as a courtesy. We could have exorcised you like some random ghost. Someone already offered to do it. So here's how it's going to go: I'm going to pour another cup of tea. If you spill it again or pull any crap like that, that's the end of this conversation. We'll call Sharon, she'll do a cleansing and banish you, we'll give the Christmas ornaments away to charity, and you'll never be able to come back here. So, think *really hard* about what you want, because this is your last chance."

Resolutely not looking at the chair where nothing was sitting, Marie got a dishcloth and cleaned up the spilled tea. Wiping the cup, she refilled it.

Throughout all this, the kitchen was silent, but she felt unseen eyes watching.

Marie put the fresh cup back in front of the empty chair. Taking her own seat, she stirred her tea clockwise, murmuring a rhyme for protection and clarity of mind. Then she took a sip, set the cup down, and looked up. "You never learned to communicate right," she said. "I don't know why, or if it was anyone else's fault but yours, but for some reason, you could only express your feelings by being loud and violent. I guess you were raised that way. Maybe your parents were like that, too. And you raised Mom that way. So, thanks a lot for that." Her fingers tightened on her cup as she thought of her mother. *That* conversation was a long way off.

"But the way you were raised doesn't excuse your behavior," she told the silence. "You had your whole life to learn better. And your afterlife. And you chose not to. You're *still* choosing not to. *Why?*" She took a few sips of tea to calm herself. "Can't you see how being that way hurt you? You ruined your relationship with Mom, Jessica, and me. We had fun with you. We loved you. But you were too dangerous to be part of our lives. That's why I'll donate the ornaments if we can't work this out—or maybe throw them away. I won't send them to Jessica. She has kids. I won't subject them to that."

The quality of the silence was beginning to change. The presence seemed to be listening now. Or at least it didn't feel as angry.

"I'd like for you to be able to stay here," she said. "I miss you, even though we had problems at the end. But if you're going to stay, there are house rules you need to follow. We have our own traditions. You must respect them. You can't throw our things around anymore, even if some of them used to be your things. And you can never, ever threaten to hurt anyone again, no matter how angry you are. You'd sure as hell better not actually *do* it. One more pinch, one more nightmare, one more broken ornament, and that's it. Understand? You've had a whole lifetime of chances. This is the last one you're going to get. This is *our* house. Not yours. You're going to respect us."

More silence followed. The fragrant air seemed to shiver. This was a deciding moment. If the spirit wouldn't agree, she'd have to be removed. It would be too dangerous to keep her around.

"Can you respect that?" she prompted. "Give me some kind of sign. I know you can. If you can't show me you agree, we're done. I'll call Sharon, she'll do the cleansing, and you and I will say goodbye."

The quiet continued. Marie imagined the spirit considering deciding if it could stand to be suppressed. She remembered how Grandma had looked during serious discussions: how her body would go still and her eyes would stare at nothing, as if she were reading words written in the air. Holly said Marie sometimes went quiet like that, too. Maybe she'd inherited it.

What was it like to be a ghost, bound so tightly to people and things you'd known in life, yet separated absolutely from them in a way that could never be breached? Maybe the ghost wasn't even listening. Maybe she'd gotten bored and let her dark attention wander off to focus on other things.

After an eternity, the empty chair moved slightly. Then there was a light pressure on Marie's shoulder, like a frail hand had just been laid there. Marie laid her hand over the same spot and felt the memory of cool skin.

In the country of her memory, cool wind shivered over a frozen pond, and a girl and a woman looked across the ice at a winter sunset. Marie's breath caught in her throat, forming around something like a sob. Then she exhaled, and it wasn't a sob at all but a deep, cleansing sigh. She smiled at the empty chair, turned without fear, and left the kitchen.

When Holly and Dis came back, Marie was in the living room, eating spice bread on the couch with the cats curled up on either side of her. The bread was warm, flavorful, a little dry. It had always been a little dry when Grandma made it, too. It wouldn't have been the same if it had come out perfectly. On the windowsill, the angel sat in sunlight. Next to it sat a framed picture of a woman who, even in death, might try to work for something higher.

A Superfluity of Nuns

JOHN KISTE

From behind the bushes, I watched a murmur of nuns trickling a jug of bourbon into the cemetery cistern while decrying its evils in sibilant whispers. As the final golden drop escaped the container, they straightened their habits, shifted their wimples, and vanished down the darkening path, leaving me cold, unseen, and most amused. Or rather, mostly amused. That had been *my* bourbon. I had rested it on a tombstone while I relieved myself in said bushes. I had not heard the crisp shuffling of the nightmare horde of zebra-hued ladies until they had already gained possession of the unattended liquor.

No matter, I was drunk enough. It was time to face my uncle.

Heavy flakes of snow had begun to flit earthward, and their swishing in the icy air muted all sounds beyond the distant gates of the graveyard. Yet here a gelid wind sliced through the leafless trees and skirted the mausoleums, keening like baby banshees still learning their craft. The many ornate stones already wore caps and scarves and mufflers of white, and in the deepening twilight I could make out a string of letters on one slouching marker. It read: RIPARIG. "Riparig?" I repeated aloud.

Suddenly, a clammy hand touched my ungloved one. I whirled about in a mad start and came eye to eye with a straggling sister. And what eyes they were—enormous and liquid and piercing blue. These disturbing orbs were truly level with mine, for the girl (and little more than girl she was) stood the same six feet as me. Her rosary beads clattered against her jet-black tunic. As I stared, frozen in body and mind, a great wisp of raven hair fell jauntily across her left eye. She nearly smiled at my fright, without actually doing so, and said in a soft voice, "It means 'rest in peace and rise in glory.'" And she was gone. I trembled along my limbs, for I could not seem to remember her going.

Still shivering, and not entirely from the cold, I picked my way to the exit gates and found the half-deserted city street a haven. This entire day of Christmas Eve had forced its peculiar, ethereal quality into my brain. All this borough was unfamiliar territory, and my alcohol-addled sensibilities oddly blended the strangeness of my physical surroundings with the nonsensical happenings that had engulfed me since I had arrived by train this afternoon. I had not been to St. Swithins in two years. A codicil of my dead father's will specified that biennially I must travel here at Yuletide and negotiate my allowance from a trust fund that was being administered by Uncle Myron, my father's only surviving brother.

This old bachelor relative had always exuded kindness and jollity, except when it came time to hand me my money. He was not a miser—hardly that; I believe it had been his idea to make the required visits at Christmas so he could share his holiday table with me. He simply despised my decadent lifestyle, and the degrading use to which I put my inheritance. At each encounter, I was forced to suffer harangue upon tirade, as though he felt personally responsible for my soul, while I personally questioned not only its peril but its very existence.

His concerns were certainly valid ones from his own viewpoint. I had been known to lose two months of that allowance during a single evening of cards. I spent more on spirits than on sustenance, and far more on prostitutes than on anything profitable. And on one night every two years I would show up at his residence as an ersatz prodigal son and debate good and evil with him until he relinquished my funds in disgust.

These musings flooded through me as I stumbled along the snowy streets, passing beautifully wreathed shop doors and garland-strewn plate glass display windows. Now *that* was a dress! I pulled up sharp before a lady's clothing store, enthralled by a blue velvet gown that shimmered just inside. Only the girl I pictured in it was no lady, nor would it remain long unravaged on her unwashed body. I paused to consider. These were the types of thoughts that so troubled dear Uncle Myron.

As I studied the curves of the material, the bright blue color seemed to drain away, and the pattern shrank and altered before my eyes. This was not a trick of faltering street lamps. In an instant, a nun's habit and cincture hung behind the glass, and I rubbed my drunken eyes and determined I was *not* drunk enough. I slapped the side of my head forcefully with an open palm, and the radiant blue rushed back into the garment. As I noted previously, the night was not a normal one. It had graduated to openly abnormal.

Far off I heard Christmas bells peal throatily from a church steeple, and somewhere in the other direction, unseen carolers sang. The snowflakes grew fatter and wetter, and the few pedestrians about me pulled collars tighter and hats farther down. Every hat glowed like a spotless white wimple in the corner of my eye, and I found myself repeatedly staring directly at shoppers to assure myself they were real, much to their discomfort. I definitely needed another drink.

I recollected from my visit two years earlier that a pub called The Penguin graced the strewn garbage of a squalid back alley. My psyche screamed for the taste of bourbon and the sights and smells of filth and neglect. Alas, as I veered into the byroad, the trash and debris eluded me. The cobblestones that were not covered by pure, untouched snow had been scrubbed fresh by some interfering committee of public do-gooders. The tavern still existed, but I was disinclined to approach it when the stuffed penguin mascot hanging over the door writhed and melted into the shape of a tiny nun before my eyes. And this time no rubbing of the bloodshot orbs could dispel the image. I fled horrified into the night.

That group of carolers whose notes had barely reached me earlier now assailed my path. "God Rest Ye, Merry Gentlemen" lilted about the tumbling flakes. But in my sight, watch chains metamorphosed into beaded rosaries, cravats became holy headpieces, songbooks dissolved into Bibles, and galoshes turned into prim, short black leather boots. This time I screamed. The singers scattered, probably believing me an escaped lunatic, which was not far wrong. For a long time I simply ran, heedless of a destination.

A half hour later found me on the old man's brownstone stoop. His ancient but efficient butler admitted me at the first ringing of the bell. As he gathered my soaked coat and scarf and waved me inside, I saw at once a huge fire in the hearth of my uncle's study, and rushed to the chair beside it to vanquish my shivers and chill. I also clung to a mad hope that the heat would aid me in recovering my senses. A maidservant brought me a snifter of brandy within seconds. A moment afterwards, my uncle entered from a rear alcove.

"I hate to enable your bad habits, my boy," he said with a

broad smile on his lined and bearded face, "but I saw you coming up the steps outside and thought you needed warming up."

I turned and regarded him in a rather different light than I ever had before. "Thank you, sir," was all I answered for some time as I attempted to regain my composure—and failed. "It has been a weird evening," I finally added.

"Perhaps the delirium tremens have caught up to you." He waggled a finger in my direction.

"Perhaps," I felt compelled to agree. "Of course I always believed they were brought on by a withdrawal from alcohol. Something I have not yet attempted."

My uncle shrugged. "Let's get some food in you."

Uncle Myron's dining room stood as a testament to the festive season. A tall, trimmed and lighted spruce topped by a massive star outlined the bay window, and shimmering candles and greenery touched every surface. The long oak table sagged under platters of ham and turkey and mounds of varied side dishes and desserts. I was reminded of Ebenezer Scrooge's room once the Ghost of Christmas Present had commandeered it. Surrounding the tree and on each chair and sideboard lay meticulously wrapped gifts with beautiful bows and tags.

"I thought I was your only relative," I mumbled with a mouthful of potatoes and gravy.

He laughed. "So you are. These presents are for the underprivileged children of St. Swithins. This has been a hard year for all of us, and they have naturally suffered the most."

I turned these words over in my head. "You are a good man, Uncle Myron," I whispered.

He was somewhat taken aback by my compliment. He pulled both his pocket-watch and his handkerchief from his ample waistcoat and noted the time as he glanced away to blow his nose and, I think, dab at his eyes. "I suppose we should get your affairs sorted, dear nephew, so you can be on your profligate way."

If I had surprised him before, he was thunderstruck by my next words. "I was hoping I could occupy the guest room tonight and greet the Yuletide with you."

His head snapped back to me. "Why boy, I have never known you to keep Christmas company with any but whiskey and whist and wicked guttersnipes. It is indeed a weird evening, as you pointed out. But of course you are truly welcome."

I stood and paced the festive room. "Well *something* has been hinting all evening that I should change my immoral and licentious ways. I am thinking such an uncharted course has merit on many levels."

My uncle snorted. "I've been flat out telling you as much for years."

I nodded. "I know, Uncle. I am quite aware of that. Somehow such hints pack more punch coming from a whole convent's worth of nuns."

The old man peered at me with steady eyes. "Nuns? Around here? Unlikely, my wild young nephew."

Now it was my turn to be stunned. "Hardly," I replied. "I've seen dozens tonight."

My uncle watched me narrowly for some minutes before stepping across to stoke the fire. His gnarled hands moved the poker with an uneasy grace. I heard him mutter to himself, "A field trip? On Christmas Eve? Highly unlikely." Over his shoulder, he said calmly, quietly, and most deliberately, "There are no sisters in St. Swithins Parish. The nunnery burned to the ground on this very night of last year. A sudden and monstrous conflagration. There were no survivors."

I sat down heavily into the chair behind me. I was very

glad it was there, for I would have sat down regardless. I could barely feel my legs. They were not cold any longer, but I could not presently move them. We did not speak as Uncle shuffled to a high shelf and pulled down a thick and recently-bound tome. He thumbed to a page in the middle and laid the volume on my lap. A color photograph of the St. Swithins's nunnery stared up at me, with all the sisters aligned in their black and white uniforms before it.

The old man had clearly been deeply affected; he spoke slowly and his tone was tinged with sadness. "Every one of these women, from novices to lay sisters to the prioress, was taken home to God exactly one year ago tonight. What His purpose was in so doing still eludes me. I would have thought He would wish them still here to guide lost souls to the path of glory."

"Perhaps they are," was all I could manage.

In the dead center of the photographed crowd, I gazed unblinking at a piercing blue eye, while the other was hidden behind a tress of falling black hair.

Reindeer Games

BROOKE MACKENZIE

J osiah eyed the pile of antlers in the corner of the room as he ate the porridge Papa had placed before him. "Eat up, boy," he had said with a grin that seemed almost insidious in its mirth (as Papa was not a mirthful person). "You're gonna need your strength today."

The antlers had been placed in front of the fire overnight to dry and harden. They had been wrapped in leather cords, which ended in braided handles at the base that the men would soon slip over their hands so their grip would be secure. The points of the antlers themselves had been carved into gleaming, unforgiving spears. Josiah had witnessed the yearly Christmas Eve ritual many times before: the womenfolk stayed up late, preparing the antlers and sneaking sips from the wine barrel, their laughter becoming louder as the night wore on. The men slept, their bellies filled with stuffed goose, pheasant, and ale, their minds plastered in the vivid colors of violent dreams. However, this time, Josiah would not stay behind on Christmas Day, helping the women as they knitted and gossiped and seasoned the Christmas cake. Josiah let his eyes fall on a smaller pair of antlers, extracted from what he could tell was a young buck. This year, having reached the age of 13 two months earlier, he would have to participate. The thought made his stomach turn and he gagged on his porridge. His mother raised her eyebrow in brief concern, but Josiah averted his eyes and continued eating.

The door opened, ushering in swirls of snow that, for a moment, made the room sparkle before the chill hit. A bearded man stood in the doorway, grunted, and gestured to the antlers. Then, in another swirl of skirts and aprons, the women set down their knitting and gathered around the antlers. Josiah wasn't sure how this choreography happened both wordlessly and seamlessly, but in a blink, the antlers were carried outside and arranged neatly in the snow. Josiah's papa placed a hand on his shoulder and guided him to the perimeter of a circle the men had formed around the antlers. This was it. The moment he'd been dreading since he was old enough to know he should. At 13, he was finally old enough to be a part of the Christmas Day hunt.

The bearded man Josiah had seen earlier that morning, Silas, cleared his throat with a juicy rattle and began speaking. The high-pitched wind carried his voice away from the group, but it had such a chilling depth to it that the words resonated in Josiah's bones. They were the same words Silas had spoken to the men since Josiah first heard them as he watched through the window from his cozy perch on his mother's hip.

"Fifty years ago, on Christmas Day, a band of Mohawk Indians came upon this village. The Mohawk crept up so quickly and quietly that the men scarcely had time to grab their weapons. As the story goes, Silas, my great-grandfather and namesake, grabbed a pair of antlers that had been cast aside after skinning a buck and ran the biggest, tallest man right through, piercing his ribcage and exposing his heart. When the other Mohawk Indians saw this, they thought Silas had some kind of magical powers and retreated, yellin' and screamin' as they ran. They must have warned the others, because after that day, the Mohawk stayed far away from my great-grandfather." Silas raised his hands—which, like the rest of the men's, were bare. Josiah's hands ached in the wind and he longed for his mittens. "And now, every year on Christmas Day," Silas continued, "we kill our game with antlers as a tribute to Silas, so that he will watch over this land and keep us safe from our enemies. And today," Silas nodded to Josiah, who felt a jolt run through him, "we welcome Brother Josiah to our hunt. Sorrel, would you do the honors for your son?"

Josiah's father nodded and wordlessly picked up the smallest pair of antlers. As he slipped the leather straps over Josiah's hands, the snow fell and the wind picked up. Josiah shivered.

"Stay still, boy, or I can't get the straps tight," his father said. Josiah nodded, willing himself to stay still. He felt a sharp pressure around the back of each hand as his father placed Josiah's fingers in the correct position for the best grip. When Sorrel was finished, he raised Josiah's arms, and the antlers extended from them like monstrous hands. Everyone in the circle made a deep hooting sound, like a pack of wild animals.

Silas helped the other men strap the antlers to their hands and said nothing. The air was filled with a solemn gravitas, even as the winds picked up and everyone's clothes were coated in powdery flakes of snow. Josiah stuck his tongue out and caught a snowflake before remembering himself.

Silas's wife helped him with his antlers, and finally, the group was ready to journey up and over the steep hill bordering the village, out of sight of the women and children they were leaving behind.

Josiah could hear only the wind and the ragged effort of his own breathing as they trudged up the hillside. He didn't want to turn to see the windows of the village, warm with firelight, disappear behind him because he feared he might burst into tears. The wind lashed at his face, and the snow had turned into punishing crystals, and Josiah's stomach roiled with the thought of the task at hand.

Josiah had spent a lot of time with animals, caring for the sheep and pigs that were raised in the village, even taming squirrels and the occasional deer with bits of bread he snuck from his supper. He had certainly never hunted nor slaughtered an animal, and from what he understood of this particular hunt, everyone had to participate in the kill. Experience had taught the men that if everyone didn't participate, the village would not earn the ancestral protections they sought and would be at risk of enemy attacks, illness, or even a failed harvest. Josiah thought of his mother and younger siblings and swallowed the lump in his throat.

He trailed to the back of the group, and after they reached the top of the hill and descended the other side, there was a brief respite from the relentless wind. He rubbed the wind-induced tears from his eyes. From where he stood he could see a buckskin-colored shape in the ravine below. The wind picked up again and the shape was obscured by blowing snow, but he could see it thrashing and struggling. Josiah squinted and saw another shape behind it. The animal was tied to a pole. Josiah groaned. This wasn't a hunt. It was a slaughter.

Halfway down the hillside on the way to the ravine, Silas turned and faced the group, raising his antlers in the air. "An eye for an eye! A tooth for a tooth! A heart for a heart! Ours is a fearsome and vengeful God. We give this offering in His Name!"

The other men raised their antlers and once again made that terrible hooting sound. Silas turned and charged down the hillside, and the other men followed suit, slipping and struggling in the snow as they went, which made their masculine movements look boyish and clumsy. Josiah dragged his feet, falling behind the others until his father, who was several yards below him, noticed that his son was no longer next to him. Josiah watched his father struggle back up the hill and detected a wildness in his eyes that he had never seen before. It frightened him.

"Hurry up!" his father yelled, but the sound was quickly carried away. The wind was blowing straight against them, making it hard to see. Combined with the snow, it made the trek down the hillside more laborious than Josiah thought he'd be able to manage. His footsteps crunched and the hooting of the men echoed menacingly in the ravine. One sound rose above it all: a woman screaming.

Josiah thought at first that it was the sound of the wind screeching in the warm spaces between his ears and hat, but the scream turned to a wail, and seemed to be coming from everywhere all at once. He scanned the group of men as they continued the trek down to the ravine—the distance between them and him growing larger by the moment—and looked behind to see if one of the women had left the warmth of the village and followed them over the hill. But the sound seemed to have no source. He saw the deer in the ravine thrash more wildly as the men drew closer, and he heard the scream again —this time, he was *sure* it wasn't the wind—and he thought he heard it taking on the shape of words. The animal reared up on its hind legs and a yellow-green sensation of sickness rose up in Josiah's throat.

This wasn't a deer. It was a woman.

Josiah lengthened his stride, the antlers attached to his arms making his gait awkward and unbalanced as he tried not to inadvertently stab himself with his own weapon. He saw the woman more clearly: she'd been draped in several layers of deerskin to make her look like a fawn; her black hair whipped wildly around her face. Her hands and feet were tied together, and the rope connecting her to the pole was tied around her waist. As Josiah heard the panicked syllables emanating from her and rising up the hillside, he recognized their distinctive quality. She was speaking a Native dialect he recognized from when the Mohawk traders came to the village. The men always spoke English in their business dealings, but the women and children would be in the background, communicating to each other in a language that sounded gentle and comforting, the way rabbit stew sounds when it is boiling on the fire. Josiah always played with the children, surpassing their communication barriers, and the villagers always offered the traders bread with butter and honey and juniper tea served in porcelain cups. The violence of the past, while damaging to both parties, had healed enough to make a textured scar of collaboration, and, if not friendship, at least a tranquil truce of mutual benefit. Seeing a Mohawk woman tied to a pole and dressed like a deer gave Josiah a shock so intense he heard his pulse in his ears, felt it behind his eyes and at the tips of his fingers.

The men had formed a semicircle around the panicked woman, and Josiah's father turned and gestured to him. Josiah drew closer but didn't join the group. He had witnessed the men returning from the hunt every year, their antler weapons bloodied, their chests puffed with pride, and their voices riddled with adrenaline, making the whooping sounds they had derided as "savage" when they had emanated from the

Mohawk all those decades ago. Surely this couldn't have been the "game" they were hunting? Surely this was a ceremonial display, and they planned to release the woman before killing an actual animal? Josiah felt his lungs crystallize as he quickly sucked in a cold breath.

"Sister! You perform a noble service today! Let ye be the sacrificial lamb to pay for the sins of your people!" Silas screamed before taking the first strike. It was a gentle one, peeling away the deer skin at her shoulder. From his vantage point, Josiah could see the woman was naked underneath. Josiah dry heaved but stopped the sound just in time. He shook his head "no" uncontrollably, unceremoniously.

Josiah's father gestured for him to join the group. Josiah took a few performative steps forward before feigning a fall in the snow and digging both sets of his antlers into the ground. The act needed to look like a fall, not outward disobedience.

He had been taught to pray since before he could speak. Twice a week in church and every night before supper. In that moment, kneeling in the snow, he didn't want to pray to the vengeful God he had been raised with as a father figure. The punitive one. The very same God that would not have approved of him shirking whatever vengeance had been commanded in the name of this violent yearly tradition. Instead, not knowing quite where to speak or how to plead, but knowing only that he couldn't bear to see this woman slaughtered, he simply uttered a word: "Please."

He closed his eyes. He knew that, after they had inflicted their violence, the men would carry the woman's body off, bearing all the markings of an animal attack—the antlers would have been so very calculated in the way that they landed—and offer their condolences to their Mohawk business partners. *The wolves are extra hungry this time of year. Keep an eye on your womenfolk when they go off to collect food.*

Josiah saw this image in his mind, an image that seemed to bear a high level of inevitability, this contradiction in the Thou Shalt Not Lie commandment that had been the motivation behind many a whipping for him, and again, he spoke his plea into the earth. *Please.*

The men worked precisely, a method perfected over the past fifty years: each man took a turn at peeling off the deer-skins in which they had dressed her. Then they clawed at her extremities. Moving in slowly, purposefully, increasing her fear and panic to arouse their own excitement. It was even more fun if she was particularly beautiful, with skin impossibly well preserved in the harsh climate. The last antler weapon blow, and arguably the most satisfying one, would be to the taut surface of her face. This, after her guts had spilled out and the bulbous tube of her intestines had been hacked into bits by the entire semicircle of antler hands. The final facial strike would be, Josiah knew, the honor reserved for Silas.

Josiah dry heaved again, and again managed to hide the primal, sick noise. Once again, he pled into the earth. He heard more antlers removing more deerskin and the nauseating screech of someone whose flesh had just been pierced.

Please.

Please.

Please.

Anyone but the vengeful God.

Please.

Josiah heard his father bellow, but it was a sound quickly carried away by the wind, the blowing snow, and the female screams as antlers pulled away the deer skins and sliced at flesh. Josiah continued to feign an injury as he pled his frantic prayer to the ground.

He didn't hear footsteps. He felt an upward swirl of snow and wind next to him, and when he looked left he saw a pair of mukluk boots—the old-fashioned kind, a style Josiah had only seen in stereoscopes—and he looked up. The man's face was ensconced in a halo of animal fur, and his dark complexion was a beautiful contrast next to the white and buckskin shades of his hood. He had somehow managed to enchant the snow into a precise, glistening whirlwind around himself.

Josiah gasped in surprise, his lungs stinging, at the unlikely image of the Mohawk man next to him. Josiah saw his open ribcage, held apart and framed by antlers in an impossible shade of pure white. He gasped. A purplish sack hung in the fleshy blackness of the chest cavity—it was the man's heart. It lay still, gleaming in the pale winter light like a doomed jewel.

Josiah tried clasping his hands together in prayer before remembering the antlers attached to them. "Please. Please, Tall Man, please." Tall Man was the only name that came to Josiah.

The man glanced at him, spoke some words in that sweet, boiling stew language, and walked toward the men. With each step, snow whirled upward in a small, inverted cyclone. He left behind no footprints.

The men took turns striking the woman with their half-beast, half-human hands. They disrobed her and slashed at her skin, breaking the surface but not yet mortally wounding her. That would come later.

The group were so occupied they didn't see the Tall Man and his snowy vortex approaching. Josiah wondered if anyone else could see the man. It didn't matter. In an instant, they were all enveloped in a swirling snow torrent. It was relentless and fast and disorienting. There were shrieks and profanities coupled with the sound of cloth tearing.

In the white blur, Josiah watched the men turn on each other, their limbs slicing frantically as they transformed into savage animals. No one noticed as the woman gathered up the deer skins to cover herself and bolted down the ravine while the men flailed and attacked one another like beasts.

A hot, prickly sensation spread throughout Josiah, and his ears rang with panic. His instincts turned primal as he listened to the force inside telling him to bolt up the hill away from the group like a scared little rabbit. He ran, slipping, falling, screaming. By the time he reached his house and the arms of his alarmed mother, the tears, snot, and melted snow gushed from him.

It wasn't until the women ran after the men and came screaming over the top hill that the fugue state lifted and the men stopped clawing at one another, their antlers speckled with globs of flesh and blood. All they could do was stare silently. The shock kept the pain from settling in for a few merciful moments as they inspected their own carnage. They had sliced each other to ribbons. Flaps of skin hung off cheekbones. An eyeball dangled from an optic nerve. An ear had been detached and blood pulsed in a meaty shade of purple from the hole. One man's forehead had been cut so deeply that a frosty strip of skull peeked through the wound.

The men were half-carried back to the village by the women who dressed their wounds. Once the blood had been contained and the whiskey had taken the edge off the pain, they told a tale of a freak wind, blowing up snow, resulting in panic and chaos. They'd carry their scars for the rest of their days.

Josiah wasn't sure if it was because they were embarrassed that their baser natures had gotten the better of them, causing them to injure each other, or because the Tall Man had worked some kind of magic, but they never spoke about that day again. That particular day—that horrible blunder of a day— was simply swept under the rugged tapestry of their challenging existence. They never slaughtered again.

Every Christmas Day in the years that followed, at the top of the hill looking down into the village, Josiah would see the Tall Man and watch his snowy vortex of movement, his chest ripped open and his heart dangling like a violent memory, as he kept a ghostly peace.

The Frostling

ELEANOR SCIOLISTEIN

I remember distinctly that it was Christmas Eve, the night the knocking came. The blossoms on the blackthorn had bloomed early that year and as that ill omen predicted, we were hit by a long and particularly harsh winter. People often talk of 'winter's bite,' but that year it did not merely bite, rather, it chewed.

The schoolhouses closed, the roads became impassable, hidden as they were beneath a thick blanket of snow, the like of which had not been seen in decades and against which the efforts of spade and pick offered little resistance. As is often the case in countries where cold weather is frequent but true frigidity is rare, the authorities were ill-prepared, and just as the blossoms had predicted, life, like the soil, became frozen solid. Fixed in a state of pristine limbo as it waited and ached for the thaw.

By the time Christmas rolled around, even that same portentous tree had been stripped of its leaves and stood, instead, clawing limply at the sky whilst we wisely chose to remain inside, comforted by the crackling warmth of the fire and the quilting glow of our wine. Children released from the yoke of lessons played and chattered in the streets with the sort of shrieking mirth that always brought the faint whisper of a smile to Anna's lips, closely followed by the inevitable pang of sadness. For as dusk fell and the cold became intolerable, the children returned to their homes, leaving in their wake a hollow space where their laughter had once been and leaving Anna, as always, haunted by the ghosts of 'never was.'

As the nights began to draw in, so Anna and I were likewise forced to draw our chairs ever closer to the flicker of the hearth, her, tangled up in her knitting like some great woolen spider whilst I pursued some volume or other with a wine the colour of rubies, ready by my elbow. We had been sitting that night in just such a manner when the curious and unexpected knock had come at the door.

At first, we simply stared at one another in silence, questioning without words, who should be calling at such an hour and on such an inclement night. I recall making some joke with Anna, suggesting that perhaps it was Saint Nicholas come to bring our presents or perhaps one of his dark left tenants come to thrash us for being wicked all year. The jest, I remember, had fallen flat.

So, rising reluctantly from my carefully constructed nest by the fire to answer this untimely summons, I pulled back the bolts and slowly opened the door on to the night. What I found was not, as expected, a person, huddled against the flurries of snow, but instead, only silence. Silence of that frozen, timeless variety that comes only with snow. A hush that suggests in its unspoken lies that the world outside was always like this, a place of unbroken stillness, held in suspension by the selfish quiet of ice.

I remember that the world outside was somehow both dark and dimly lit. The sky, stretched out in a furious rage of black, was punctured with stars and showed only the thinnest sliver of moon and yet, the ground, seemingly in defiance of the dark, appeared almost to shine and glimmer in perfect, crystalline stillness. In other circumstances perhaps, I might have described the scene as beautiful, for there was undoubtedly, within this untarnished paralysis something oddly ethereal. As it was, however, having been roused from my seat for no good reason, I was in no mood to be so generous with my appraisal. I looked around from side to side, searching for the caller, but found nothing but the blasted snow.

I waited for a moment, searching the hedgerows and the path beyond for any sign of movement. I spied the blackthorn tree, its thorns jutting outward as if it wished to snag the wind upon itself, saw beyond the hedge the sloping shouldered outlines of snowmen that waited patiently in the lane. They were present, but there was no one else.

I even called out to whomever might be there and, though I waited, received no answer, my words instead being swallowed by the stillness that remained. I decided at length to go back inside and had I not, for whatever reason, looked down at that very moment, I might not even have remembered this strange incident. Though of course I did look down and as I did, I noticed something very odd.

Looking at the stretch of ground that extended between the hedges and the house I was surprised and not a little shocked to find that I could make out no visible footprints leading to the door. No indentations, no rifts or crumpled piles, no disturbance at all. The snow, I thought, must have fallen very quickly indeed, to so completely cover the tracks of whomever had knocked, what seemed like but a moment ago. I looked again, but sure enough, the snow lay thick and undisturbed like the surface of a well-iced cake.

Closing the door and cursing as I did the whirling eddies of snow that had somehow managed to creep by me and into the house, I was prepared to dismiss the sound as a mistake. If there were no footprints, there could have been no knocking. It was that simple. Perhaps, I thought, we had been mistaken, the sound was not in fact the door, but the echo of some far-off clatter that through a strange distortion of the acoustics, no doubt caused by the snow, had sounded far closer than it was.

It was only as I approached my chair and the fire that the second knock came. More insistent than the first. This time, there could be no mistake, for the door itself reverberated slightly on its hinges with the rapping of frozen knuckles against the wood. I looked across at Anna who had ceased her knitting in the expectation of a visitor and was staring back with a vacant quizzical expression that seemed to ask how I had managed to miss our visitor the first time. Again, I moved to open the door, mouthing and muttering admonishments beneath my breath. I opened it once more, but again found nothing there. Or, rather, not precisely nothing.

 For whilst, there was nobody to be seen, either at the door or upon the road, there was an object. For laying on the doorstep, clearly delivered by some unseen hand now hastily departed, was the perfectly carved figure of a baby. Made up entirely of ice and snow.

Now I do not wish for you to understand that this figurine was something akin to a snowman. Or that it in any way resembled those hastily constructed effigies made by the local children and which, with their black, coal-studded eyes and palsied, half-melted smiles, stood, sentinel-like, at fixed intervals along the path. This was nothing of that sort. This was, in short, a masterpiece.

The odd figurine was a carving, so pristine and delicate, so carefully, perfectly and almost lovingly wrought, that were it not for its brilliant whiteness and the hard, icy cold of its surface, it might well have been mistaken for a real human babe. The head, domed to a subtle curve and polished smooth like the surface of a great white pearl, fell in a soft crescent like a frozen rose to cheeks full and lively, framing lips that were gently pursed. The eyes were closed, but upon the seam, where the lids met, slender stems of frost of such fragile delicacy that they could have been removed with a single breath, curled softly upward to form the shape of lashes. Anna, who had come to join me at the doorstep, was taken with him immediately.

Lifting the strange sculpture, its skin so magnificently white that the shadows seemed an icy blue, she cradled it in her arms as if it were alive, a sight that I will admit made me feel horribly uneasy, tightening as it did a knot in the pit of my stomach, so that it flipped and broiled as if slowly chewing itself from within. We had never been blessed with children and the sight of Anna with a babe in her arms, even one composed of snow, filled the hollow inside me with ice.

Once she held him, Anna became inexplicably agitated. Moving to the coal hole, the small cupboard space beneath the stairs where we stored our fuel, she placed the infant lovingly down onto the frozen stone floor. She did so knowing that this was the coldest point in the house and in a state of near panic at the prospect of the child melting or as she put it, 'wasting away.' Turning from the tiny sculpture she screamed at me in a high, keening wail, demanding, despite the cold that had crept in through the open door, that I cross the room and immediately extinguish the fire, something I dutifully set to, noting as I did that before she closed the coal hole door, Anna kissed the tiny foundling tenderly on the forehead. I, of course, did not.

In contrast to Anna, who had become almost instantly

enamored with the sculpture, I was instantly repulsed. I reasoned, from the workmanship, that the effigy could only have been made by one man—Austin, a carpenter of great skill and acclaim who lived not half a mile from our house and whose work on the stalls of the nearby cathedral, lurid as they might have been, had earned him some measure of fame. I reflected that with this effort he may have surpassed even his own greatest work, though what he meant by leaving this thing of such hideous beauty at our door, I could not guess, until later.

Despite having retired to bed at a far later hour than was our usual habit, I found that my sleep was far from sound. The disruption to our usual routine was partly due to the strange arrival and partly due to Anna's obvious reluctance to venture upstairs or, more bluntly, to be parted from the child. Indeed, her knitting progressed not a single loop once she returned to her chair by the reignited fire and she instead, as if distracted, stared solemnly and intently into the fire or else turned, seemingly every few minutes, to look back over her shoulder and toward the tiny door, behind which the child of ice slept soundly.

When I finally persuaded her to come with me to bed, she insisted, before doing so, upon opening the door of the coal hole once more, so that she might be allowed to look upon the little carving and in her words "Say goodnight.".

Once tucked beneath the blankets, however, Anna fell asleep almost immediately, resting, so it seemed to me, with a strange half-smile of satisfaction upon her lips. I, meanwhile, remained awake for many hours. When I finally was able to drift off, my rest was disturbed by any number of horrible dreams, the worst of which was so vivid and so perfectly clear as to be indistinguishable from my waking thoughts. In it, I found myself sitting up in bed, roused no doubt by some unfamiliar sound within the room. Turning to my right, I looked at Anna, still sleeping soundly and still wearing that strange smile, and then out into the darkness of the room, where though faint, I could clearly pick out a very distinct sound. Whether it is a symptom of having never fathered children myself I do not know, but I confess that the innocent phrase 'the patter of tiny feet' has always held for me a certain degree of lingering horror.

Whilst I am all too aware that this phrase is meant to imply the joy experienced by new parents upon hearing the pad of their offspring's feet echoing in corridors and along floors, for me the phrase always conjured images of something far more sinister.

For me, the 'patter of tiny feet' conjures vague notions of some little scurrying thing, neither necessarily a child nor an animal, sporting rows of minuscule teeth and flitting with an almost imperceptible quiet from one shadowy corner to another, the only trace of its presence being the aforementioned patter of its tiny, bare-soled feet against the naked floorboards.

In my vision, the feet that make such sounds are of a gray rubbery texture, like the flesh of a long-dead fish. Plump, firm, but always and ever cold. They would pitter patter lightly with a soft, cushioned, and almost whispered suggestion of sound, sparse, but certainly, undeniably there. In the dream, it was just such a sound that disturbed me.

Propping myself up on my elbows I stared blankly into the dark, trying to discern from which direction it had come, to pick out shapes within the gloom. The edge of a chair by the nightstand, the wardrobe, and to its left another curious shape, this one low to the ground. Its curved sloping edges were smudged and ill-defined in the thickening ink of the blackness. For long moments I peered at it, waiting in silence, as a cold electric crackle flashed across my scalp, tightening the skin and forcing the hair to attention. Was it a chair perhaps? Some piece of furniture onto which Anna had carelessly flung her clothes, leaving them to droop and sag into strange lopsided shapes? I glared at the shape, willing it to move, yet deathly afraid that it might.

All at once, far louder and more deliberately than before, the sound came again. A rush of tiny footsteps before and around the bed. A hurried, pattered scramble of footsteps across the floor by the end of the bed, disturbing the blankets hanging over the edge like a draft, caused by movement.

Sitting bolt upright I called out, asking who was there, certain in that instant that it had been the force of a hand upon the bedclothes that had caused them to stir. Nimble fingers tugged at the blankets as the culprit scampered by. I remember feeling, at that moment, that my own insides seemed to have turned to ice. Surely, I thought, there could be nobody inside the house. Certainly no child or infant playing barefoot in this room at this hour. But what then? If not a child, scurrying blindly and mischievously around the room, then what?

I was close to rising from the bed, reluctant and yet determined to investigate, when the bedroom door, a door which I would happily have sworn under oath that I had both closed and locked earlier, slammed shut with a force that woke both myself and Anna and made us both sit, startled, bolt upright. As the sound, which somehow bled between the dream and wakefulness merging one with the other, faded to an echo, I could not help but imagine the key in that lock being turned. Turned awkwardly at a reaching stretch by a pair of tiny hands.

Reassuring Anna that there was nothing the matter, that it was only a draft that had caused the door to slam and that I had locked or rather re-locked the door, I pulled the blanket up to my neck and turned away, more determined than ever to sleep. No sooner had I begun to drift off, however, than I was disturbed by another strange sound, this time, I fancied, from elsewhere in the house. Turning back toward where Anna should have been sleeping, I found only a cold, empty space and looking up, saw that the door was once again wide open.

Not a little vexed by this, I fumbled for a candle and having lit it, descended the stairs in search of Anna. When I found her, still wearing only her nightdress she was seated, cross-legged and shivering on the floor. On the other side of the room, the fire, partly extinguished, glowed in its final throes, filling its small corner with an orange glow, never strong enough to reach Anna where she sat. Surveying this strange scene, I was initially at a loss as to what to say or do, until that was, I noticed that Anna's nightdress was open, that she was holding the snow baby to her breast and sobbing frantically, insisting that, "Our baby has grown cold." It was an 'our' in which I was not included.

It was at that moment that I allowed myself to wonder. Wonder about Anna's frequent visits to 'call' upon Austin the carpenter. How her deep admiration for his skill and talent had led her to spend many hours alone with the artist in his workshop and how it was only when she returned from these visits that she had ever worn the smile I had seen her sporting earlier that evening. I wondered too about those weeks, some months ago, when she had been sick. So sick in fact that she vomited almost every morning. Finally, I wondered about her visit, ostensibly because of this sickness, to Mother Eastrum, the cunning woman in the village. A woman whose garden was filled with strange figurines and half-scratched symbols. A woman who was also known to 'fix the problems' of young maidens by some dark, unholy means.

Angered by the thought, the suggestion, of such a betrayal

and by Anna's absurd and hysterical behavior, I snatched the effigy clean from her hands and with a single wrenching throw, tossed it onto the dying embers of the fire. For as long as I live I shall never forget the sound. The awful popping hiss as the snow hit the coals, drowned out and buried beneath the terrible screech of a child, screaming.

Broken Vows

V. CASTRO

Hampton Court Palace is beautiful year-round, but it's especially magical during Christmas. The aroma of hot apple cider, roasting peanuts, and hot chocolate fills the air around the outdoor ice skating rink. Blood red poinsettias and fresh pine wreaths decorate the entire premises. However, the grand palace on the banks of the Thames River can appear imposing and cold at times with statues of various creatures baring their teeth while holding coats of arms and a deep moat positioned at the entrance. It also cannot escape its dark history. Built during the reign of Henry the VIII, it is said that two of his wives haunt the grounds. One died in childbirth and the other beheaded. He loved his women . . . until he was through with them.

Nell just began her new post as a security guard at Hampton Court Palace a month before Christmas on the condition she worked Christmas Eve and Christmas Day. No one wanted to roam around the vast deserted grounds and inside the meandering hallways and rooms instead of celebrating with family over a cheeseboard and wine. In fact, most of the people who did those shifts quit by never bothering to return. It was a dream job for her while she finished writing her dissertation on Henry the VIII and The Reformation. It gave her a feeling of what it might have been like to live like royalty. And it wasn't mentally too taxing while she studied.

On Christmas Eve, Nell entered the palace grounds through the rear gardens. Despite it being winter, it felt serene and had a quiet barren beauty. The swans continued to float in The Long Water canal and the statues were even more striking against the clouded dark skies. The only sound were her footsteps crunching across the pebbled path before entering the palace.

People liked to say there were ghosts here. They had ghost tours to talk about the history and experiences some claimed to have had. Nell thought it was great marketing considering the high cost of maintaining the aging palace. But not once did she experience the faintest tingle of the supernatural. The creepiest things were the portraits of dead royalty who seemed to follow you with their eyes. She wandered through the chocolate room, wine cellar, and gigantic kitchen with a hearth big enough to fit an entire cow. Nothing to report except she would write the best damn dissertation after having this fantastic opportunity to be a part of history up close. And she loved history more than the holidays. Plus, flights back to The States were crazy expensive that time of year.

She finally reached the gallery where Catherine Howard's ghost was meant to be found. At the end was a chapel. The door was shut. Many of the rooms with art were kept dark to avoid the sunlight from degrading them further. Her steps were brisk as she just had to look into the chapel to give it the all-clear. A creak made her whip her head towards the gallery hall entrance. All these old places made sounds that seemed more sinister than they were. Old plumbing and settling wood were hardly the ghosts that were rumored to wander the corridors. She continued to walk towards the small chapel where supposedly Henry prayed on his knees while the king's guards dragged Catherine Howard away as she begged for her life. He had already found someone new to give him an heir and only needed to discard Catherine before he could marry again. Three months later Catherine was beheaded.

Nell reached for the door. She imagined the terror Catherine must have felt unable to open this door to plead for her life. Her hand touched the cold bronze and opened it a crack. The musty scent of copper hit her nostrils. It wasn't like the other rooms taking the fragrance of handmade Christmas decorations. Her stomach turned. Maybe it was decaying flowers or wood. Incense? The darkness retreated as the light crept in as she opened the door wider. She peered to the left and nearly jumped with the image of a life size oil painting on the wall catching her eye. The black background seemed smudged into the darkness of the room with the image popping to life. The scent was stronger. She stepped in and looked to her left. Her entire body quaked and stomach cramped with the need to vomit. She blinked her eyes to make sure it was real.

On the altar at the front of the small room was the severed head of a woman she didn't know. Half of her blond hair lay matted with blood and her mouth open with an orange spiked with anise seeds stuck inside. Nell screamed and turned to run though the gallery the way she came. She reached the main wide winding staircase and jogged down, careful to not trip over her own feet. She would call the police as soon as she got as far from the palace as possible. She turned a corner and bumped into Charles, one of the gardeners she met only once who kept to himself. He apparently was an expert on The Great Vine in the garden. It was a huge patch of dirt protecting the roots of the oldest and largest grape vine in the world.

"Fuck sake!" she cried. "I thought no one was here. You have to help me!"

He gently touched her forearms. "What's going on? Are you okay? Management didn't want to lose another guard this year. I was meant to see why."

She shook her head and stepped back. "There is a dead . . . a head, I mean."

Charles looked puzzled. "Look, come back to the garden cottage. Have something warm to drink and sit down. We will call the police together. If you sound like this, then they might not take it seriously."

Nell glanced up the stairway and back at Charles. She wanted to show him, but at the same time she didn't want to see that sight again. The garden cottage wasn't far. "Okay." Her entire body trembled as she walked next to him and wondered if she imagined it. Why the hell did she agree to be there at Christmas?

Nell sat in a lumpy green armchair in the small room that had a short kitchenette to make basic food, a single table, and two chairs. It smelled of mud and dry leaves. The lit wood stove fire felt good and the lights twinkling on a tiny three-foot tree comforted her. He brought her a mug of mulled wine. It smelled delicious. "Here. This will calm your nerves. Now tell me again what exactly happened."

She shut her eyes and took a sip. The heat and alcohol helped her compose her thoughts. "I was doing the rounds, entered the chapel, and a severed head was on the altar. We have to call the police."

"Are you sure?" he pressed. "Maybe it was the ghost."

She took a larger sip. "No. This was real."

"Okay. I believe you. Let me call. It will come from the landline here and the police can track the call and know it's not a prank." Charles picked up the ancient looking phone.

Nell managed another gulp. The warmth went straight to her head. She took off her coat. "May I use the bathroom?"

He nodded his head. "Just down there to the right."

Nell excused herself to use the toilet. She passed a door that led from the hallway to a smaller storage cupboard and stopped. Her blood ran as cold as the wind outside. There were a pair of muddy wellington boots and bloody hedge clippers with hair clinging from the blades. Nell felt dizzy, like the world was collapsing in on itself. The mulled wine curdled in her stomach and the scent of spices reminded her of the orange stuck in the woman's head. She stumbled back to feel Charles behind her. "You…" she whispered.

He squeezed the sides of her arms and whispered in her ear. "Yes. You think King Henry killed his wives simply so he could marry another? It was a ruse for a greater purpose. He wanted immortality. He wanted to stay great and not die before having a male heir. He would be his own heir. Jane Seymour didn't die after birth. Her life was taken."

Her words were fuzzy in her brain and came out slurred. "But he . . . he died and was sick . . ."

Charles squeezed her arms to the point of causing pain. "Because he didn't complete the ritual. I will, and immortality will be mine. I've studied the history of all the grand warlocks who tried and failed. I will be the first."

"Why Christmas?"

He hoisted her over her shoulder and walked into the storage room, grabbing the hedge clippers. "Because this dumb holiday began as the celebration of the Unconquered Sun. It heralds the longer day. And with the right ritual, longer life. Henry had no problem departing from the church because he studied all the pagan rites before Christianity. Also, no one is ever around to hear the screams at Christmas. They are too busy watching TV or stuffing their faces, some travelling. It is the perfect time to commit murder. And no one has ever looked for bodies beneath the vine."

Nell slumped over his shoulder and tried to respond but words came out as a dry croak. She thought of everyone in their homes. No one would be out to hear her scream. Without her coat she felt every drop of spitting raindrops on her back and arms. Her neck was wet. They entered the palace that possessed the quiet of a tomb. Charles lumbered up one of the main staircases. Through blurry vision she could see herself being carried through the gallery hall and into the small chapel where she found the head. Her mouth felt dry as she tried to scream. It felt like she had the worst bout of sleep paralysis. She attempted to lift her head as her body bobbed up and down. As she blinked, she thought she could see a woman. She blinked again. It was a woman in a white lace nightgown. Her skin nearly matched the light fabric, a bright red welt across her neck. Nell tried to reach for her, but her muscles could barely move. The woman placed one index finger over her lips. Nell recognized the face. But it couldn't be . . .

As they entered the chapel, Nell felt herself wanting to vomit upon the sight of the severed head again. He tossed her to the ground. "You will be my second sacrifice tonight, and this is my tenth year. The ritual will be complete. The problem the king had was he had no patience to do it correctly. Distracted by his lust."

A loud clatter made them both dart their eyes towards the gallery. One of the spears from the suit of armor on display had fallen over. He looked at Nell, then back at the gallery. He raised the clippers overhead when the entire suit of armor collapsed to the ground. This time he rushed towards the gallery. Nell tried to move. Her muscles had the weight of oversized logs, but her mind was becoming clearer. Charles whipped his head side to side. "Who's there?"

The head in the chapel fell to the ground and rolled to the threshold of the door. Charles looked back. The eyes snapped open and the orange jettisoned out of the head's mouth, hitting him in the chest. "What the . . . ?"

A burst of laughter filled the gallery. He looked around with clippers raised. Then in the entrance of the gallery *she* appeared. Nell knew that face from a painting. It was Catherine Howard. Blood leaked from the wound across her neck. She took slow steps towards Charles. Droplets of blood fell and stained the carpet like poinsettias in bloom. "You're dead!" he shouted.

She smirked. "Not anymore. Every life you took gave me the power to come back stronger than ever. Before I was a mere apparition, watching you kill. Now I am so much more." She raised a hand and the fallen spear levitated towards her. Charles opened the clippers. "I'll kill you, too."

Her eyes filled with fury and vengeance. With a swipe of her hand the spear sailed straight through his skull. He fell back, dropping the clippers. Catherine walked over to his body and looked down at his punctured skull. Her pale pink lips curled into a smile. Her gaze shifted towards Nell.

"Catherine! Thank you. I am so sorry for what happened to you."

She calmly walked towards Nell and kneeled next to her. "So am I. But now I can find salvation, on the day of new life of all days."

"You can rest in peace now." Nell managed to give her a smile.

Catherine extended an icy finger towards Nell's cheek. "You can rest now too . . . Forever. You are just the one I have been waiting for. Perfect age."

Nell's eyes widened with panic as the ghost of Catherine Howard leaned closer towards her until their foreheads touched. The ghost pried Nell's mouth open with her fingers until the spectre began to evaporate with the lightness of smoke from a snuffed-out candle. Her form slipped into Nell until nothing remained. Nell's body convulsed; tears formed in the corners her wide-open eyes. Her arms and legs thrashed as she tried to fight the ghost's invasion of her body. Then she was still again. Nothing moved. Nell rose from the floor and surveyed the room before walking out. She passed the portraits and giggled and danced through the empty corridors. When in the main outdoor courtyard, she stood before the large Christmas tree. She inhaled a deep breath of air. "I always loved Christmas."

The Lieutenant

ЛЕЙТЕНАНТ

TIM MCWHORTER

The lieutenant steps from the cover of snow-crested trees. Night has overcome the sky. He stands at the edge of a vast, rolling field. A moonlit blanket of unblemished white stretches over the winter wheat field before him. Spruces, firs, and indigenous pine frame the field on three sides. It is familiar landscape, this rural area. It reminds him of the barley fields that surround the home he shares with his wife just south of Moscow. He thinks of his Kira riding out the winter in the Big Village so far away. He thinks of their two young boys, Dmitriy and Mikhail. It is the first Christmas he has spent apart from his family. Maybe next year, he tells himself, if the war goes well. Maybe next year they will be together.

From where he stands, half frozen and covered in blood, next year feels a long way off.

Nothing moves. No small creatures scurry through the snow; no birds flutter above. The only sound beyond the ring in his ears is the angry and lonely howl of the wind tearing through the treetops. The bitter December air chills even his bones. Wet, white flakes sting his face. He nestles his coat's fur collar further up his neck and buries his hands deeper into his pockets.

Off to the right, a split-rail fence lines one side of the field. It leans awkwardly from years of use and poor construction. He squints against blinding snow and wind. He follows the fence with his eyes. It rises over a slight hill, then disappears before eventually continuing on the other side. A quarter kilometer farther, backed against a thick copse of evergreens, a small farmhouse stands like a mirage amid the foul weather. Its roof wears a thick layer of snow. Its stone and mortar chimney releases a steady plume of gray smoke into a night sky that hasn't always been so quiet and still.

The mission went as planned. Right until it didn't. Right until things went horribly wrong. They believed their provisional base to be secure as they launched short-range missiles toward the city of Makivka. Then all hell broke loose. An enemy air defense rocket missed its target, but found his base, setting off explosions and launching errant missiles in every direction. Casualties were swift and high. The attack killed nearly every soldier in their small, makeshift quarters. Nearly, because he alone survived. The fortunate died quickly. A few of the less fortunate died slowly and agonizingly in his arms.

With communications down and lacking the desire to become a prisoner of the Ukrainian army, he began to walk. Images of Kira and the boys occupied his thoughts, pushed him onward. He trudged through falling snow for hours. Could only guess how many. His head throbbed. His ears replayed the sounds of never-ending explosions. Pain entangled his body with icy, sharp tentacles. In a moment of weakness, covered in a comrades' blood, he prayed for death to come for him, as well. With all feeling gone from his extremities, he could only wonder if his prayers would be answered.

Kira. Dmitriy. Mikhail.

He has to continue, has to keep going. Even if he must walk all the way back to Moscow.

With the distant farmhouse his more immediate destination, the lieutenant slogs through ankle-deep snow toward the fence. He is anxious to move beyond the trees toward something more akin to preservation. It will mean losing the shelter from the biting wind, but a farmhouse means shelter from it all —the cold, the snow, *and* the wind.

The lieutenant follows the fence up and over the hill toward the modest abode. His footing is consistent, mindless, one frozen foot after the other through drifts that are at times knee deep. He comes upon an occasional scorched area. Remnants of missiles that fell well short of their target. Blemishes upon a country caught in a fight they never asked for. At his position, he must keep emotion at bay, yet empathy for the innocents knocks on his heart's door.

As he draws near the farmhouse, an equally modest, welcoming barn stands to the left. The building's split gray siding allows the elements to infiltrate in several places. For a moment, he considers the shelter, flaws and all. After all, he is the enemy in this part of the world, and entering the house means walking into an unknown situation. What type of reception can he expect? What or who might await him within those walls? He instinctively pulls his hand from his pocket and rests it on the cold, steel butt of the standard issue MP433 Grach at his hip. He looks once more to the barn. Something about the house beckons him. A candle burns like a beacon in the front window, and he turns toward it.

Cautiously, he approaches. He peers through the glass.

His eyes widen. His chapped lips part and his mouth falls open.

The window frames a festive holiday scene, not unlike those he has shared with his own family in years past. A long, wooden table sits in the middle of a large room, displaying an abundance of food and drink. Breads, bowls of what appear to be stews, jars of pickled cucumbers, tomatoes, and sweet peppers. Christmas decorations, traditional in this part of Europe, adorn the table and walls. A *didukh*—a sheaf of wheat stalks tied with a blue, white, and yellow towel—rests on the table, while another sits perched beside two framed photographs atop the mantle. A fire blazes from the hearth beneath. And in a far corner stands a sparsely decorated pine tree, its spiderwebs handmade from paper and silver glitter, glistening in the firelight. Joyful but muted sounds emanate from inside the home. Laughter accompanies the angelic voices of children in song. A teenage girl with blonde hair, a younger boy with black. A mother and father. Both stand nearby, both wear proud smiles.

Kira. Dmitriy. Mikhail.

It isn't them, but it's their faces he sees in his mind.

The wind strips some of the lieutenant's tension. He relaxes by a measure. There are no armed landowners awaiting him, ready to defend their home and country. No enemy soldiers holed up to escape the harsh elements. There would be no ambush.

The lieutenant's empty stomach grumbles at the sight of all the food. His extremities yearn for the warmth of the fire. Gifts from God Himself. He peels himself from the window and makes his way through the snow to the homestead's heavy wooden door. There, he knocks twice. His fist is so frozen, he doesn't feel the impact.

Inside, the chorus of song continues uninterrupted. The father joins in with a hearty hoot. The mother adds a bit of laughter.

With no answer or reason to believe they heard his knocking, the lieutenant repeats the act, pounding the door even harder.

Still, no one answers.

He is wasting time, he tells himself, and the frigid conditions aren't improving.

As he reaches for his pistol to shoot through the lock plate, a thought occurs to him. It isn't unheard of for farmers to leave their doors unlocked, especially in the middle of nowhere. He tries the door, which opens.

The chorus of song bursts forth. A rush of light draws him in. He stomps through the snow piled in front of the door, tracking it into the entryway. He slams the door closed behind him. The howling wind dies a swift and sudden death. Without hesitation, he pulls his pistol from its holster and spins around.

The lieutenant expects to be greeted with quizzical, even shocked expressions.

The occupants afford him neither.

None of the family members so much as flinch at the sudden intrusion. The mother wraps her arms around her still-singing daughter, and with much merriment and cheer, kisses her atop the head. The father busies himself with buttoning his young son's vest.

Even as the lieutenant points a pistol in their direction, no one turns his way.

How could it be? Surely the rush of cold air grabbed their attention. The sudden braying of wind. The bloodied soldier barging through their doorway. Any one of those circumstances should have whipped their heads around, yet they acted as if their celebration hadn't just been crashed by a lost, half-frozen stranger.

The lieutenant stands dumbfounded; brow furrowed. Have they been instructed to ignore him? Is this how they have been told to greet the enemy should they encounter one? The lieutenant focuses his gaze on the children. He watches them for a moment, searching for a crack in the façade. He finds none. He marvels at how well they hide their fear.

As the family goes about their holiday preparations, the lieutenant brushes snow from his shoulders and stomps it from his boots. He addresses the father.

"Sir, I am Lieutenant—"

A faint whistling reaches out from the back of the house.

The lieutenant stops, turns his attention to a wooden door on the room's far wall. Where does the door lead? Where is the whistling coming from? He has taken a step in its direction when the teenage girl finishes her song.

The ensuing silence brings the lieutenant's attention back to the family.

All eyes are on the teenage girl. On the table, she places a small, braided ring of bread atop two other, larger ring-shaped loaves. In the middle of the stacked rings, she nestles a red candle identical to the one burning in the front window. She retrieves a match from a small box and strikes it along the side. She touches the flame to the wick. Once the candle is lit, she blows out the match and places it on the tray where the bread sits.

"The *Sviata Vecheria* is almost ready, Anna," the father says. "Would you like to check for the star?"

The teenage girl crosses the room, brushing past the lieutenant without so much as a glance up. Remarkable, he thinks. Poor child must be terrified. Where she stands at the window, only three meters separate her from him.

"Papa!" An excited Anna points through the frosted glass at the night sky. "I see it. The first star."

"Mary's star." The father smiles. "Come now. Come sit so that we can pray and begin this celebration of the birth of our

Lord, Jesus Christ."

The father turns to the mother, and with a smile, pulls a chair out from the table. *"Moya lyubov."* After the mother is seated, he pats her shoulder, then pulls out the chair beside her and waits as the young boy climbs upon it. The father slides the boy's chair up to the table. The teenage girl also sits and slides her chair in. The father sits in his own chair beside a fifth, empty chair where the sheaf of wheat stands, the empty setting reserved for the spirits of deceased relatives.

The lieutenant watches this all from just inside the doorstep. How wonderful a scene. Yet how bizarre for them to not notice him. Not a glance. No trembling hands to betray their fear.

They act as if he doesn't exist.

His annoyance grows from being ignored, something a man in his position is hardly accustomed to. The lieutenant stomps over to the table. He makes as much noise as possible. With hungry eyes, he devours the trays and bowls filled with holiday bounty while deciding what to partake of first. He recognizes many of the traditional dishes of the twelve-course *Sviata Vecheria*. The large ceramic bowl of *Kutia*, the Christmas supper's main dish. A bowl of boiled cabbage and potato-filled dumplings. Fish balls and marinated herring. A jug of stewed fruit *uzvar* sits nearest him, the staple drink of the holiday feast.

"God has favored us with good health," the father says. "Let us give thanks." Taking a piece of bread, he dips it in a bowl of honey and places it on a small saucer. He passes the plate to Anna, who passes it on to her mother at the other end of the table. They repeat the process until all family members possess a saucer with a piece of sticky bread.

"Let us pray," the father says, and watches until all at the table have set down their saucers, clasped their hands, and bowed their heads. Only then does he close his eyes and lower his head. "Our Father, which art in Heaven . . ."

The lieutenant cannot believe what is happening. He stands there, hovering over the family like an impending storm. And yet, they don't break. Should he sit? Despite his weariness, he does not feel like sitting. The food and drink, however, beckon him. Partake of us, they say. His grumbling stomach encourages the same.

The lieutenant crouches until he is eye level with the father. With eyes closed, the man continues praying, asking the Lord to bless their meal. The lieutenant shouts into the man's face. "Hey! Fool!" The man doesn't flinch. A steady flow of words spills from his mouth. Rising, the lieutenant pulls his pistol from the holster on his hip. He swings the end of the barrel around, points it directly at the man's ear, and cocks the hammer.

"And forgive us our trespasses, as we forgive those who trespass against us."

"Ridiculous!" The lieutenant re-holsters his pistol. He grabs the jug of wine by the neck, brings it to his lips, and drinks. The liquid is cool. It goes down smooth but has no flavor.

"Your wine lacks the taste of simple water, Comrade."

The lieutenant drops the jug onto the table in disgust. He reaches for the top ring of bread and tears off a piece. He dips the chunk of bread into a bowl of what he hopes is *borscht*. Dripping purple broth across the white tablecloth and the front of his coat, he stuffs the bread into his mouth.

As much as he chews, no flavor emerges. "Madam," the lieutenant says, tossing the half-eaten hunk of bread onto the plate before her, "pig's slop tastes better than your bread." He spits the chewed mouthful onto the floor.

The mother remains as stoically ensconced in prayer as before being addressed.

"For thine is the kingdom," the father continues, "the power, and the glory, for ever and ever."

In one voice, the family provides the prayer's coda. "Amen." All four open their eyes and raise their heads.

The lieutenant has had enough. He sets his jaw, places both hands on the table, and leans in. He roars at the father, spewing spittle from his mouth. "By God, look at me!"

As fierce and abrupt as it was, his outburst is ignored.

"Even now," the lieutenant bellows, pounding the table, "after drinking your wine and eating your food before you, you miscreants refuse to acknowledge my presence. You refuse to show me the respect a man of my stature deserves." He slams his hands on the table once more before turning away.

With hands and feet far from thawed, he seeks the heat of the glowing fireplace across the room. He stands with his back to the fire. His mind races, determining ways to best impress himself upon the obstinate family. He watches as they turn their attention, not to him, but to the table's bounty, and begin to eat. Silver scrapes pottery. Glass clangs against wood. Sloppy, open-mouthed chewing fills the room until the mother gently lays her hand on the young boy's knee with a whisper.

When after several minutes the lieutenant still cannot feel his feet, he turns and steps closer to the fire. He stretches his hands toward the flames. So close, he fears his wool sleeves might catch fire if an errant spark were to leap in his direction.

Even with his hands mere centimeters from the fire, its warmth eludes him. The lieutenant grabs a log from a nearby small pile, and after stoking the fire with its end, tosses it atop the blaze. He thrusts his hands even nearer the fire than before. Flames lick his fingertips.

The only warmth he feels is the fiery rage growing within. His face flushes. Frustration tugs at his fringes. He looks once more to the family. He pulls his pistol, raises it, and fires a shot into the ceiling. Dust and shards of wood fall to the floor.

Still, the family acknowledges nothing more than the food they consume.

The lieutenant fires three more rounds into the ceiling.

When that fails to elicit a response, the lieutenant lowers his pistol and shakes his head. He has no other recourse than to let go of his anger. Concern replaces it. That these people could maintain their act with shots fired from mere feet away is not possible. No will is that strong, especially that of a child's. Something else is at work here. Alternative explanations elude him. A burgeoning fear grows within him. Is he losing his mind? Or worse? Is he . . .

One thought cements itself in his gut. He can hardly bring himself to indulge it. Is it possible? Is he . . . dead? Does he no longer breathe the same air he once did, the same air as the others in the room? The argument for this is substantial. Spirits, he allows, aren't easily acknowledged.

Kira. Dmitriy. Mikhail.

His heart races. His blood pumps through his still-frozen veins. No! It cannot be! He cannot be dead! What of his beloved family?

The lieutenant paces before the fire. Three steps, turn. Three steps, turn. Three steps—

A long, sustained whistle billows from the back of the house.

The lieutenant stops. He glances first at the family dining at the table, then at a door leading to what he assumes is the rear of the house. What is that infernal noise? Is someone in the next room? Are they taunting him? Attempting to signal him? The family? If so, they appear not to hear it any more than they hear him.

The lieutenant leaves the light of the fireplace and

approaches the wooden door. With his pistol at the ready, he places his other hand on the knob. Without regard for the family's privacy, he turns the knob. He pushes open the door.

Pistol front and center, he rushes into the next room.

At least what remains of it. One wall is gone. In its place, a large, blackened hole glares at him. The jagged brick and stucco frame reveals a view of the forest behind the house. Trees with broken trunks lean awkwardly beyond the opening. Cold air rushes past. Snow and ash flutter about the room. A missing section of roof allows it to accumulate on the rough-hewn floor. Drifts as deep as a boot encircle a large, black crater in the floor.

A bed sits against one wall, piled high with brick, rock, and what used to be shingles. Underneath the debris, snow and ash, stained a deep red. Within it, body parts lay in a tangle, their identities unknown, yet familiar. A teenage girl with blonde hair, a younger boy with black. A mother and father.

Kira. Dmitriy. Mikhail.

It isn't them, but it's their faces he sees in his mind.

The lieutenant's heart shatters. His stomach recoils as he recognizes the damage his own missiles can do. He raises a hand to cover his mouth. It can't hold back the vomit. He spits out the last of it, hands on his knees. His knees buckle under the crushing weight of responsibility.

Eager to escape the scene, the lieutenant scrambles and retreats to the front of the house.

The brightly lit and festive home he entered minutes ago is no longer brightly lit; the atmosphere is no longer festive. Darkness now shrouds the room. A cold and lonely tomb. No candles burn on the table. No light beckons from the window. Bowls and plates of spoiled food collect dust on the table. The fireplace stands cold, nothing burning within but the passing seconds.

The family of four stands beyond the table, hands joined, their solemn faces cast downward, their skin and clothing translucent and fading. Within seconds, they disappear altogether.

The lieutenant stands aghast. He knows now why the fire provided no warmth, the food and drink no taste.

And as the wind whistles through the hole in the wall behind him, the realization he is not dead does not come as a relief but as a bittersweet taste in his mouth.

Midnight Bang

HAILEY PIPER

New Year's Eve melts beneath a studded tongue. Candace wonders briefly if the tab would absorb faster had she taken the piercing out, but the night already juices in her spit, in her blood.

She has maybe moments to freshen up in the ladies' room of the club before the world thrums into a rainbow of Saturn's rings. Black tiles make kissing noises under her sneakers. The white-tiled walls jitter in place. By the time she's washing her hands, her skin has gone fuzzy. It forgets where flesh ends and the chilly air begins. The restroom's stark coldness would feel lonesome if not for the pleasant balloons climbing her bloodstream into her brain.

Moments after shutting off the faucet and thrashing damp hands at the wall, Candace notices the mirror. Cracks web through its glass in black lightning bolts. Most of its surface is useless except for a small intact slab at the center. Candace should see a twenty-three-year-old with heavy black eyeshadow, a silver stud in her nose, and gray eyes already swimming with joy.

She instead finds a young woman with short sky-blue hair

and a pale face. Purple makeup circles her eyes, and her lips are painted black.

"Already losing myself," Candace says, laughing. A tinny sound, her uvula replaced with a small bell.

She raises a hand, the nail polish black, and the other woman raises hers, each fingernail violet, her arms coated in black fishnet sleeves. When Candace smiles, the other woman stares blank. Candace prods with one finger, and the woman on the other side pokes back with two. She feels cold and hard, like a restroom mirror should.

Candace giggles. This high will be exquisite, she can already tell. Time to forget her roommates, forget both her jobs, and soak up sweet feelings all the way through midnight and into the new year.

She leans toward the glass, and the glass leans in return. The ladies' room tilts, but she defies its angles, its gravity, gripping the sink basin and peering closer, close enough to feel the blue-haired woman's breath on her face. Two violet-painted fingers aim out, as if to press against Candace's lips. She shuts her eyes and awaits a kiss in the cold.

A whisper strokes her mind. *Orange, green, might OD.*

Candace thrusts her eyes open, emerging from a whirlpool of darkness. She faces gray eyes, black eyeshadow, her own dark hair haloing pink cheeks. Her reflection has returned to the mirror's unblemished center, encircled by a storm of broken glass.

A sudden *clack* stiffens her spine as the door bangs open, inviting a herd of drunk girls into the ladies' room. They crowd around Candace, at first sharing the usable fragment of mirror to adjust their own hair and makeup, and then compliment her wavy hair, her soft-featured face, her black wardrobe lined with silvery spikes, studs, and grommets.

"You're so badass," one says.

"You have such pretty eyes," says another.

"Everything's so tiny in here," another adds, studying the narrow stalls, the miserly section of mirror not cracked to hell, the vent near the ceiling across from the door. It almost looks like a person could fit inside, but it's probably too small.

Candace gazes at the vent's reflection, refracted across a dozen chips of mirror glass. Could there be a person in there? Is that why she imagined the blue-haired woman? She almost sees the darkness move behind steel slats.

But then everything is moving, and the drunk girls have their hands on her, their fingertips coiling into her nervous system. For a moment, they're all one creature. Candace laughs with them, that ringing bell again, and then she makes to leave, get back to the dance floor. New Year's Eve won't last forever.

With the door half open, she takes one last glance at the mirror. It shows the stalls, that vent, the other girls, her face.

The cracks in its surface form a hundred glass daggers aimed at her reflection.

THE CRAMPED ALTERNATIVE club flashes every color Candace's eye can perceive. Its insides swim around the few dozen contorting figures. A circular skylight gazes down on the dance floor, dark with the winter night, and its glass reflects every pulsating indoor light. The air swirls with smoke of mysterious origins. Everyone is full of piercings, covered in tattoos, humanity in a mosaic of sculpted forms and radiant eyes.

Candace squeezes between a beautiful round woman and a bony guy with oversized, over-belted pants dripping off his hips. She smiles at them both, and the woman grins; the guy nods. They let her pass to the bar and then ease back to dancing.

Linda notices her visitor as she serves two crimson drinks to a couple of mohawked young men. Their hair seems to wave at Candace, and her hand responds in a sluggish greeting.

"Hey there, astronaut," Linda says, bubbling with New Year's cheer. "Still heading to space or making a landing? Those tabs can get pretty unpredictable."

"Orbit," Candace says.

She grips the bar to steady herself while her hips slide side to side with goth-techno beats. Part of her wants to swim with the room, part of her wants to dance, but a more crucial part needs to ask Linda a question.

"Ever see somebody else in the mirror with this stuff?" Candace asks. "Or do I have short blue hair and lots of violet on my face?"

"You look like you," Linda says, raising her voice where the music thunders. "But blue hair and purple paint? That sounds like Erin."

Candace licks her lips, tastes the name. "Erin."

"Were you coming here back then?" Linda fetches a water bottle from beneath the bar and passes it to Candace. "I'd only started the month before, even thought about quitting when it happened. Mariska *did* quit. She was the one who trained me, but that was it for her."

"What was it?" Candace asks, slurping down water. Her mouth has never felt so parched.

"Finding a dead body," Linda says. "Erin died in the ladies' room last New Year's Eve."

The club briefly stills, holding Candace in place. She wants to believe she's found her recreational substance sea legs, but she recognizes the steel vice of momentary sobriety.

And then the music shifts to some industrial tune, the lyrics in Japanese. The floor wobbles, and Candace jolts from the bar and starts laughing, looking around, eyeing the dancers for any sign there's been a death from a year ago haunting this grungy friendliness.

Short blue hair flashes beneath the club's now-magenta glare. Someone wearing fishnet sleeves. Violet eyeshadow.

"Can't be the same girl then," Candace says. "I see her there." She tries to point, but her finger arcs wide, gesturing to most of the dance floor.

"That's that, then," Linda says. She encourages Candace to polish off the water bottle and then returns to her other customers.

Candace takes a breath, eager for the club to fill her lungs, and then she staggers toward this blue-haired woman who is not Erin. Or must at least be a different Erin.

She stands at the center of the dance floor, not dancing, only waiting expectantly at the deepest valley of what should be a flat surface. Candace reaches her and begins to sway, to gyrate, to lean close and smile. Every impulse is a good idea right now, and she can't help her tongue.

"Linda tells me you're dead," she says. "Or you look like somebody dead."

The Erin lookalike tilts her head, no expression on her lips. Club lights flare and darken around her in time to growling guitars, and her violet makeup sinks through her face to form a bright-eyed skull.

That melodic whisper strikes again. *Violet, blue, strangle you.*

Candace jerks back, her hazy eyes fixed on Maybe-Erin. "The colors—they'll do what?"

Erin/Not-Erin cocks her head to the other side. She then raises two violet-nailed fingers to her temple in a makeshift gun.

A loud *bang* pauses the club's music in anticipation of a beat drop, and the dance floor dives into momentary pitch blackness. Candace holds her breath.

The club then swells with strobing azure and purple. The music roars alive again, and every dancer twitches and twists in the fresh light. But none of them stand with Candace.

Erin is gone.

THERE'S no such things as ghosts. Ridiculous that Candace even has to think it. Erin was there, then gone, the club equivalent of a hitchhiker who turns out to have been dead all along, a Ghost of Christmas Whenever who's arrived a few days late. Candace wouldn't give this a second's credit while sober. She should give it even less while her blood feels like it's grinding to the club's rhythm.

But that glimpse in the restroom mirror is like a speck of dust stuck in her eye. She can't quit seeing it, and so long as it stings, she can't stop thinking about it.

Someone else besides Linda must know more. Candace roams the dance floor, asking the other dancers what they know of blue-haired Erin who died last New Year's Eve.

"Ghost peppers?" one asks. "Only on pizza."

Candace doesn't correct this misunderstanding, only moves on to the next dancer.

"Curses?" another asks. "They're only really in baseball. And maybe hockey."

Most dancers either mishear her or ramble nonsense, but she meets a pair in their mid-twenties, one in a long black coat, the other wearing a studded choker from which dangles a steely chain.

"Ghosts?" Choker asks with a smile. "There's no dead or alive on New Year's, kid."

"What?" Candace blinks hard, and the club's colors pulse against her eyelids. "Why not New Year's?"

"All is one on New Year's. It's liminal." Choker waves a gloved hand as if parting clouds. "When the past won't love you and the future looks bleak, New Year's is a bridge between all things. Not a natural liminality, and not ancient. It exists because we believe the year changes. On a temporal scale, you are always alive and dead. Don't you know physics?"

Candace shakes her head. She doesn't see a bridge; she sees a halo cast by neon lights. Her mind spins with goth-techno heartbeats and synthesizers playing minor keys.

"Lay off a sec," Blackcoat says, nudging Choker aside. "You're asking about Erin then? I used to know her a little. You're wondering what happened?"

Candace isn't sure anymore, but her body sways forward and back, forcing her head to nod.

"The old bartender found her." Blackcoat makes an indiscernible sign with one hand. "Erin liked small places. Cramped rooms, cozy spaces. She used to squeeze through gaps in unfinished construction walls and mellow out with the wires and the rats. Like it was a warm embrace. I used to think she was agoraphobic, at least a little."

"Agoraphobic." Candace's mouth feels tight, like there's a tiny Erin wedged beneath her tongue.

"But she wasn't," Blackcoat goes on. "She just liked cramped places to hide, like that balmy attic studio where she used to live. In fact, she liked it too much. Last New Year's, she scuttled up into that vent in the ladies' room, like some raccoon looking to hibernate for winter. It looks bigger than it really is, and she got stuck. Probably panicked. Her place to hide became a place to die. The old bartender found her sometime after midnight, quit the next day. That was the end of Erin."

"How'd she die?" Candace asks.

"A bad high, a good scare, you can trick yourself into dying. When they pulled her out, she had her fingers aimed at her head, like a gun. Everyone else getting a midnight kiss, Erin gave herself a midnight bang." Blackcoat demonstrates with two fingers pointed at her temple. Or her eye. "An act of true faith. She believed in her death enough to make it happen. Scared into cardiac arrest or something."

Choker pushed into Candace's throbbing field of vision. "True faith in a wrong-way transcendence."

"You need to stop," Blackcoat said, a warning in her voice.

"Erin meant to make her living self and dead self meet across the temporal liminality of New Year's," Choker says in a conspiratorial tone. "That's *my* theory. But she died at an odd angle, offset the liminality. Must've passed on seconds too early, or a half-second too late."

"Enough. You're too stoned for strangers." Blackcoat grabbed Choker's chain and tugged to one side. Her wary eye fell on Candace. "Careful. You can find a lot of hurt poking at what everyone else has best left alone."

CANDACE BECOMES a small and furtive creature at one corner of the dance floor. She began the evening intending to ride her high through midnight, straight on to New Year's Day, but it might be better to sleep off this particular trip. Its road felt potholed and dangerous.

A fast-paced drum pushes the dance floor into thrashing limbs and nonsensical screams, and Candace twitches to thrash with them. This isn't right. She's been needing a night away from her personal wasteland of three spiteful roommates and sixty hours of shit work for weeks now. A night to be herself.

Maybe Erin felt the same last year when she crawled into that vent. Craving a place removed from the outside. From everything. A tiny space hugging her on all sides, somewhere to make her own.

Someone dances too close, brushing Candace on the left, and then another dancer passes on the right, and then a third figure leans behind her. She tries sliding out of their way, but the presence sidesteps, sticking to her back.

A fishnet-coated arm encircles her waist. The skin is pale, and violet polish colors the fingernails.

"Erin?" Candace whispers, but she can't hear herself speak beneath the amplified drums and thumping bass.

Another arm snakes at Candace's left, bicep to bicep, elbow to elbow. The hand forms a two-fingered gun. It rises up Candace's side, and Candace's arm rises with it, as if unseen strings bind together a ghostly puppeteer and her living puppet. Colors flash in Candace's black-painted fingernails, as if gleaming off a real pistol, and an earthquake rocks her chest. She feels a chill in her fingertips, as if she's again touching the restroom mirror.

Red, black, heart attack.

Candace charges two steps forward, trying to escape the whisper and the touch. When she turns around, no one's there.

Merry squeals and delighted gasps draw her attention to the dance floor again. The dancers are watching the world above them, where a swirling snowstorm descends against the skylight glass. It rarely snows in January anymore, and the descending flakes almost feel like a miracle. The dark sky becomes a pupil, the snowfall becomes white flesh, and the strobing colors turn the ceiling into a kaleidoscopic eye gazing down on the dance floor.

Lights flash scarlet, orange, pink. Everyone is dancing, some with tongues sticking out as if they can catch snowflakes.

Midnight is watching from the future—Candace feels it, exactly as Choker warned. They've almost reached it. Stay on this dance floor a little longer, and the countdown and music will shake her into next year.

The music holds its breath, and the club goes black.

When the beat drops and the colors roar in again, everyone has stopped dancing. Candace is surrounded by stiff figures. Each face has turned to a bright-eyed skull, with their fingers forming makeshift flesh guns aimed at their heads. Blackcoat and Choker stand by the bar; Choker's gun is a leather glove. Even Linda isn't safe, a bottle in one hand, the other aiming at her head.

Every dancer's fingers slide over skin, as if their temples aren't good enough, and the fingertips need to blast them in the eye. They're only waiting for a midnight bang.

Candace shrieks and backs away from the dance floor.

The lights strobe in violet, then green, and everyone is dancing again. As if nothing has happened. Some of them scream along with Candace, mistaking terror for excitement.

They're all alive, and they're all dead. It isn't time that's turned liminal; it is life and death beneath the shadow of a coming midnight. Candace questions if Choker is right that Erin failed at some transcendence last New Year's.

Or if in dying, she has succeeded.

THE LADIES' room throbs with color as if Candace hasn't left the dance floor behind. She never should have taken that tab from Linda. What exactly is coursing through her system? She has no idea, but it isn't a sweet feeling, more the anxiety she could get at home around her roommates, the exhaustive stress of work.

Now she would rather be anywhere but here. She wants to vomit the drug onto the black tiles, scrape it from her tongue, only she's hours too late if the problem is a drug. A year too late if the problem is a ghost.

Candace catches the restroom mirror out the corner of one eye. The reflection is skewed. Maybe that's Candace's face, flashing with every imaginable color.

But it might be the dancers out in the club, each trapped in a different reflective shard between the many lightning bolts of that cracked mirror. They aim finger-guns at their heads. It's a vision stuck in Candace's eye, and she watches an act of true faith inspire the dancers toward reality.

A midnight bang crashes through their skulls, up to the skylight, where it shatters into a thousand pieces and spills killer glass and miracle snow across the dance floor.

Teal, maroon, stab wound.

"No!" Erin shrieks, rushing for the mirror. "What do you want? Why are you doing this?"

The illusion of dancers has vanished. Only her own reflection haunts the mirror's central slab. The hundred remaining glass daggers reflect the rest of the ladies' room in tiny, harmless fragments.

Until something moves in the mirror's upper-righthand corner. A shard twitches with a reflection of sliding steel, dots of violet, and stark blue locks.

Erin's hand has pushed the vent open near the ceiling, across from the door. Her head peers out, half hidden by shadow. She's looking at the mirror. At Candace.

A shrill moan climbs Candace's throat as she whirls around, ready to shriek again.

The vent is shut. No one's pushed its steel cover open from the inside. No head peers out, watching the ladies' room.

Heart pounding, Candace settles against the sink basin. She turns around again to splash cold water on her face, desperate to wake up from this miserable high.

Her face is gone from the mirror. Erin's pale visage fills the glass.

Candace flinches, meaning to retreat, but she's locked in place. Her fingers have hooked to the sink basin, and no matter how hard she tugs, they won't let go.

Erin leans toward the glass from within, and the world seems to screech in pain as her face emerges from the mirror. Two fingers jut out, their violet-tipped pistol aimed for Candace's head.

Twin visions fight between her eyes. One shows the moment earlier this evening when she prodded the mirror, reaching out for the ghost. The other shows a woman crammed into a restroom vent, seeking the smallest place she can squeeze herself into.

Erin leans closer, her fingers and face nearly touching Candace. She thinks she hears a countdown thundering from the dance floor, the noise surging through the ladies' room wall. A few dozen mouths chant in near unison.

Ten! Nine!

Almost midnight. Why did Erin die last year, and what could it possibly get her? What the hell does she want? Her face is blank; she gives nothing away.

Eight! Seven!

Candace's skin stirs at the touch of cold breath. Think, figure it out. What does Erin want? What did Blackcoat say about last year? *Everyone else getting a midnight kiss, Erin gave herself a midnight bang.* And then Erin died.

Six! Five!

Candace can change that for the ghost. Swap that death memory for a kiss. Everyone wants closeness, affection. That has to be why Erin sought out tight spaces. To hide, and feel held.

Four! Three!

Ghostly fingers blur at the edge of Candace's sight. She shuts her eyes and pushes herself forward, won't let the moment be interrupted this time.

Two! One!

Her lips seek Erin's, but a whisper strokes her thoughts, clouding out cries of Happy New Year.

Pink, gray, midnight bang.

No lips cross Candace's. Instead, sharp violet fingernails pinch one of her eyelids and yank it up, peeling the thin flesh from her eye. Not a makeshift gun, but a pincer for keeping an eye open.

Candace can't yank herself from this needle-tipped grip, can't turn away without tearing her eyelid off. Erin's placid expression fills the world, too close, too blurry.

And then she drives herself into Candace's eye.

Candace jerks backward, at last wrenching her hands from the sink basin, and she crashes to the black floor. Her fingers claw at her face, her eye. The eyeball screams inside its socket, like she's caught a fingernail in the white flesh, a mirror shard in the pupil, something she can't get out. Every thrashing spasm makes her clothing's silvery pieces clink against the restroom tiles.

She lies there for some time, maybe a minute, maybe a whole year longer, as the high from Linda's drug finally begins to fade.

One hand gropes at the sink basin, and she feels it lurch in the wall as she pulls herself up. She doesn't care. Something is wrong with her aching eye.

The mirror shows her a familiar grimace and narrowed eyes. She forces them wide open. One doesn't hurt, and its iris is gray as always.

The other stings, and its iris has gone violet.

Candace blinks. Her eyelids move out of sync. She does it again, shuts them hard, hoping to get them back in rhythm.

Darkness slides away as the violet eye flashes open and moves against her will. It glances left, then right, painful with each forceful thrust, and it scans every corner of the mirror.

Candace screams through her teeth and tries to force the eyelid shut. She can't be seeing this. It can't be *doing* this.

The seditious eye resists her, staring open even as a teardrop forms at its corner. Its white flesh turns red, and the violet iris pulsates around the black pupil. There's a pressure against the eyeball, like inner-skull fingers clutching a nerve and guiding every movement from behind.

Or from inside the eye. A cramped little corner, where a ghost might like to hide.

Midwinter Tales

JONATHAN JANZ

DECEMBER 24TH, 1881 LANCASTER, VIRGINIA

As the fire crackled in the hearth and his grandchildren leaned forward, elbows on knees, married children watching from their spouses' sides and youngest daughter resting her head against the gilded epaulets adorning her fiancé's shoulder, Mr. Julius Rhodes spun out his tale.

He took his time. Haste was the enemy of a fine story. One must luxuriate in the waiting, must remember that one's audience, be they three years old, like his youngest grandson, or a septuagenarian like Rhodes himself, craved an experience.

Rhodes tossed his listeners a morsel here, a crumb there, and reveled in their startled expressions as they solved first one mystery, then another. That's what all good stories were, he reflected. Mysteries. And all good storytellers understood that they were but suppliers of the necessary clues and that the audience, if treated fairly, would not only unravel the narrative's convolutions, but rejoice in the unraveling.

He paused to sip his mulled wine. The taste, though reminiscent of the clementine oranges he'd relished since childhood, carried none of the sweetness it had only a month earlier, when his dear Josephine was still alive.

"What happened, Granddad?" one of his nine grandchildren asked.

Rhodes pretended to study his goblet. "An accident."

A hush descended on the children. They exchanged wide-eyed glances.

"Because the brother and sister had wandered onto the ice in the middle of a snowstorm," Rhodes explained, "they quickly lost their way. Being twins, they understood the need to stay close to one another." He paused for effect. "They also knew they were in danger of freezing to death."

Rhodes's daughter-in-law shifted on the settee, a hand clutching the pale-blue linen at her breast. "Are you sure this is a proper story for children?"

Rhodes's only son placed a soothing hand on his wife's knee. "Father's yuletide yarns are parables, dearest. You know that."

She smiled weakly. "Must they be so macabre?"

Yes, Rhodes thought but did not say. He'd learned long ago that for a tale to leave any sort of mark on a young mind, it needed to have teeth.

"As I was saying, the brother and sister were alone on that pale-gray sheet of ice. At first they laughed and frolicked, the experience being new, and the wind's bite not yet troubling their cherubic faces."

"What's cherubic?" one of his granddaughters asked.

Tommy, the oldest grandchild and his son's only son answered, "It means chubby. Now listen to the story."

Rhodes caught the muffled laughter of his adult children. He glanced over his shoulder at Agatha, his youngest daughter, beheld the warmth in her gaze, and understood that when her time came, she would be the best parent in this room.

Better than Rhodes himself, better than the rest of her siblings. There was always something special about Agatha. No one deserved happiness more. When she'd reached her mid-twenties without finding a suitable match, he'd worried she'd descend into spinsterhood. And then, as though providence had discovered some gross oversight, into their lives had marched this broad-framed soldier.

Rhodes took a moment to assess Mr. Grayson. Though a bit older than Agatha and a decorated member of the Army of the Potomac, there was something youthful about the man, a vibrance, almost a mischievousness, that rendered him the ideal partner for his cherished daughter. After an expeditious courtship, the two had decided to be married in the spring.

"Did they stay lost, Granddad?"

Rhodes blinked at Tommy. Though the lad was eleven, his eyes twinkled with the same expectant fervor gripping his younger siblings and cousins. Rhodes frowned, but before their chattered promptings overtook him, he snapped his fingers. "Ah, yes. Lost on the lake. Lost in the snowstorm."

The kids settled into complacent silence. Pale orange flames twirled and crackled in the hearth.

"They wandered that way for who knows how long. Ten minutes? An hour? When old Jack Frost whips up a tempest and the world goes white, there's no way to know. But the twins staggered on until, some distance ahead, they discovered a shadow on the lake."

"Was it a ghost?" a granddaughter asked.

"A creek," Rhodes said. "Just a tributary. The twins made for it, as they should have, but when they found themselves within the encompassing trees and the wind's breath no longer tore at them with such violence, they decided to tarry longer on the ice."

His grandchildren exchanged solemn looks.

"But this was bad ice. The sister, though born the same day as her brother, was the more responsible of the two. She urged him to return home with her. He refused. Safely sheltered from the howling storm by the sheer creekbanks, he endeavored to test the ice, going so far as to stomp on it as a means of frightening his sister."

Fathomless dread gripped the faces of his grandchildren. He'd heard tell of Tommy luring his little sister onto the ice last week, and it was on Tommy that he needed to impress an appropriate fear of such behaviors.

"The brother continued clowning despite his sister's entreaties. She seized his arm and ventured to drag him toward shore, but he only laughed and resisted. His laughter was so loud, she barely heard the first crack."

Rhodes paused and stared into his goblet, where the firelight danced in hexagonal red prisms. "You see, children, December ice is the worst ice. Brittle, like cheap glass. The sister feared her brother was about to break through. She lunged for him, but in doing so, her little boot happened on a fissure, and before she knew it, the freezing creek water had swallowed her whole."

Several grandchildren gasped. His daughter-in-law shook her head and hurried from the room. Rhodes glanced at his son, who grinned crookedly and gestured for him to proceed.

"The brother was, as you might imagine, despondent. He went to bed that night not even caring that it was the eve of our Savior's birthday. He no longer wondered what sort of presents Father Christmas might deliver, nor what sweets their mother might bake. You see, the concept of *their* no longer existed. His only sibling, no matter how much they had bickered, was gone, and gone along with her was part of the brother's soul. The only remnant of her was the empty bed beside his."

Rhodes sat back in his chair and rested the goblet on his belly, which though still ample, had shriveled somewhat in the month since Josephine was taken from him. "The brother lay awake deep into the night. His parents had not explicitly blamed him, nor did they need to. The lad did that himself. He closed his eyes and buried his head in his pillow, yet neither the sight of his sister's frightened eyes plunging into the murk nor the shrill scream silenced by the water would fade from his memories. Her body had not been retrieved, for there was a current under that devilish glass, and the brother could not help imagining his sister's poor body gliding ceaselessly through the lake, her frail fingers caressing the entombing ice."

"*Father*," Agatha said with a rueful smile.

Rhodes winked at her.

"What happened then, Granddad?" Tommy asked, not at all sounding like he wanted to know.

Rhodes swept the assembled grandchildren with a serious gaze. "Then the brother heard a rustling sound at the foot of his bed."

The grandchildren held their collective breath.

"He closed his eyes and pretended it was imagination. For a minute or two, this worked. But when he felt the covers about his ankles stir, he could no longer pretend it was mere fancy."

Tommy's little sister nestled into her brother's side; Tommy slid an arm around her. Rhodes smiled. Earlier that day Tommy had been chasing her around the backyard with a frozen rat, but there was no such meanness in his heart now.

"A smell rolled over the brother," Rhodes said. "The odor of black mud. Of dead fish." He eyed Tommy. "Of regret."

One of the grandchildren whimpered.

"The sheets stirred. The brother would've drawn up his feet, but they would no longer cooperate. It was as if his body had turned to ice. Whatever it was in the bedroom with him began to inch its way up his spine. The smell intensified, gagging and dank. Something twitched over his knees. His hips. Wet claws dug at the skin of his belly."

One of his grandsons buried his face in his hands.

"The room was dark, but the brother didn't need to see his visitor. He knew who it was, for he could feel her crawl up his chest, her cold, clammy clothes soaking his skin. When she reached his face and her rank, fishy breath puffed over his trembling mouth, he could bear the tension no longer. He opened his eyes."

Rhodes paused. His grandchildren sat forward.

Tommy licked his lips. "What happened then?"

Rhodes opened his mouth to answer but caught a glimpse of Agatha from the corner of his eye. Though these were only her nieces and nephews, her pretty forehead was seamed with concern.

Rhodes gave her a little nod. "When the brother opened his eyes, it was morning. Yellow sunlight blazed through the windowpanes and made the frost whorls sparkle."

Tommy expelled pent-up breath.

"What about the visitor?" a grandchild asked.

"Gone," Rhodes answered. "Along with the smell. The brother sat up and swiveled his head around to peer at the bed in which his sister once slept."

Tommy's voice was scarcely a whisper. "Was it empty?"

"It was not."

Several grandchildren gasped.

"His twin was there, sleeping soundly, but very much alive. The brother rushed over to the bed and his embrace was so fierce he nearly broke his sister's bones. She awoke, blinking, and looked up at him. 'Is it Christmas?' she asked. Her brother wiped away the tears in his eyes, smiled down at her, and answered, 'It is.'"

The grandchildren broke into applause. Two of them piled into his lap and peppered him with kisses. Rhodes chuckled and spared a glance at Tommy, who was hugging his little sister with a potency previously undreamed of. Only one grandchild—Tessa, a most precocious six-year-old—looked sour. "Just a dream," she murmured. "What a cheat."

Rhodes permitted himself a grin, then rose to help wrangle the kids into their coats and mittens.

SOMETIME LATER, with most everyone departed to rest up for the festivities and Agatha retired upstairs for the night, Rhodes poked at the fire while his future son-in-law reposed near the hearth with a brooding expression.

"I hope I didn't bore you," Rhodes said. "The tradition of the Christmas Eve story is one I hold dear. Been telling them for ages. Ever since Josephine and I were first married."

A shadow slipped across Grayson's face, and Rhodes regretted mentioning his late wife. Unfortunate that Josephine had suffered her fatal collapse on an ill-advised hike to Grayson's country home. Even more unfortunate that his future son-in-law had been the one to discover Josephine's lifeless body . . .

Rhodes returned the poker to the tool rack and hobbled over to his favorite chair. The leather groaned as he lowered into it.

Grayson sipped his Hennessey cognac. "With respect, Mr. Rhodes, you did commit a fatal error."

Rhodes nodded. "The hazards of improvisation."

"It isn't that. You're perfectly capable of spinning out a pretty tale."

With an effort, Rhodes maintained his smile.

Grayson cupped the goblet in both hands and peered into it, reminding Rhodes uncomfortably of a fortune teller he once encountered near a Boston wharf. "When you reached the ending . . . you flinched."

"I wanted the children to sleep tonight."

"Yet death is real," Grayson answered. "I understand that more than most."

Rhodes raised his goblet. "You helped preserve this fragile union. Thank you for your service."

Grayson frowned. "The ghosts remain. They've followed me to my homestead."

"I have no doubt." Rhodes shrugged equably. "But I'd imagine your memories of the war grow more distant in a bucolic setting. Perhaps that's why you took up farming rather than some other trade?"

"You're mistaken," Grayson answered. "The countryside is too quiet. At night I hear their screams."

"War is a hellish business," Rhodes agreed.

"It is not war I refer to."

For a long beat, the soldier's gaze bore into him. A pine knot popped in the hearth and made Rhodes jolt. He slapped palms to knees. "It's nearly midnight and I must retire." He stood, his joints cracking nearly as loudly as the seething logs. He hobbled toward the staircase, but paused at Grayson's chair to clasp his future son-in-law by the shoulder. "I'll trust you to extinguish the fire."

Grayson stared straight ahead, his jawbone rigid. Rhodes removed his hand from Grayson's shoulder, his fingers gone cold. Under the stiff fabric of the soldier's uniform, the muscles had been as hard as lead. Rhodes opened his mouth to say something, he knew not what, for it was obvious he'd given his future son-in-law offense. But it was late, he decided, and whatever ill will he'd enkindled in the younger man would gutter in the frosty darkness of sleep.

Yes, he thought, moving toward the stairs with scarcely concealed haste. Rest was all they needed. On the morrow they would be exchanging gifts. His daughters would be preparing a feast. The grandchildren would be roughhousing in the backyard snow. And the men would be shooting billiards over scotch and cigars. It would be a proper Christmas, albeit his first without Josephine. He could hardly believe she was gone.

It's the holiday, Rhodes thought as he clumped up the steps. *The season brings out melancholia in even the most sanguine temperaments.*

He sighed as he entered his bedroom. For all he knew it could be the cognac that had sharpened the soldier's tongue. For some, drink was a mellowing agent; for others, it had the converse effect. He'd once known a good-for-nothing named Fredrick whose mouth ran away from him whenever he imbibed, and that poor soul had come to a bad end. Thinking of that long-dead drunkard, he chuckled, eased onto his bedstead, and began the job of removing his shoes.

"Leave them on," a voice behind him said.

Rhodes whirled and beheld the figure in the doorway. The candleless room was murky, but the winter starlight glinted off the soldier's medals and shining dark eyes. Rhodes placed a hand over his galloping heart. "My God, Grayson. You gave me a fright!" He bent toward his shoes.

"I said leave them on," Grayson commanded.

Rhodes's lips went firm. "I should think you'd want to remain in your father-in-law's good graces."

A steel click rang out. Rhodes's limbs went rubbery.

"Up," Grayson said.

Though Rhodes knew what the click had been, it was still a

surprise to find himself peering into the obsidian eye of a Webley revolver.

"My coach," Grayson instructed.

Rhodes couldn't take his eyes off the revolver. "Your fiancé is across the hall. If she hears—"

"Grab your topcoat on the way out."

Rhodes finally managed to meet Grayson's pitiless gaze. "Is it money you want?" He couldn't suppress a sneer. "An ampler dowry?"

"I want to give you something."

"A good scare?"

Grayson shook his head. "A story."

THE DECEMBER WIND WAS BEASTLY.

Lancaster was inland enough to avoid the howling depredations of the Chesapeake, but this winter, either due to his finally crossing the seventy-year mark or from some meteorological anomaly, nature's merciless breath pierced deeper, the chill penetrating his very bones. And of course Grayson's coach was open-air.

Rhodes muttered, "When do I hear your demands?"

Grayson's slack hold on the reins moved not a jot. Rhodes might as well not have been occupying the same bench. They trundled out of town, and Rhodes was unsurprised to find not a single candle burning in the homesteads there. All were silent, all were asleep. As one should be on Christmas Eve.

He ran his tongue around his mouth. "At least tell me why the hell you bothered to ingratiate yourself this past year if in the end you merely intended to extort me."

Grayson glanced at him. "Do you have some past sin for which you could be extorted?"

"I do not," Rhodes answered gruffly.

"Mm."

Rhodes crossed his arms. The worst part of this, other than the betrayal, other than having to explain to his darling Agatha, his baby girl no matter her age, that her fiancé was a scoundrel, was the base humiliation of it. Grayson's Webley was holstered away from Rhodes, so to reach the bastard's left hip Rhodes would have to lunge across the reins and wrest it away. But couldn't he simply give the charlatan a shove, send him toppling from the coach, and goad the horses down the forest road himself? Grayson was no doubt a capable shot— one had to be to survive a war—but the man would have to recover from the fall first, marshal his wits, and take aim. And all in the dead of night under the veil of a shadow-choked sky and the primeval forest enshrouding the coach and its duo of Dutch mares. A very difficult shot indeed, Rhodes judged.

He *must* do it, he realized. The further they drifted from town, the more challenging it would be to navigate the snow-heaped roads. There was also the matter of reaching the constable before Grayson cut him off.

He turned and discovered Grayson watching him. Watching him and smiling.

"What in God's name is so amusing?" Rhodes snapped.

"You're an open book."

"I've no idea—"

"You're hoping to overpower me," Grayson interrupted. "You're working yourself up to it, thinking if you catch me unawares you can commandeer my coach and like some Byronic hero, save your daughter and your reputation."

Rhodes couldn't bear the gloating face. For the first time since embarking on this accursed errand, Rhodes was grateful for the concealing darkness.

"Agatha doesn't need saving," he finally managed.

Grayson merely smiled his droll smile.

Rhodes crossed his arms. "Whatever you have planned for me, leave my child out of it."

The soldier made no answer. The mares bore them deeper into the forest, the sky a memory now. All around them the snow-laden evergreens and the ice-glazed oaks formed impenetrable ramparts. Rhodes knew there must be a crossroads ahead, but his aging eyes had lost the loom of the path. The only sounds were the stifled clopping of hooves on virgin snow.

Grayson said, "I once heard an account of an incident at the Governor's Palace."

The bench seat seemed to fall away beneath Rhodes.

"It involved a young man from an affluent Williamsburg family," Grayson continued. "Fredrick, we'll call him."

Dear God, Rhodes thought. A pulsing throb began in the base of his skull.

"Fredrick was a wastrel," Grayson explained. "Too much too soon and all that, you know the old story. His father, an important man in Virginia politics, was bewildered by his son. 'Industriousness,' Fredrick's father used to say, 'is the path to the divine.' But Fredrick cared not for the divine, nor for the well-paying positions his father arranged for him." Grayson chuckled, but there was strain in the sound. "Fredrick would leave the office early and spend the evening carousing. He took up with artists and painted ladies." A glance at Rhodes. "Even writers."

Rhodes did not answer. He scarcely noticed the cold because he could no longer feel his extremities.

"Fredrick was a disappointment. To society, to his dear mother—an indolent woman, though good-hearted—and most of all to his father. So his father attempted a new gambit: to marry Fredrick off to a girl from a respectable family. Fredrick resisted, but in the end he went along. *I can pretend to be married*, he thought. *My wife and I will simply lead separate lives."*

Grayson paused. "But there was a problem."

Stop him, Rhodes thought. *Go for the gun or knock him from the bench, but for pity's sake, stop this damnable tale.*

"You see," Grayson went on, "the woman—we'll call her Josie—was already in love. I'll bet you know her suitor's name."

"Whatever you're playing at—"

"Julius," Grayson said. "Julius Rhodes."

It knocked his wind out. Rhodes could only slouch there, his thin breath skirling in ghostly wisps as the mares conveyed them through the lusterless night. Though he would not—could not—look at Grayson's face, the pleasure was evident in the man's voice. "Would you care to take up the narrative?"

"There was an accident," Rhodes murmured.

Grayson went on as though Rhodes hadn't spoken. "Julius was a climber. A schemer. Josie admired Julius's ambition. She wanted stability. Prestige. All the things she knew Fredrick would never give her."

Grayson snapped the reins taut, and the mares lurched through a knee-high drift. "Josie entreated Fredrick to give up his marriage suit, but Fredrick was indifferent. He knew if his father didn't entangle him with this girl, he'd do so with another, and Josie was at least attractive. Fredrick appreciated her feminine charms, her plunging necklines—"

"Don't talk about her," Rhodes said through his teeth.

"I can appreciate devotion," Grayson answered. "What I cannot countenance is murder."

It acted on Rhodes like a slap.

Grayson went on. "The desperate lovers—or should we call them co-conspirators?—attended a ball at the Governor's Palace. The evening began as all such evenings do: with pomp and formality. But as the hours lazed by, the lavishness of the affair took on carnal colorations. The very air became charged with debauchery. And as always, Fredrick partook of the venal delights." Grayson glanced at him. "As Julius and Josie knew he would."

"I don't know where you heard this story, but it's time—"

"For you to hear the truth," Grayson cut in. "Yes, though you know the tale well, I doubt you've allowed yourself to acknowledge the particulars." Grayson's lips twisted in a sneer, his dark eyes aglitter. "As you've floated through life . . . scribbling your narratives . . . rearing children . . . playing the proud patriarch to your adoring grand-whelps . . . I doubt you've paused to ruminate on the events that made possible your good fortune. On the blood that stains your hands, old and leathery though they might be."

God damn him, Rhodes thought. He couldn't bear this any longer.

"The accident was easy enough to stage," Grayson continued. "Fredrick was inebriated. Scarcely upright. Josie lured him to the atrium balcony. She smiled and laughed with him. She leaned into him and whispered words of love."

A sheen of sweat broke on Rhodes's forehead despite the frigidity of the night.

"And then," Grayson said, "Julius appeared."

"I will not be blackmailed."

Grayson ignored him. "Josie told the men she needed to step outside for some air. When she was gone, Julius congratulated Fredrick and patted his back manfully. Julius even toasted Fredrick! They drank to Josie and Fredrick's happiness. Julius wished him long life and prosperity."

"I didn't—"

"Then he shoved him over the balcony."

Rhodes's guts clenched.

"You know the Governor's Palace well, Julius. It's a three-story drop onto unyielding marble. Fredrick's bones shattered like porcelain."

Rhodes spoke under his breath, as though there might be listeners in the forest. "Even if this . . . *fantasy* were true . . . the events you're describing occurred forty-five years ago. You're in your early-thirties, Grayson. You were neither present for this incident, nor could you reasonably credit any secondhand account. Statements were taken from everyone that night, and all who witnessed the unfortunate man's fall corroborated its accidental nature."

"So you admit to it."

"I admit to nothing," Rhodes growled. "Yes, I was present when Fredrick Wycliffe fell, and yes it was a tragedy. But it was not, as you so erroneously insist, premeditated murder."

Grayson was silent a moment before saying, "You're right. He wasn't murdered at the Governor's Palace."

Rhodes shot him a look.

"He was murdered at the hospital."

Rhodes's innards coiled into knots.

"He mightn't have lived through the night," Grayson said. "His injuries were severe, and even had he survived, the doctor was certain he would never walk again. In addition to his myriad injuries, a lung had collapsed. He was scarcely breathing."

"Grayson—"

"*Silence!*" Grayson thundered.

Rhodes felt not seventy, but seven. A child sitting before the hearth as a ghastly tale unspooled.

"Because it was a July evening in a city as vibrant as Williamsburg, doctors were hard to come by. Fredrick was rushed home, but despite his father's reputation, he had to make due with a midwife, who had been summoned to his family's estate to deliver the child of a housemaid's daughter. Hostage to his broken body, Fredrick heard it all through the adjoining wall. The shrieks of the young mother seemed to the suffering man like the keening wails of the damned."

Gastric juices churned up Rhodes's gullet. "Please stop the coach."

"The young mother's cries assaulted Fredrick for hours. Fredrick writhed with as much strength as he could muster, yet he couldn't give voice to his anguish. You see, he was too weak…"

"Please—"

"…too weak to call for help when the figure emerged from the shadows of his room…"

Oh my God, Rhodes thought. *Oh my holy God.*

"…too frail to summon the midwife. Fredrick watched the apparition float nearer. It was grinning."

"Grayson—"

"It was Julius, of course. Julius who'd followed Fredrick home to consummate the injury he had inflicted. Fredrick could do nothing but watch his executioner draw closer. As he wreathed Fredrick's throat with his callow fingers. *As he throttled him to death.*"

Rhodes vomited over the side of the coach.

Grayson said nothing for a time, and it was just as well. Rhodes's mind could no longer function rationally. He thought he might swoon from terror.

"But then," Grayson explained, "something unexpected happened."

"Dear God," Rhodes panted, "dear God."

"Have you ever studied Norse mythology, Julius?"

"Just tell me what you want."

"The Norsemen believed that their *hugr*, their essence, could be transferred to a newborn upon their death." A bloodless chuckle. "I taught a lesson on the subject at William & Mary."

Rhodes glanced at him. "I didn't know you were a professor after the war."

"Before," Grayson corrected. "Before the war."

Though he could only discern fleeting glimpses of his captor's face, Rhodes had the impression the man sitting beside him had lost his mind.

"Impossible," Rhodes said.

"Is it."

"But that would make you—"

"Forty-five years old," Grayson finished. "Forty-five this past July."

Rhodes stared at him with dawning horror.

Grayson nodded. "Here we are."

They trundled down Grayson's lane, bypassing the stone cottage. Grayson led the mares through the dooryard and into the stable.

Once inside, Grayson climbed down and fired a lantern, but Rhodes remained where he was. As Grayson unhitched the mares, Rhodes surveyed the tack on the hooks. Bridles, halters, brushes. His eyes lingered over a pitchfork. He could reach it, he was sure, before Grayson could stop him. But could he complete his ambush without being fired upon? Grayson was a Civil War hero. If he'd really killed as many rebels as his reputation suggested, he would make short work of an old man with a pitchfork.

Grayson finished housing the mares and disappeared through the barn door. Distantly, Rhodes thought he heard the faint cries of some animal, but it might have been the winter wind. He toyed briefly with the notion of setting off into the night, but that was a fool's errand. Grayson would merely track his prints. Or Rhodes would become lost in Stygian darkness and would perish before dawn.

Rhodes slouched on the bench. There was nothing to be done.

Shivering, he stuffed his hands into the pockets of his topcoat. He should have taken the time to grab gloves. The combination of the cold and his arthritic ache—

Rhodes sat up straight. His benumbed fingers had happened upon a slender object in his coat pocket. He remembered the letter he'd been hoping to receive from the Williamsburg solicitor, the confirmation of the Bruton Parish Episcopal Church for his daughter's wedding. He'd trudged to the mailbox each day for weeks, always remembering to bring his letter opener . . .

And here it was now, in his pocket. A meager weapon, perhaps, but more practical than a pitchfork.

Grayson reappeared through the outer door. "Move, Julius. We don't have much time."

Rhodes obeyed, as he did noting how Grayson's eyes gleamed. There was a briskness in his manner that hadn't been there before, a fervor. Rhodes left the letter opener in his pocket. He must wait for the perfect time.

Grayson seized his arm and compelled him into the night. Rhodes staggered along beside him, the shin-high snow biting his bare ankles and causing him to stumble several times. The wails grew loud enough that Rhodes could no longer persuade himself it was the wind. Grayson's homestead lay to their left, but he steered Rhodes toward another outbuilding.

"Is your plan to freeze me to death?" he demanded.

Grayson smiled but did not answer. The wails that slashed the night air intensified. They were coming from the modest shed toward which they were slogging. Grayson swept the door open and shoved him inside, the soldier handling Rhodes as easily as Rhodes would one of his own grandchildren. A musky odor swam over him, sweat and flesh and bristling fur.

No, he corrected. *Not fur.*

Wool.

Several pairs of black eyes studied him in the gloom. Beyond them, a shape stirred, plump and grayish.

"Why have you brought me here?" Rhodes demanded.

A shrill wail echoed through the sheep pen. Grayson stepped toward the wooden gate, lifted the latch, and drew it open.

"In you go," Grayson said.

Rhodes shook his head.

Grayson sighed, drew his revolver, and asked, "Must we do this?"

Rhodes could do nothing but enter the pen.

THE EWE BELLOWED. Lying on her side, the woolly creature agitated her head, her black eyes catching the lantern light. Rhodes kept his distance.

Grayson's voice was close enough that the tiny hairs on the nape of Rhodes's neck stirred. "Something troubling you, Julius?"

The ewe tossed her head back and wailed.

Rhodes swallowed. "What's wrong with her?"

Grayson perched the lantern on the railing so that it cast a fulvid glow over the animal. Rhodes's eyes wandered to the ewe's swollen midsection, which showed swatches of pink flesh beneath curls of wool.

"She's in labor?"

"Lambing," Grayson corrected. "We call it lambing."

"I don't give a damn what you call it. I'm done with you."

But the moment he turned to push past Grayson, the

soldier shoved him so hard he tumbled backward into the hay. It did little to cushion his fall. Pain lanced his left wrist and his tailbone cracked the wood hard enough to make his spine tingle.

"What the hell is wrong with you?" he demanded.

Grayson stood over him, his face a gloating mask. "Stay where you are."

The ewe on the floor beside him let loose with a yodeling cry. Rhodes made to get up.

"Last warning," Grayson said and placed the Webley against his forehead.

Rhodes sank down next to the ewe.

"So this is about humiliation," he said. "Someone who knew Fredrick blames me for his death and wants me to wallow with the lowliest creatures."

But Grayson was no longer watching him. His glittery eyes had shifted to Rhodes's left.

Where a tiny lamb stood gazing at him. Under other circumstances Rhodes might have been touched. The lamb's coat was an ethereal white, on its face an expression that might almost be called a smile. He watched in some amazement as it wandered closer, dipped its head, and nuzzled his shoulder.

"She fancies you," Grayson said softly.

The lamb crowded closer, its moist snout nudging his cheek. He hadn't the energy to repel her advances.

"Pet her," Grayson instructed.

Rhodes responded with a muttered oath.

Grayson twitched the revolver toward the lamb. "Do it or I'll put her down."

Rhodes stared up in amazement. "Are you such a sadist? To murder a defenseless animal?"

Grayson thumbed back the hammer.

With a sigh Rhodes stroked the lamb's back. It buried its

head between his armpit and the dusty hay. A couple feet away the lambing ewe let loose with an anguished scream, and Rhodes gave his little companion an involuntary squeeze.

Grayson was laughing. "No shame in feeling squeamish, Rhodes. Labor is a trial for any creature, particularly these final moments."

Rhodes had to suppress a wave of nausea. He'd been raised in the city and had never witnessed a birth of any kind. In his imagination they were blood-drenched, gory affairs that often culminated in the deaths of both mother and child. Flesh crawling, Rhodes made to turn away from the ewe, but the lamb who'd befriended him gave out a plaintive bleat.

"Kiss her," Grayson said.

"Gods damn you," Rhodes growled, "I've had enough—"

The blast of the Webley made him yelp. It was as though someone had thumped his thigh with a mallet. Then the pain rushed in, and he realized Grayson had shot him. Rhodes bellowed and pawed at his leg.

"Enough puling," Grayson snarled. "Drag your mossy old body closer to the ewe."

Rhodes did as he was bidden. The conflagration in his leg was unholy. Blood sluiced between his fingers. He'd never walk without a limp again.

Grayson hunkered down to inspect the ewe. "Nearly time now."

"This is madness," Rhodes moaned. "Even if such a thing were possible, how could you know the precise moment—"

"The window lasts a few minutes."

"You're a fiend," Rhodes said. The light was too poor to afford him a proper view of his leg, but he could feel the hot blood pulse between his fingers, the torn pants slimy in the chill December air. *Bleeding out*, he thought.

"Your wife didn't even put up a fight," Grayson said.

"My wife died on the way to your house."

"She died here, among the sheep. Then I dumped her body on the road."

When Rhodes only gaped at him, Grayson nodded. "That's how your dear Josephine looked at me when I told her who I was. Like all the strength had left her body."

Rhodes licked his lips. "You're not Fredrick."

"She went willingly from my home to this sheep pen. I explained how the memories of my past life seeped in slowly, mostly in dream."

Rhodes watched him with dawning incredulity. The agony in his thigh had dulled to a thudding drumbeat.

"Often it would manifest as a *pull*," Grayson said, "a magnetism toward certain places. Or objects. Do you remember Fredrick's favorite drink?"

"Cognac," Rhodes whispered.

"*Hennessy* Cognac." Grayson massaged the ewe's flank and frowned. "She's closer than I thought. It's time."

"What are you—" Rhodes began to say, but his protest was extinguished as Grayson cinched an arm around his throat and dragged him into his lap. The indignity of the position—resting between the man's splayed legs as if the two were sunset-gazing lovers, for Christ's sake—was quickly outdistanced by the horror of what he was witnessing.

"What's wrong with her?" Rhodes asked.

"She's delivering," Grayson answered, "and you're proving as docile as your wife."

The words hardly registered. The ewe's hindquarters were arranged in the most unfortunate way, as though Rhodes were some skittish veterinary student made to observe this grisly biological miracle in order to pass a final exam.

"When Josephine learned who I was and what I remembered," Grayson said, "she went slack all over. The ewe screamed bloody murder, but as Josephine passed out of her body and into her new one, she never made a sound."

Rhodes's gaze shifted to his own lap, where the white lamb had fashioned itself into a ball against the crotch of his pants. The blood seeping from his leg soaked into the lamb's white wool, darkening it to the hue of communion wine.

"You're insane," Rhodes said.

"You've not heard the best part," Grayson murmured at his ear.

The ewe's vulva dilated wider. The ewe tossed back her head and bellowed. Rhodes was almost frightened enough to avoid gagging.

"You'll soon be reunited with Josie," Grayson said.

Rhodes attempted to swallow, but Grayson's forearm prohibited it. "Even if this is possible," he managed. "Even if you can somehow . . . transfer me to this . . ." He eyed the dilating ewe, caught a glimpse of tiny forefeet, and felt a wave of lightheadedness. "What then? My wife and I . . . we live on in these bodies? Is that where all your machinations have led? This is your grand vengeance?"

Grayson's voice was almost tender. "Josephine no more knows who she is than I did as an infant. It took me decades to grasp what had happened to me."

"Then you admit it's pointless!" Rhodes cried. He pawed at Grayson's imprisoning arm, but Grayson redoubled his grip. Tears oozed from the corners of his eyes, his airway capillary-thin.

"But she does know *something*," Grayson said. "Look at her, Rhodes."

Rhodes did. The lamb had rested her downy chin atop his crotch. She gazed at him adoringly.

"When you join her," Grayson went on, "she'll befriend you. The two of you will sense something in the other."

And staring into the lamb's ardent eyes, Rhodes could almost believe it. His mouth twisted into a bitter line. "So we'll be happy! We'll frolic in the goddamned meadow!"

"For a year," Grayson agreed. "But then I'll bring your son and your daughters here next Christmas Eve. Your precious grandchildren."

Rhodes's eyes widened.

"And to commemorate your passing," Grayson said, "I'll assist them in selecting two lambs to roast on Christmas Day."

Rhodes whimpered and bucked, but the soldier's grip was as implacable as his voice.

"You and your wife won't understand entirely," Grayson said. "Dumb beasts have not the intellect to comprehend all that the human mind can." His voice lowered to a growl. "But a trace of you will exist, and you will see in your loved ones' faces your final demise. They will *devour* you and your wife, Rhodes."

The ewe's birth canal yawned wider, the lamb's forelegs sprouting like asparagus shoots from dewy earth. Rhodes's vision blurred. *No air*, he thought, then remembered his bleeding leg. *No more blood either*. He reached into his coat pocket.

"It is time," Grayson said, "for you to join your dear Josephine."

Grayson's hand clamped over Rhodes's nose and mouth. Rhodes screamed, but the sound was bottled by Grayson's calloused skin. The soldier's voice echoed down to him as though Rhodes were coffined in a slowly-filling grave: "Just as you smothered me in that damnable hospital, I now deliver you to your new body."

With the last of his strength Rhodes thrust the letter opener up. Grayson jarred and his hand fell away. Rhodes pitched onto his side and gasped for air. Grayson coughed and gagged.

Rhodes attempted to crawl away, but his wounded leg no longer worked. The lantern light revealed a smeary puddle of crimson beneath him.

So we're both going to die, Rhodes thought. The notion brought a queer species of comfort. His vision dulled, the honey-colored light fading to a dreary gray. *One of us becomes the lamb*, he thought. *The other simply dies.* He closed his eyes and nearly laughed at the absurdity of the idea.

A choking sound brought Rhodes's head up. Grayson was indeed dying. Rhodes had aimed true when he'd plunged the letter opener into the bastard's throat. A glistening bib of burgundy darkened Grayson's chest. Yet despite his growing paleness, the soldier's eyes remained fixed on the lambing ewe.

Rhodes followed Grayson's gaze and saw the viscous matter trailing from the ewe's birth canal, as well as the pair of shapes that writhed in the glistening heap of afterbirth.

Rhodes uttered a weak laugh. "Two of them. I guess you'll be joining me and Josephine."

The white lamb eased down beside Rhodes's face. He drifted off to the sensation of Josephine's pink nose nuzzling his own.

A minute later, he awoke to the same sensation.

Ghosts in Glass Jars

STEPHANIE M. WYTOVICH

E dith walked up the attic stairs, a cup of hot elderberry tea in one hand, a piece of buttered toast in the other. The soft glow of the morning's light reached through the windows, beckoning her to the workshop table, a dark slab of smooth wood covered in cotton balls, small glass jars, and littered with different colored paints, pencils, strips of felt, and several baskets filled to the brim with twigs, dead leaves, rocks, sea glass and an assortment of other mismatched goods from the earth.

The attic was a quiet place. Outside of Edith and maybe her bulldog Gladys, there wasn't much reason for anyone else to find themselves there: not her son, not her grandbabies, and certainly not her vapid daughter-in-law, Justine. No, this was a place just for her, and she found great comfort in making it her own. There was a rocking chair and an end table near the west-facing window, and Edith liked to sit there and work on one of her many crochet projects or just let her mind wander among the sound of cars skidding on ice. If she was particularly lucky, she'd get to listen to an argument or watch someone slip down their front porch stairs in the morning. Coffee everywhere, shirt ruined. Definitely late for work.

But that morning, she took her time getting settled, her body a stiff byproduct of its 77 years. She stretched and rolled her shoulders, bent her neck from side to side. Her knees cracked when she walked, and her hip ached, which caused her to reach for her cane while she prepped the room and warmed up her bones. Edith took a sip of her tea first, tasted the sweet tang of the local honey she'd picked up earlier that week, and then turned on a myriad of lamps, preferring the soft wattage of low lighting.

First, she tended to the bells.

Sometime in her early thirties, Edith started collecting bells. She picked them up at estate sales, antique shops, yard sales. The only rule was that she'd only buy them used—never new —so its spirit, *its song*, stayed intact. She kept them on a book-shelf she dusted daily. Before she rang each one, she lit a bundle of rosemary to cleanse the space and protect her from whatever she might wake up.

Next, she lit the candles.

There wasn't a lot of furniture in the attic, but there was enough. Either way, she preferred using individual candle-sticks or candelabras—if she could find them cheap—and she liked to set them directly on the floor. Something about fire and grounding and working magic from the feet up always resonated with her, plus she liked the threat of being burned alive while she worked. All it would take was the wrong movement or a distracted mind, and the whole room could be up in flames before she had a chance to escape.

The thought thrilled her.

After the room was awash in the faint smell of smoke and the distinct smell of dripping wax, Edith sat on her workbench and closed her eyes. She wore four silver rings on her right hand and an assortment of raw crystals in varying sizes on her left. She thumbed them while she meditated, focusing hard on the tourmaline piece she never took off.

Images slipped in and out of focus, and she worked to grab them when she could. Her neighbor's kid throwing trash in her yard. The mailman leaving her packages on her front steps in the rain. Her stomach growled as she mentally grabbed the memory of a woman screaming at her children at the park last week, and when Edith opened her eyes, she thought she had enough to work with.

She grabbed her grandmother's sewing kit from underneath the table. There was a pincushion in there she favored that was shaped like a tomato. She took out one of the pins and pricked the middle finger of her left hand. A bubble of blood slid out from beneath her skin, and she ran it along the opening of a small glass jar she'd selected. She did this three times, counterclockwise.

And then she spit inside it.

Outside, snow fell in big, soft clumps, and it had started to collect on the roof. Edith watched it, transfixed, as she took a bite of her toast, some of her blood mixing with the butter.

She smiled and looked at the jar, her thoughts turning to car crashes, broken ankles, unexpected illnesses near the holidays. She opened the window and scooped a little bit of snow into the jar.

"Maybe I'll get lucky and this one will cause a death," she whispered to no one, her tea going cold on her desk.

CREATING a haunting was hard work but collecting ghosts had always come easy to Edith. It was something she'd been doing unconsciously since she was a child, and it wasn't until her mother noticed the little girl next door screaming in her backyard—she was alone and pointing at the swing—that she sat Edith down and explained to her how the whole thing worked, why she needed to be careful.

Her mother used words like *thin* and *in-between* to describe the place she sometimes went to in her head, talked about how if she concentrated hard enough, she could bring something back: a friend, a foe, a servant. This explained why her mother talked to walls and took her tea in the parlor in the afternoon, all the chairs pulled out, a pot of empty tea in the middle.

Her mother was lonely, so of course she brought back friends.

Edith wasn't, though.

She was angry.

She spent most of her childhood alone in her room, eyes closed, palms open, just walking through the dark places in her head. She met people in shadows, shook hands with *things* scratching under the floors, and she took careful notes of their histories, all the crimes they'd committed, all the blood they still craved. When she came to, she would carefully remove her clothes, place them in the laundry basket, and then take a long, cold shower. She'd rub her skin raw with salt, careful to get any spectral marks or fingerprints off her body. Before bed, she tucked a piece of amethyst under her pillow and placed a glass of water on her bedside table. It was important to her the spirits knew who was in charge, and if her charms and rituals didn't work, she had tourmaline and selenite above her door and a thin layer of brick dust and eggshells at every entry point in her room.

Now all these years later and none of those old habits were necessary anymore. Maybe it was because she no longer had anything they envied or wished to take because she was just as haunted and trapped as they were. Or maybe it was because she scared them rather than the other way around. Either way, life had become about biding her time, keeping busy, seeing how much hurt she could cause before the wound of life opened her up and swallowed her whole.

It was bleak, but she had to admit, she still found it fun.

Edith took a cotton ball and began to gently pull it apart. She wanted soft wisps and untethered edges, and when she had the shape she wanted, she grabbed some clay and textured fabric, some gauze, and worked to complete the clichéd look of a white sheet hovering in the air. When the mold dried and firmed up, she took out her mortar and pestle and placed two small pieces of raw labradorite and smoky quartz into it. She ground them up until they were a thin layer of dust and then she poured some of her tea into the bowl to help make a dark paste. Edith dipped a paintbrush into the sludge and drew uneven, different sized eyes on the ghosts. When she was satisfied, she eased it into the jar, watching it, still transfixed, as it seemed to float.

Behind her, the flames doubled in size, and while no one held a single bell, they rang like a carillon, their echoes lingering in the room like an early morning fog. Edith leaned over the jar and spoke a string of soft whispers into it. Then she pulled out one of her eyelashes and dropped it in, too.

FOR A SMALL TOWN, the post office was forever busy, and Edith wondered when the building had time to breathe. The two women who usually worked the front desk were middle-aged with bad attitudes and even worse hair, and no matter what day or time she stopped by, the one could be found popping her gum the way a cow chews its cud.

Disgusting.

Edith leaned her walking stick against the wall and sat her package on the counter. It was small and wrapped in brown paper, adorned with a slim candy cane string and no return address. A green wax seal with a faint imprint of mistletoe held the edges together.

"Hello, Edith," the woman said, her voice monotone and unpleasant.

Edith ignored her. "Same-day shipping. And no, I don't care if it's more expensive, and yes, I want tracking on the package."

The woman glared at her and pulled a tissue out of her cardigan. She blew her nose. "Anything fragile in there," she said, motioning to the box.

"Yes," she replied, point-blank.

While the woman rang her up, Edith snuck a look at the people around her. Everyone was either checking their phones, yelling at their children, or audibly sighing to get across how inconvenienced they all were. Their discomfort made her smile. It was one of the reasons why she was always sure to carry a mason jar full of change when she went out to run errands. These younger generations were all about speed: self-checkouts, automated payments. Did no one balance their checkbooks anymore? Did anyone even carry cash?

"Edith? You here with me? I said that will be $23.95," the woman said. "Do you need stamps or anything else?"

"No, I'm fine," Edith said, taking her time to count out her change. No one would yell at an old woman, especially one who looked like she was sending out some holiday cheer. She took advantage of this and asked the cashier if she could repeat the total again.

Give me your anger, she thought. *Give me your rage.*

By the time she finished counting out 95 cents, mostly in

nickels and pennies, the room buzzed with tension. Edith took her receipt, placed it in her purse, and then took a second to put on her scarf and button up her jacket. By the time she left, everyone was red in the face and ready to burst.

SHE DIDN'T SEND ghosts often, but when she did, she liked to make a day of it. Edith walked to the coffee shop a block or two down the street and purchased a peppermint hot chocolate, her usual. She didn't tip, not even when the young boy went out of his way to give her extra whipped cream and snowflake sprinkles. On her way home, she stopped at the Cheesecake Shop, an ironically named bakery considering they almost never had any cheesecake available. She ordered a raspberry scone and sat next to a faux fireplace and watched the snow fall outside while she unpacked the rest of her bag.

Edith opened her journal—a cheap, well-loved black notebook she'd picked up at the bookstore a few years back—and wrote down the day's date, time, and intended recipient of the ghost.

Wednesday, December 20th. 1:45 p.m. Chesley Vandercourt, Pittsburgh, PA.

She took a sip of her drink and savored the rich creaminess of the chocolate. The cold aftertaste of the peppermint. She let a bit of whipped cream linger on her upper lip while she scribbled down a few more notes and then took a healthy bite of her scone.

"Excuse me," a soft voice said. "Is anyone sitting here?"

Edith ignored the person and continued to write, hoping they'd go away, get the hint.

They didn't, and after a few seconds of anxious contemplation, they sat down instead. A bit of their overpriced latte dripped on the table.

"Well, don't you look all cozy sitting here and writing while it snows. If I didn't know better, I'd think I was in the beginning of one of my favorite cozy mysteries," the woman said, a sweet but ultimately unsuccessful attempt at conversation. "I just love this time of year. Peppermint everything!"

Edith gave a weak smile and nodded her head.

The woman took out a well-loved book and opened it to a dog-eared page. "Have you read anything fun lately? I've been loving Ellery Adams myself, but I always seem to come back to Agatha Christie this time of year," she said. She took a bite of her cookie and accidentally smeared chocolate on her crushed velvet Christmas-themed blouse. "Oh, fiddlesticks, will you look at that?"

Insufferable woman.

The fire flickered in front of them, a soft dance against the light café jazz playing in the background. Edith's legs felt heavy like they were sinking into the floor. This was common after she delivered a ghost. The exhaustion, fatigue. Walking with the spirits took a lot out of her, and this time, even her jaw clicked, her joints swollen, inflamed.

She made a great effort to cross her legs. The hem of her long black skirt dusted the floor. The bones in her right hip popped as a chill passed through her body. Edith dropped her pen as her head flew back against the chair. It froze there at a bent angle, her mouth open, her eyes glazed.

"Oh, goodness," cried the woman next to her, her latte now on the floor. She jumped to Edith's side and cupped her face. "Ma'am, can you hear me? Ma'am?"

Edith's vision tunneled as she moved with the ghost, her world dark, clouded, but beginning to open. The rustling of paper filled her ears and was followed by loud rips and tears. As the twine was cut, her gums started to bleed.

She watched as Chesley opened the box and removed the

jar. Her right eye—the one missing an eyelash or two—began to twitch as the man examined the ghost, a confused look pouring over his face. Inside the box was a note, an inscription Edith had taken meticulous care to write.

What wakes you nightly, what scares you most. I gift you this haunting, bequeath you this ghost.

He read it out aloud—they always did—and once the words left his mouth, Edith gasped and sat upright in her chair, the spittle from her raucous coughing fit showering the Yule-clad woman who looked possessed by fear. The paramedic who kneeled at her side ushered the barista for a glass of water and then spoke in a slow, gentle tone.

How long had she been out this time? Fifteen minutes? Twenty?

"Ma'am? Can you hear me? Are you okay?" he asked. Truth be told, his face was a tad pale, too.

Edith removed a forest-green handkerchief from her sleeve and spit out a tooth. She folded it up—out of sight, out of mind—and then used it to dab the corners of her brows and alongside her neck.

"Oh, yes, yes. I'm fine," she said, fanning herself. She had some trouble disguising the smile spreading across her face.

"If you're okay with it, I'd like to take your vitals, make sure everything is in order?" the man half-asked.

Edith laughed and a bit of blood slid out the corner of her mouth.

She had a good feeling about this haunting. She felt it in the redness of her cheeks, in the bruising that quickly spread across her ribs.

"No. That won't be necessary," she said, brushing him off with her hand. "In fact, I think I'd prefer you leave. I quite like my space and I'd prefer you *all* to respect it." She stared at all the wide-eyed fools who had their phones pointed at her. They were like statues the way they all stood there, their mouths agape in shock.

Edith made a move to grab her cane, the phones came down, and a glass of water appeared at her side. Everything felt tense, awkward. People didn't know what to do, where to go. The owner tried to turn it around by turning the music back on and offering everyone a free sample of their seasonal latte: gingerbread with whipped cream and a sprinkle of mini gumdrops.

It didn't take long for the distraction to work, and for a moment, Edith missed the building pressure of the crowd.

The woman from earlier sat back down and tried to compose herself. She rubbed her eyes and smeared even more of her mascara across her cheeks. Her hands were shaking, but she tried to clean up her mess: the spilled latte, the crumbled cookie pieces on the chair.

Edith observed the woman as she reached for her book when a touch of wickedness spread through her chest. She thought better to ignore it.

She leaned over to the woman and extended her wrinkled hand. "I'm sorry. You've been so kind since you sat down, and I've been nothing but distracted this whole time. My name is Edith. Let me buy you another latte for giving you such a scare."

The woman seemed to relax then, her shoulders drooping, her eyes lightening in the glow of the fire. She smiled then, a gentle, kind smile, and then let out a big sigh of relief. *Trust.* Edith read it all too well.

"Oh! That would be mighty friendly of you, Edith. Thank you," she said, extending her hand. "My name is Shirley."

Shirley, Shirley, Shirley.

"Well, it's lovely to meet you, Shirley. Thank you for taking such good care of me during my fit. I look forward to getting to know such a kind soul more."

Edith smiled and got up to order her new friend's drink.

In her head, she imagined what it was like to hear her scream.

Last Year's Man

RAMSEY CAMPBELL

As Santa headed for his grotto a man lurched into his path. "Think you're the real thing, do you?"

Laurence glanced around the Shopping Stop precinct to make sure no children could hear. "So long as the youngsters believe I am."

The man hugged his Better Bottle carrier, which was extruding a pair of glass necks. His breath suggested the wine shop had a constant patron. "What do you reckon you know about kids?"

"I teach them."

"Then you should be getting on with it, not putting people out of a job."

"I don't have any bookings now until next term. Anyway, if you'll excuse me—"

"Don't you want to hear about the crowd you're working for? They all want a piece of you." His scowl veered away from Laurence to range over Butchest The Butchers, the Bet Your Life betting shop, the If I Had A Hamster pet emporium… "They use you up," he said louder and more loosely, "and guess what Santa gets after all he's done for them? The sack."

His voice brought the precinct manager out of his office at speed. "Claude," Ben Denton said, "you were asked not to come back."

"That's me, Santa Claude. Shows I was meant for the job."

Denton emitted a sound summarising both a grunt and a sigh. "Please don't start bothering people again."

"Just giving your new man a chance to make himself scarce."

Laurence wasn't about to feel threatened by somebody a head shorter than himself and bulky less with muscle than with puffy piebald flesh. "Better be taking your purchases home, Claude," Denton said. "You know you can't drink here."

"See, that's all we means to them. Soon as they've sold you they want you gone." He focused his disgust on Laurence to add "But you still want to be part of them."

"Sorry you had to hear that," Denton said as Claude stumbled at the exit doors so precipitately they barely had time to sidle aside. "You can see why we had to replace him." The sight of Laurence ducking into Santa's economically proportioned hut prompted him to comment "We built that for him. You should be all right sitting down."

Con from the Thanks To Planks hardware store had constructed the dinky cabin. A surreptitiously rickety picket fence in front of the doorless entrance enclosed a yard sporting a Christmas tree and a clump of giant red plastic toadstools spotted white. There was just enough room in the shed for the occupant's chair and its attendant bulging sack. The unvarnished squarish wooden chair was too low to be wholly comfortable, and acknowledged Laurence's weight with a tentative stagger. Soon enough a woman led a little girl to him, having scanned the barcode on the side of the hut to pay for a present. At least the child's arrival on his knee didn't seem to trouble the chair. "What's your name?" he said.

He asked the question often as the day advanced, and "What do you want for Christmas?" He had to wonder if he was repeating not just himself but his predecessor. He greeted every newcomer with a smile too pronounced for the beard from Inhabit The Habit to hide. Each visitor's reward was a present from the sack, packages bound with a pink bow for girls, blue for boys. Whenever nobody was watching he massaged his thigh to ease an ache.

He counted Christmas trees in windows as he walked home. He'd done without a tree since electing to live by himself. The microwave spun him a curry, and then it was time for a seasonal film. An angel showed James Stewart how badly off the world would be without him, and hadn't Laurence earned the right to feel a fraction of the same? He needed no more than the glass of wine he'd had with dinner to bring him a decent night's sleep.

In the morning he was at the precinct well before it opened. The staff toilets doubled as a dressing-room. Some of the shops had refilled his sack. He was practicing a chortle in preparation for the first customer when the entrance doors let in a wind and a man made straight for him, or at least as straight as his unsteadiness permitted. "Keeping them happy, are you?" Claude said like a wish for the reverse.

It was all he managed before Rod from security intercepted him. "Ben says you're barred. Don't give us any grief."

"Just let me go to Better Bottle."

"Can't do it, chum. You'll have to buy your liquor somewhere else."

"Don't they want my money any more? They've had enough of it."

"Right, they've had enough and we have. Now be a good feller and get lost."

"You've had enough of me, have you?" This was aimed at Laurence. "You've not had all you're getting," Claude said.

Rod watched him and the doors perform a series of hesitant advances and retreats before his determined lurch persuaded the glass halves to complete their separation. "Give us a shout if he comes back," Rod said.

Close to noon on the following day a chill wind through the gaping entrance made it plain that Claude had. The wind flapped Santa's sack, and as Laurence clutched his costume about him he saw Claude had sprouted pallid stubble like a bid to compete with the Christmas disguise. "That's what Santa's meant to feel like," Claude called, merging some of the consonants into mush, and stumbled back and forth to prevent the doors from closing until Rod stalked to confront him. Glimpses kept making Laurence think Claude had sneaked back into the precinct, but it was always some member of staff crowned with a drooping Santa cap. He didn't see the man again until the start of Christmas week.

On the Sunday he was on the way to don his costume when Denton detained him. "You'll need to start wrapping presents now. It's our busiest week, and nobody's got time to do an extra job."

"Aren't you asking me to? You never mentioned it when you hired me."

"I didn't think it needed mentioning. Just get here however early it's going to take."

"I don't get any elves, then."

Perhaps Denton heard the hope underlying the debilitated joke. "Claude managed by himself," he said.

The chair in the grotto was heaped with presents together with wrapping paper and scissors and ribbon. Laurence bore the cumbersome armful to the food court and dumped it on a table outside What's Up Wok. Which colour of ribbon went with each item? A colouring book and a banded bunch of pencils, a cheap wristwatch, a jigsaw—he disliked the last item as thoroughly as packaging presents, because he'd never been much good at either task. He folded paper around item after unhelpful item and struggled to pin the lumpy haphazard wrapping down while he attempted to secure it with whichever ribbon came to hand. He was sweating with frustration and exertion well before all the presents were parcelled, however unevenly. He left the ungainly pile on his chair in the grotto while he dashed off to costume himself.

He'd stowed paper and ribbons and scissors under the chair and was making to fill up the sack when his fingers encountered a soft moist shapeless object that felt like a thick wad of cobweb. Had somebody taken the sack for a bin? The item was a false beard, stained in a way he didn't care to ponder. He fished it out and hastened to dispose of it in the nearest bin. As he glared about in search of the perpetrator of the prank he glimpsed a figure among the fancy dress in Inhabit The Habit, rubbing the lower half of his face as if to magic the features away. When Laurence turned for a better look he couldn't see the fellow. No doubt he'd been appraising something, and his Santa hat came with the time of year.

Laurence had barely finished filling the sack when Denton opened the doors to the public. As visitors lined up outside the grotto Santa's festive questions began to feel automatic. A lull allowed him to massage his thigh, and then a little girl clambered aboard. "What's your," Laurence said and did his best to pretend he hadn't hesitated, "name?"

"Lisbet."

He produced the most convincing chortle he could summon up. "What do you want for Christmas, Lisbet?"

Dolls were the answer, which went with her extravagantly frilly dress, another aspect of the image her mother was determined to promote. He found her a package elaborately ribboned in pink, trusting the contents would be to her taste. As she ran to her mother she declared "Mummy, he sounds just like Mr Curtis."

"I'm sure your teacher wouldn't play a trick like that," her mother said, staring hard at him.

He was hoping he hadn't disillusioned the child when he heard a low voice close to him. "Maybe you weren't such a clever idea after all."

He glanced around to see Denton making for his office. The comment must have come from him, though the blurred voice hadn't sounded much like his. Laurence thought it wise to pretend he hadn't heard. The rest of the day brought no problems other than the intermittent wobble of the chair and the ache that kept rediscovering his leg. At home a second glass of wine after his microwaved chili accompanied Bing Crosby and his dream of a white Christmas, all of which helped Laurence not to dream.

Next day a taller stack of presents awaited him. By the time all of them were wrapped he'd found several words to intone under his breath. He replenished the sack until it bristled with angular bulges. The mirror in the small room redolent of disinfectant showed him Santa recovering his image piece by piece. White gloves provided the finishing touch. He fished them out of his fat pockets and inched his hand into the right one, only for his fingertips to flinch from whatever thin sharp objects had preceded them.

He shook them onto his palm, where they gathered in an unappealing heap. He might have taken them for false nails if they hadn't been so discoloured and irregular. He flung them in the toilet and shook the other glove over it, dislodging a second set of five. Who could have played such a prank, and why? On his way to the grotto he searched for hints of guilt—surreptitious watchfulness, concealed amusement, ostentatious innocence. He'd located none by the time his first visitors came to consult him.

"What's your name?" "What do you want for Christmas?" He could only hope the questions and his manufactured chortles distracted everyone from the compulsion to flex his fingers in bids to dislodge a sense of lingering intrusion in the gloves. It left him furiously determined to identify the culprit. As his first queue petered out he crouched forward for a better view, and caught sight of an intruder. Claude was slouching against the window of Nailed You, and sent Laurence a smirk from within a mass of whitish stubble like an embryonic Yuletide beard while he waggled all his fingers to display how incomplete their tips were. Laurence stood up so fast his head collided with the low roof, sending a shudder through the cabin. He ducked out with a snarl of pain and saw the guard across the precinct. "Rod," he called, then shouted "Rod."

The guard's look grew quizzical as he approached. "What's up with your head?"

"Never mind that." Laurence gave up rubbing it to point at Nailed You, only to falter. "He was there. He'd sneaked in."

"Who did?"

"Claude whatever the rest of him is. The chap who had my job last year. He must have run off when he saw you."

"He won't be coming back."

"I hope not. He played a trick on me I don't even want to talk about."

Rod gave him a stare that did duty as some kind of question. "He's gone."

If the guard was undertaking to ensure it, Laurence ought to be satisfied. His next customers were twin girls who proved to be identical in their wishes too, not to mention their weightiness that made the chair creak in sympathy with his ache. As the second girl bore off a parcel he'd failed quite to match with her sister's, Denton tramped over to him. "Rod says you hurt your head."

"Thumped it on the roof, that's all. This place isn't really my size."

"I said it wasn't made for you. What are you saying it's done to your head?"

"I'll survive. I was in a hurry because I'd seen the chap you barred. He'd sneaked in while Rod wasn't looking."

"I doubt it."

"I wasn't criticising Rod. He must have been busy elsewhere."

"I'm telling you you couldn't have seen Claude. He's gone to the grotto in the sky."

"One of us has to be mistaken."

"Yes, and I'm looking at him. Claude's as gone as gone can get."

"How gone is that? How do you know?"

"The police wanted to know if we'd set him off somehow. Whoever's fault it was, it's certainly not ours." Having glanced about to establish nobody was nearby, Denton nevertheless lowered his voice. "God knows what he thought he was trying to prove or who to," he said. "He must have been drunk out of his skull to do all that to himself. I don't know how he could even bear to watch. Before he stopped he couldn't do that either."

Despite Denton's exhibition of dismay, Laurence suspected he relished recounting the events. As a parent brought a little boy to put an end to the information, Denton muttered "So long as you didn't do anything worse to your head."

He meant Laurence had only fancied he'd seen Claude,

which must surely be the case. Laurence didn't need to hear any more about the man's demise. Presumably he'd stolen into the precinct to secrete his contributions in the gloves, and that had worked on Laurence's imagination. He couldn't afford to take offence at Denton's tone while he needed to earn all he could. Discomfort close to loathing made him peel the clammy gloves off and thrust them in the pockets of the jacket now that Denton wasn't watching him.

None of his visitors or their parents appeared to miss them. He was still aware of them, and eventually abandoning the costume on the chair came as a relief. Lingering distaste hindered his enjoyment of the risotto the microwave delivered, and rather more than a second glass of wine weighed his mind down so much he lapsed into a dull doze before Lillian Gish could rescue the children from the preacher with the knife in time for Christmas. He shouldn't have succumbed to slumber in the chair, because he slept very little in bed.

His eyes felt swollen with the dull grey of the sky when he trudged to the Shopping Stop. He almost dropped the entire pile of presents left for wrapping as he carried them to the food court. Well before the task was done he wished he could have stayed in bed. He stuffed the sack and went behind the scenes to don his festal outfit. What were the lumps in his pockets? Santa's gloves, of course. While he had no intention of wearing them, perhaps he could turn them in for replacements.

The left one was reluctant to emerge, having snagged on an obstruction, or its contents had. No, the contents were the hindrance, and began to squirm, flexing all the digits of the glove as Laurence dragged it forth. Had an outsize spider found its way in? Then the spider must be short of almost half its legs. Panic that came close to blinding him sent Laurence to jerk the token window up and fling the swollen writhing glove into the alley behind the precinct. A sensation of intrusive restlessness reminded him that he was still holding the other glove, which had begun to convulse as an arrival struggled to fit within. He hurled it after its twin and slammed the window, then rested his forehead against the chill tiles of the wall. He didn't need to think about the incident—he very much preferred not to—as long as he'd dealt with whatever had to be. Once he'd gone some way towards persuading himself he fled into the mall.

He'd hoped to feel safer among people. "Ho ho ho," he told anyone who drifted near the grotto, but fell short of enticing many of them. He was turning his head back and forth like a beast in the cage that his hut had begun to feel like when he glimpsed someone waving to him. No, the man was pointing at the butcher's window, indicating it with just an arm. As Laurence twisted to look the chair gave a spavined lurch beneath him. The intruder had gone, but he could see it had been indicating a meat cleaver. He was striving to fend off any thoughts this prompted when Denton hurried over. "What's the problem now?"

However he'd betrayed there was one, Laurence felt desperate to conceal what he yearned to think he hadn't seen. "The chair. It isn't safe."

"Mind out. Let's see what you've done, for God's sake." As Laurence ventured out of the grotto and cast a nervous glance around the precinct, Denton dumped himself in the chair. "Nothing wrong with it, and you've only got another day," he said, then stared at Laurence. "Where's your gloves?"

"I lost them."

"Lost them," Denton said as if the words themselves were an offence.

"I wore them on the way home," Laurence improvised desperately, "and now I don't know where they are."

"Wait there and I'll bring you some more. And if we don't get the others back they'll be coming out of your money."

He returned from Inhabit The Habit with a pair he thrust at Laurence, and lingered to watch him edge his apprehensive fingers in. At least nothing was waiting to be encountered. In time Laurence gave up glancing nervously about in search of an intruder, though he felt trapped in the hut with the chortles he was driven to emit. Surely he could stand one more day of this, and then it would be Christmas.

The remains of the risotto were more than enough of a dinner, and required quite an amount of wine to wash them down. He would have liked to feel Judy Garland was wishing him a merry little Christmas, but perhaps he was as merry as he could achieve just now. He stumbled off to bed before he could slump into a doze, only to jerk awake and discover he was mumbling "What's your name?" For a moment if not longer he feared hearing an answer in the unlit bedroom.

"See it's your best day," Denton urged or warned him as he let Laurence into the precinct. "You owe it to the kids." He watched Laurence bear the latest stack of presents and wrapping paraphernalia to the food court, and eventually left him alone with the task and his throbbing dry-mouthed head. By the time the final package was wrapped and equally haphazardly ribboned, he had just minutes to resume his costume. He found nothing untoward in the pockets or the sleeves or the gloves or, as a last reason to be wary, the beard. As he returned to the grotto he felt able to wave to the customers Denton was admitting to the mall. Surveying his surroundings whenever he had the chance reassured him nobody unwanted had crept in. He might have relaxed into feeling safe if the chair hadn't revived its creak.

It emitted a complaint whenever a child boarded his knee, and he felt it shift beneath him. At least its ailment didn't seem to be progressive. Surely it could survive the day—and then Laurence saw a boy far too broad for his years plodding towards the grotto. Wishing him away didn't prevent his mother from magicking an admission from the barcode on the cabin. "What's your name?" Laurence said as the child advanced on him.

The question didn't halt the approach. "Teddy," the boy said.

"Stay there, would you, Teddy? You're too big a chap to be sitting on anyone's knee."

This was meant as a compliment, but perhaps Teddy heard it otherwise. "Everyone else did."

"You sit on Santa's lap," his mother called. "That's part of your treat, so don't be shy."

"He says I can't, mum."

"That's ridiculous. We've paid for it," she said and glared at Laurence. "What exactly is the issue here?"

"My leg," Laurence said in desperation. "It isn't quite up to the job."

"Then you shouldn't be doing it. Come along, Teddy, and we'll speak to whoever's in charge."

"Doesn't he want his present?" Laurence said in a wild bid to save the situation. "Wait and I'll find you a special one, son." The largest package tied in blue was topmost in the sack, and he knew what it must be. "Do you like jigsaws?" he hoped aloud.

"Sometimes."

"Let's make this one of them, then." As Laurence caught the parcel by its ribbon, a pair of unexpected objects nudged his fingers. He'd wrapped a bag of marbles donated by Employ A Toy, but how had these escaped? He closed his other hand around them, only to find they were too soft for marbles —sweets, then, except he'd put no sweets in the sack. "Be quick and take your present," the woman said, which made him raise his eyes to her. Beyond her, outside the Be Seeing Us opticians, stood a figure he knew all too well. It was winking at him, but why did this look so unnatural? Because each wink —left, right, left, like attempts to establish whether they still worked—made the eyelid cave in.

Laurence flung away the contents of his hands with a cry that left any words behind. The parcel thumped the boy's chest, and he blundered backwards as he caught it. "Come out of there," his mother cried. "We'll be seeing someone about this."

No amount of fearful staring showed Laurence any dreadful items on the floor, and he couldn't see a loiterer outside the butcher's or anywhere else in the mall. He upended the sack in front of him, and was trying to convince himself that it contained nothing uninvited when Denton marched over. "What in Christ's name are you playing at now?"

"Just checking I've enough left. I don't want to upset anyone."

"Too damned late for you to start caring about that. I've just had to give a woman back her money because you said her kid was overweight and chucked his present at him."

"That's not quite how it went. I told you this chair wasn't safe."

"You won't be in it much longer. I've had people complaining their kids recognised you from school as well. If we had anyone else I'd be giving you the boot right now."

"Maybe there is," Laurence felt driven to blurt, "but I don't think you'd like him."

"No idea what you're raving about. Now for Christ's sake put all that stuff back where it belongs and don't lose us any more cash."

Laurence might have fled the job, even abandoning his pay, if he hadn't been unwilling to disappoint children. He took a nervous time to scrutinise the packages before refilling the sack while a queue gathered at the picket fence. "Just doing the job my elves should have done," he called, which failed to amuse anyone much. He did his utmost to reduce his weight on the chair, but it greeted every new arrival with a creak like his ache rendered audible. "What's your name?" he had to keep saying, and "What do you want for Christmas?" while he struggled to ignore a figure dressed in red. Or was the colour a costume? He mustn't look, not least for fear that his reaction would disturb the children. He might have taken the intruder for an upright piece of meat in the butcher's window if he hadn't glimpsed how it kept mouthing his words. Whenever he summoned up a bout of chortling, the object quivered to imitate him.

There were just enough presents for his visitors. As the sack sagged flat Denton's omnipresent voice announced that the precinct was about to close for Christmas. Laurence watched the shoppers leave but couldn't tell when the intruder had departed. He was returning his costume and the sack to Inhabit The Habit when Denton brought him a thin envelope. "There's your pay less that woman's refund and the money for the gloves you said you lost. Good luck finding another job."

"Don't be like that, Ben. Remember when it is," Lydia said from behind her counter. "Forget the gloves. I can stand the loss." Less benevolently she added "I'll give him the balance and you can pay me back."

They left Laurence feeling sufficiently festive to wish them both a happy season. If anything continued to haunt the precinct, he hoped at least it wouldn't trouble Lydia. Soon the new year would take him back to teaching. He distributed Christmas greetings to everyone he met on the way home. He meant to pass out more tomorrow at the restaurant where he'd booked his Christmas dinner.

When he let himself in, the house was dark and silent. The stairs creaked underfoot like a reminder of the chair that was no longer his. He was halfway to the top floor when the parsimonious timer put the light out, and so he didn't see who wished him a merry Christmas, though the voice sounded familiar. Or had the wish been intended for him? Now he realised a door had muffled it, presumably why he hadn't been able to judge its tone. "Have one yourself," he said, searching with his key for the lock.

The apartment door swung inwards, revealing his unlit hall. He had to take a pair of strides to reach the inconveniently located light switch, and was about to press it down when the voice spoke again. "Here's your last package," it said. The words dismayed him almost as much as its location, because it was in front of him. As he stumbled backwards he collided with the door, which slammed behind him. He had no time to decide which would be worse—opening the package that awaited him or trying to put it together—when his present came shuffling and groping through the dark to find him.

Meet the Contributors

K.G. ANDERSON is a late-blooming writer of horror and dark fantasy who hails from the foggy coast of the Pacific Northwest. Prior to finding her speculative fiction muse, she reported on politics and crime, reviewed hundreds of mystery novels, and wrote about pop music for the iTunes Music Store. Her short stories appear in magazines and anthologies including *The Mammoth Book of Jack the Ripper Stories*, *Weirdbook*, and *Galaxy's Edge*, as well as on podcasts such as *The Overcast*. For links to more of her stories, visit http://writerway.com/fiction.

———

RAMSEY CAMPBELL is an English horror fiction writer, editor and critic who has been writing for well over fifty years. Two of his novels have been filmed, both for non-English-speaking markets. Since he first came to prominence in the mid-1960s, critics have cited Campbell as one of the leading writers in his field: T. E. D. Klein has written

that "Campbell reigns supreme in the field today," and Robert

Hadji has described him as "perhaps the finest living exponent of the British weird fiction tradition," while S. T. Joshi stated, "future generations will regard him as the leading horror writer of our generation, every bit the equal of Lovecraft or Blackwood."

———

V. CASTRO is a two-time Bram Stoker Award nominated author of Aliens: Vasquez, The Haunting of Alejandra, The Queen of The Cicadas, Goddess of Filth, Hairspray and Switchblades and Out of Atzlan. She is a Mexican American ex-pat living in the UK for the past 16 years. As a full-time mother, she dedicates her time to her family and writing. Visit her at www.vcastrostories.com.

———

CLAY McLEOD CHAPMAN writes novels, comic books and children's books, as well as for film and TV. He is the author of the horror novels THE REMAKING, WHISPER DOWN THE LANE and GHOST EATERS. He also co-wrote "Quiet Part Loud," a horror podcast produced by Jordan Peele's Monkeypaw for Spotify. Visit him at claymcleodchapman.com.

———

ADRIENNE CLARKE's writing dream began with a childhood love of fairy tales that made her want to create her own stories. Since then, she has written short fiction, novels, poems (and quite a few fairy tales in between). Her first YA novel, *Losing Adam*, garnered a silver medal in the 2018 Independent Publisher Book Awards and was selected as a finalist in the Eric Hoffer Book Awards. When she's not writing, Adrienne can be found searching for faeries (and other enchanted creatures) with her daughters, Callista and Juliet.

———

DOUGLAS FORD's short fiction has appeared in a variety of anthologies, magazines, and podcasts, as well as two collections, *Ape in the Ring and Other Tales of the Macabre and Uncanny* and *The Infection Party and Other Stories of Dis-Ease*. His longer works include *The Beasts of Vissaria County*, *Little Lugosi (A Love Story)*, and *The Trick*, his newest from Madness Heart Press. He lives on the west coast of Florida.

———

JONATHAN JANZ is the author of more than a dozen novels and numerous short stories. His work has been championed by authors like Josh Malerman, Caroline Kepnes, Joe R. Lansdale, Stephen Graham Jones, Brian Keene, and Jack Ketchum. His ghost story THE SIREN AND THE SPECTER was selected

as a Goodreads Choice Awards nominee for Best Horror. Additionally, his novels CHILDREN OF THE DARK and THE DARK GAME were chosen by Booklist and Library Journal, respectively, as Top Ten Horror Books of the Year. He is represented for TV & Film by Ryan Lewis (executive producer of BIRD BOX). Jonathan's main interests are his wonderful wife and his three amazing children. You can sign up for his newsletter, and you can follow him on Twitter, Instagram, Facebook, Amazon, and Goodreads.

————

JAKE JEROME lives in Philadelphia, PA with his wife and two cats, Herman and Princess Penelope, who are his editors. Although...he's beginning to suspect their incessant meowing isn't construc-  tive criticism. His work has been published with Black Hare Press, 34 Orchard Magazine, The Horror Tree's *Trembling With Fear*, and Writer's Digest Magazine. You can visit him at his website: jakejeromewriter.com.

————

JOHN KISTE is a horror, sci-fi, and mystery writer who was previously the president of the Stark County, Ohio, Convention & Visitors' Bureau and a Massillon Museum board member. He is a double-lung transplantee and organ donation ambassador, a McKinley Museum planetarian and an Edgar Allan Poe impersonator who has been published in Flame Tree Press's Terrifying Ghosts, A Shadow of Autumn, as well as dozens of other anthologies, magazines, and publications. He won the 2020 Dark Sire Award for Best Fiction and is an active member of the Horror Writers Association. He can be found at johnkiste.word-press.com.

———

DARREN LIPMAN is a high school mathematics teacher and writer in Milwaukee, Wisconsin. His poetry has appeared in Strange Horizons, and his fiction has appeared in the Eastern Iowa Review. When not writing, he enjoys drinking coffee, playing board games, and spending time with his Alaskan Klee Kai, Hoonah.

———

BROOKE MacKENZIE is the author of the short fiction collection GHOST GAMES, which Kirkus Reviews called, "[a]n indelible batch of nightmarish tales," as well as the upcoming horror poetry collection, THE SCARY ABECEDARY. Her short fiction and poetry have been published in numerous magazines and anthologies, and she has been known to win the occasional horror writing contest. She grew up in a haunted house, and so there is nothing she loves more than a good ghost story. She currently lives in a delightfully haunted town in Northern California with her husband and daughter. For more about Brooke, visit www.bamackenzie.com.

———

TIM McWHORTER was born under a waning crescent moon, and while he has no idea what the significance is, he thinks it sounds like a very horror writer thing to say. A graduate of Otterbein University, he is the author of the horror-thrillers, *The Opening, Shadows Remain, Bone White*, its sequel, *Blackened*, and a  collection of short stories, *Let There Be Dark*. He spends his days landlocked in a suburb outside Columbus, OH, but his nights dreaming of sun, surf, and getting sand in all those uncomfortable places.

———

Seth Ryan

LISA MORTON is a screenwriter, author of non-fiction books, and prose writer whose work was described by the American Library Association's *Readers' Advisory Guide to Horror* as "consistently dark, unsettling, and frightening." She is a six-time winner of the Bram Stoker Award®, the author of four novels and over 150 short stories, and a world-class Halloween and paranormal expert Her recent releases include *Haunted Tales:*

Classic Stories of Ghosts and the Supernatural (co-edited with Leslie S. Klinger), and *Calling the Spirits: A History of Seances*. Lisa lives in Los Angeles and online at www.lisamorton.com.

————

HAILEY PIPER is the Bram Stoker Award-winning author of Queen of Teeth, A Light Most Hateful, No Gods for Drowning, The Worm and His Kings series, Your Mind Is a Terrible Thing, Cruel Angels Past Sundown, Unfortunate Elements of My Anatomy, and Benny Rose the Cannibal King. She is also a Locus Award Finalist and an active member of the Horror Writers Association, with articles and stories appearing in Tor Nightfire, CrimeReads, Library Journal, Pseudopod, Vastarien, Cast of Wonders, Cosmic Horror Monthly, and various other publications. She lives with her wife in Maryland, where their occult rituals are secret. Find Hailey at www.haileypiper.com.

————

ELEANOR SCIOLISTEIN is the pen name of Vincent Heselwood, a writer of gothic horror from Manchester, UK. Recently nominated for a 'Saturday Visiter Award' by The International Edgar Allan Poe Association, Vincent makes the majority of his income working as a ghostwriter for other successful horror authors, but plans to step out of the shadows and release work under his own name this year.

KATHERINE TRAYLOR is a US-born writer currently based in Prague, Czech Republic. Her work has previously been published in *Dangerous Waters* (Brigid's Gate Press), *Once Upon a Wicked Heart* (Fiction-Atlas Press), and *Gods & Services* (Critical Blast Publishing), as well as by  *MYTHIC Magazine* and JMS Books. Her writing is often fairy-tale-inspired with a strong focus on transformation. She shares a home with her beautiful partner and three four-footed sons. Follow her on Twitter (@amongthegoblins) or at her website, katherinetraylor.com.

 **CHET WILLIAMSON** has written horror, SF, and suspense since 1981. Among his many novels are *Second Chance, Ash Wednesday, Reign,* and *Psycho: Sanitarium*, the authorized sequel to Robert Bloch's classic. His two most recent novels, *Murder Old and New* and *A Step Across*, were co-written with his wife, Laurie. Over a hundred of his short stories have appeared in *The New Yorker, Playboy, Esquire, The Magazine of Fantasy and Science Fiction*, and many other magazines and anthologies. He has won the International Horror Guild Award, and has been shortlisted for the World Fantasy Award, the HWA's Stoker, and the MWA's Edgar.

STEPHANIE M. WYTOVICH is an American poet, novelist, and essayist. Her work has been showcased in numerous magazines and anthologies such as Weird Tales, Nightmare Magazine, Southwest Review, Year's Best Hardcore Horror: Volume 2, The Best Horror of the Year: Volume 8, as well as many others. Wytovich is the Poetry Editor for  Raw Dog Screaming Press, an adjunct at Western Connecticut State University, Southern New Hampshire University, and Point Park University, and a mentor with Crystal Lake Publishing. She is a recipient of the 2021 Ladies of Horror Fiction Writers Grant and has received the Rocky Wood Memorial Scholarship for non-fiction writing. Follow Wytovich at http://stephaniewytovich.blogspot.com/

———

Assistant Editor

 **JOHN PALISANO**'s novels include *Dust of the Dead, Ghost Heart, Nerves*, and *Night of 1,000 Beasts*. His novellas include *Glass House* and *Starlight Drive: Four Halloween Tales*. His first short fiction collection *All that Withers* celebrates over a decade of short story highlights. He won the Bram Stoker Award© in short fiction for "Happy Joe's Rest Stop" and Colorado's Yog Soggoth award. More short stories

have appeared in anthologies from *Weird Tales, Cemetery Dance, PS Publishing, Independent Legions, Space & Time, Dim Shores, Kelp Journal, Monstrous Books, DarkFuse, Crystal Lake, Terror Tales, Lovecraft eZine, Horror Library, Bizarro Pulp, Written Backwards, Dark Continents, Big Time Books, McFarland Press, Darkscribe, Dark House, Omnium Gatherum,* and many more. Nonfiction pieces have appeared in *Blumhouse Online, Fangoria,* and *Dark Discoveries* magazines and he's been quoted in *Vanity Fair, The Writer* and the *Los Angeles Times.* You can find out more at: www.johnpalisano.com

———

Executive Editor

GABY TRIANA is the Cuban-American author of 25 books for adults and teens, including *Moon Child, Island of Bones, River of Ghosts, City of Spells, Wake the Hollow, Cubanita,* and *Summer of Yesterday.* Her short stories have appeared in *Classic Monsters Unleashed, A Tribute to Alvin Schwartz's Scary Stories to Tell in the*

Dark, A Conjuring for All Seasons, Novus Monstrum, and *Weird Tales Magazine*. She has co-authored ghosthunters Sam & Colby's horror novel, *Paradise Island*, and edited the ghost anthology series, *Literally Dead (Tales of Halloween Hauntings; Tales of Holiday Hauntings)*. As a ghostwriter, Gaby has penned 50+ novels for bestselling authors in every genre. Her own books have won the IRA Teen Choice Award, ALA Best Paperback, and Hispanic Magazine's Good Reads Awards, and she writes under several pen names, including Gabrielle Keyes for her paranormal women's fiction. She lives in Miami with her family and the four-legged creatures they serve.

Dear Reader . . .

If you enjoyed this anthology, please:

🌲 *Leave a rating/review on Amazon and Goodreads;*

🌲 *Post a book photo on social media. Tag the authors and Alienhead Press;*

🌲 *Join the Alienhead Press newsletter to receive updates, notices for open call submissions, and more.*

Thank you for your support!

- Alienhead Press

First in series

LITERALLY DEAD
TALES OF HALLOWEEN HAUNTINGS

Edited by
GABY TRIANA

Featuring Jonathan Maberry, Gwendolyn Kiste, Tim
Waggoner, Lee Murray, Sara Tantlinger, Catherine
Cavendish, Jeff Strand, Alethea Kontis & more!

Literally Dead: Tales of Halloween Hauntings

SAMPLE CHAPTER
THE CURIOSITY AT THE BACK OF THE
FRIDGE BY CATHERINE CAVENDISH

Welcome. Welcome.

It is indeed most gratifying to see so many of you here today. I am sure you are all eager to hear why I have invited you, aren't you? Well, your waiting is at an end. So, gather round, everyone, because the story I am about to tell you is a strange one indeed.

I was introduced to "it" by an old man who lived on the edge of our village. His name was Robert Clements, but everyone called him Bobby Clem. Of course, most of you are far too young to remember him.

Bobby Clem lived in a tumbledown cottage atop a small hill. If you passed by during the day, you would swear it was derelict and long abandoned, but at night, a candle burned in every window. I never found out why.

What's that, you said? Why didn't I ask? Ah, sometimes it is better not to ask too many questions. You might not like the answers. No, it was simply the way things were. It is a tradition I have chosen to keep alive.

I first met Bobby Clem when I was a small boy. Indeed, I

was small in every way. At nine years old, I was shorter than the seven-year-olds—a shy, only, motherless child. She had died when I was a mere baby. Dad and I lived alone together, and my father would work all hours trying to keep food on the table and clothes on my back.

On school holidays and weekends, I was left to my own devices while Dad was at work and I took to wandering off on my own, exploring the many country lanes and shady pine woods.

One day I came across a man with a shock of white hair. He was bending over a trap, releasing a dead rabbit. Job done and prize retrieved, he stood and towered over me, but I was used to craning my neck. The man's unkempt beard covered his face and neck, leaving only piercing blue eyes and a kindly smile. Dirty, old corduroy trousers were tied at his waist with frayed string, while a threadbare overcoat and grimy shirt completed his appearance.

"What's your name, lad?" His voice sounded gruff but not unkind. Despite having been repeatedly instructed never to speak to strangers, maybe it was something about his eyes—an innate benevolence. Suffice it to say, I made an exception in his case.

"Brian," I said.

"Well, Brian. Do you want to come and share some rabbit stew with me?"

I had nothing else to do, and rabbit stew was one of my favorites. Like any boy of my age, anytime was dinner time.

On the short walk to his home, he questioned me about my life. I told him everything, from losing my mother to being bullied at school, taunted because of my height and poverty. All the other kids seemed to have so much more than I did. I told him everything, but all I learned about him was his name.

Bobby Clem. And I kind of knew that anyway. He was spoken of in hushed whispers by grown-ups. Robert Clements who used to be a professor at the university. Now reduced to the local down and out. "Stay away from Bobby Clem," we children were told. "Or no good will come to you." But I didn't have any friends. No one wanted to play with me. Bobby Clem was the first person who had taken an interest in me, and I so wanted a friend of my own.

I had passed his cottage many times but never paid it much heed. Now, Bobby pushed open the door and it groaned, swinging wildly on broken hinges, revealing a sparsely furnished room, its rickety table sporting a leg supported by ancient, moldy books. Galvanized buckets stood like sentries awaiting the next heavy rainfall which otherwise—judging by the gaping holes in the roof of the one-story building—would cascade down, flooding the place.

Bobby Clem led me through the room into the kitchen, such as it was. My new friend slapped the rabbit down on a none-too-clean pine table. From the sink he selected two of the least dirty plates and a vicious looking knife. He then proceeded to skin and butcher the rabbit. I looked around in vain for a cooker, but only a fire burned in a small range. A cooking pot, like a witch's cauldron, hung suspended over it.

I thought there was no electricity, but a sudden, clanking buzzing told me otherwise. In the corner of the room, an ancient, massive fridge stood, plugged into a single socket. Bobby saw me looking.

"Ah, there's a story behind that fridge," he said, as he carried on preparing our meal. "One Halloween, years ago, a man knocked on my door. It was a raw night, a blizzard blew, and this stranger stood on my doorstep, dripping from head to toe and shivering. I brought him in, sat him by the fire, gave him dry clothes, a blanket and something hot to eat and drink. In the morning, the storm had blown over, and the sun was shining. The man was so grateful for my hospitality, he wanted to repay me.

"I refused to take payment, and he made to leave. He called me outside, saying he needed some help with his van. It was a big, old cranky thing, and it wouldn't start. I used to tinker a bit with cars when I was younger, so I checked his engine. Sure enough, there was a loose cable. Once I reconnected it, the engine turned over fine, and the man was away. I went back inside, and there it was." He pointed his bloodied knife at the fridge. "How he got it in here… let's put it down to one of life's mysteries, because it got here somehow, didn't it? I opened it, and it was piled high with everything you could want for a delicious Halloween feast. Turkey, all the trimmings, even pumpkin pie. I'd never eaten that before. Have you eaten that, Brian?"

I shook my head.

He smacked his lips. "Delicious. Hey, it's Halloween in a few days, maybe your father will let you come and eat pumpkin pie with me."

I doubted that, but as Halloween was on Friday, and Dad was working nights all weekend, he wouldn't have to know, would he?

Bobby chopped up the meat, added carrots, potatoes, herbs, and onion and dumped the whole lot into the cooking pot, along with fresh water he drew from a hand pump by the sink. "There, we'll let that stew for an hour or so. Are you hungry, Brian?"

My stomach gave a growl. Bobby laughed, and I liked the sound. It was tinkly and sincere.

"Now, let's have a look in that fridge. Is there anything in there, I wonder?"

He opened the door wide. I stared at the empty shelves. It was certainly the cleanest thing in that house, except… "What *is* that?" I pointed to a large black blob that looked a bit like a jellyfish, stuck to the back wall.

"Oh, that's my friend. The Curiosity, I call him. As it's so close to Halloween, I thought he might come out. But no." He slammed the door shut. "Must leave him to his privacy. He doesn't like to be disturbed."

"But—"

Bobby put a finger to his lips. "No questions, Brian. You'll meet him right enough. At the proper time. But it must be on his terms. Do you understand?"

Of course, I didn't, but I nodded and hoped that would suffice. It seemed to.

Whatever else Bobby Clem was, he cooked a delicious stew, and, a couple of hours later, stuffed to the gills, I made my way home with promises to return on Halloween.

OCTOBER 31ST. It rained. All day, torrents of it poured down. A river ran down the road at the end of our path. Small children cried as their trick-or-treat costumes were ruined or parents decided it was too wet to venture out. I didn't care. They never included me anyway, and for once, unlike them, I had plans I could keep.

I arrived at Bobby Clem's cottage where the aroma of a delicious meal set my taste buds tingling and my mouth watering even before he opened the door.

"Welcome, Brian," he said. "We're all ready for you. Look what a feast we have."

I stared. Bobby had moved the kitchen table into the living room. It was heaving with a roasted turkey—its skin golden brown—little chipolatas wrapped in bacon, dishes of roast potatoes and vegetables. There was gravy and the promised pumpkin pie. I never questioned how he managed to create all that in one cooking pot. No questions, remember? Not ever.

Bobby Clem had cleaned the room so that it shone. Even the floor revealed polished floorboards. The only evidence of the dilapidated state of his cottage was provided by the buckets into which rainwater dripped.

"Some people spring clean. I do mine on Halloween. It's my 'thank you.'"

I pondered that while I took my place at the table. "Oh, you mean a 'thank you' to the man who gave you the fridge?"

"Not entirely."

It was then I noticed a third place setting.

"Is someone joining us?" I was a little disappointed. I suppose I wanted to keep my new friend to myself.

"Our benefactor," Bobby said. "Now you can meet the Curiosity."

I blinked. There was no one there, but a slithering noise came from behind me, moving closer.

"Don't be alarmed by his appearance, young Brian. He can't help that any more than we can help being quite hideous to him."

I swallowed and dared to look down as the Curiosity slipped past me. It moved on pseudopodia—I had recently learned that word at school where we had studied the life cycle of an amoeba. It thrust out its jelly-like protrusions and made its slow way round to its place at the head of the table. A few seconds later, its head—if you could call the blob a head—emerged. Bobby sat down and proceeded to load the Curiosity's plate with pumpkin pie.

"He doesn't like turkey," Bobby said, setting the plate down in front of his friend. "He has other…tastes. But he adores pumpkin pie. Now, Brian, help yourself. Tuck in and eat. The Curiosity has provided all this fine food for us. Don't ask me how. It's enough that he does it. Every year. But only at Halloween. The rest of the year he keeps himself to himself, and I...look after him."

I tried to work it all out in my nine-year-old head. "So, the fridge is his?"

"That's right. The stranger— I never did learn his name— looked after him. For some reason, the Curiosity prefers to live in there. I suppose the temperature suits him, and he is left alone, which is what he likes. He can turn very nasty if you disturb his slumber."

Bobby Clem rubbed his hand, and I noticed a scar where his little finger should have been. Odd that I hadn't noticed it before.

"He sleeps for most of the year. And before you ask, I don't know what type of creature he is, where he came from, how old he is, or any of the usual things. I know that he exists. That he *is*. And that's all you need to know, too, Brian."

From that day on, every year at Halloween, I joined Bobby and the Curiosity for a sumptuous feast. I grew up. Dad died, and I moved into the cottage. Years passed, and the place was falling down piece by piece, so I built us this nice new home with our own generator. We took care of our friend and bene-factor together until Bobby Clem passed away.

I see we have another question. You there, the little boy at the back. You remind me of... never mind. You want to know what I've learned about the Curiosity over the years? Well now, that would be telling, wouldn't it? But as you asked so politely, I'll tell you...some of it, at least.

When Bobby Clem lay dying in his bed, he seemed to shrink a little more each day. His skin took on a strange transparency that I'd never seen before. Sometimes it was as if I could see the blood pumping through his veins but becoming thicker and more sluggish with each passing day.

Meanwhile in the old fridge, the Curiosity was positively blooming. He pulsed as if infused with fresh blood. No longer black, he shone with a reddish radiance. It was like he was tapping into Bobby's impending demise, maybe helping him on his way.

Then one day, Bobby slipped into a coma. During our last conversation, he had made me promise not to seek any kind of medical help. "Not under any circumstances," he said, "and when it's your turn, you mustn't either. The Curiosity will take care of everything."

I asked him what he meant by that, and with a great effort, he said, "My time is over, so I see more clearly now. I understand more. The Curiosity is not one being. He is made up of many who have gone before, and on All Hallows' Eve, they provide for the one who is their current guardian. Hence the feast. When I'm gone, you'll see them, but only on the first Halloween after my passing, and the glimpse will be so fleeting, you'll think it was a dream."

Those were his last words, but he was right. That first Halloween, soon after I'd buried Bobby's body out there in the woods, I saw them. So many shadows, ghostly figures busying themselves cooking, baking…and there, among them, was Bobby Clem. He smiled and waved at me, as he put the final touches to the pumpkin pie.

He was right, though. I have never seen them again. As for the Curiosity and I…we carry on as before. The feast appears as if by magic once a year. To this day I don't know if I dreamed that legion of ghostly cooks, but I certainly love their pumpkin pie. As for my mysterious friend, he asks so little in return. Merely that I provide him with food for the rest of the year.

And that, my dear ones, is where you come in.

————

Read more in:
LITERALLY DEAD: Tales of Halloween Hauntings

————

Also by Alienhead Press

HORROR:

LITERALLY DEAD: Tales of Halloween Hauntings

MOON CHILD

ISLAND OF BONES

RIVER OF GHOSTS

CITY OF SPELLS

PARANORMAL WOMEN'S FICTION:

WITCH OF KEY LIME LANE

CRONE OF COCONUT COURT

MAGE OF MANGO ROAD

HEX OF PINEAPPLE PLACE

YOUNG ADULT:

KIMBO

UNRAVELED

CAKESPELL

ALIENHEAD
PRESS

Printed in Great Britain
by Amazon